"THEY HAVE DARED THIS TIME, MASTER CHIUN, AND THEY HAVE SUCCEEDED."

Chiun's face blanched. "Do not tell me the private garden was violated."

"It was."

"Emperor, what of my dragon?"

Smith shifted uneasily in his seat. "We don't know yet, Master Chiun. We believe that there has been some sort of break-in at the facility. The security systems would suggest as much. A substantial break-in."

"Emperor, do not mince words. What of my dragon?"

Smith waved his hand open and helplessly, and said, "The dragon is dead."

Chiun's eyes blazed.

D0836597

CREATED BY WARREN MURPHY & RICHARD SAPIR

THE DESTROYER

DRAGON BONES

A GOLD EAGLE BOOK FROM

W🌐RLDWIDE.

TORONTO • NEW YORK • LONDON
AMSTERDAM • PARIS • SYDNEY • HAMBURG
STOCKHOLM • ATHENS • TOKYO • MILAN
MADRID • WARSAW • BUDAPEST • AUCKLAND

If you purchased this book without a cover you should be aware
that this book is stolen property. It was reported as "unsold and
destroyed" to the publisher, and neither the author nor the
publisher has received any payment for this "stripped book."

First edition October 2006

ISBN-13: 978-0-373-63260-2
ISBN-10:   0-373-63260-6

Special thanks and acknowledgment to Tim Somheil
for his contribution to this work.

DRAGON BONES

Copyright © 2006 by Warren Murphy.

All rights reserved. Except for use in any review, the
reproduction or utilization of this work in whole or in part
in any form by any electronic, mechanical or other means,
now known or hereafter invented, including xerography,
photocopying and recording, or in any information storage
or retrieval system, is forbidden without the written permission
of the publisher, Worldwide Library, 225 Duncan Mill Road,
Don Mills, Ontario, Canada M3B 3K9.

All characters in this book have no existence outside the
imagination of the author and have no relation whatsoever to
anyone bearing the same name or names. They are not even
distantly inspired by any individual known or unknown to the
author, and all incidents are pure invention.

® and TM are trademarks of the publisher. Trademarks indicated
with ® are registered in the United States Patent and Trademark
Office, the Canadian Trade Marks Office and in other countries.

Printed in U.S.A.

And for the Glorious House of Sinanju,
at www.warrenmurphy.com

1

The *harruunukking* was too insistent to ignore.

"Ten more minutes."

Harruunukk.

"All right, I'm up!"

Still tired, she sat up and rubbed her eyes. The clock on her desk told her it was almost one-thirty in the morning. Breakfast number one was late. No wonder there was so much complaining.

Huh-huh-harruunukk.

The willowy blond woman rolled out of the tangled sheets on the portable cot and trod barefoot from the cramped office into the large research laboratory. As soon as she appeared, the abominable noise stopped and turned to impatient snuffling.

"You could let me sleep through the night for a change."

Dr. Nancy Derringer stepped to the rail and held up a hand. The great beast in the auditorium-sized, plant-filled pen stretched its serpentine neck and pressed its cheek against her hand.

The head was small by comparison to the many tons of body that stretched many feet behind it. Its skin was orange and black, and glimmered with moisture. Hunger had motivated it to emerge from its low, swampy pond in the middle of its habitat. Its long neck was orange banded in black, and along the ridged back were fat orange splotches.

The creature's eyes were still as big as a human head, but they were watery and edged with thick lashes, like the eyes of a giant goat or a hideous but gentle cow.

"You poor thing," she said lovingly. "You really do look like a simpleton, but you're smart enough to know when it's time for breakfast."

Nancy was dressed only in her oversize sleep shirt, but no staff were due for another hour. She didn't even bother putting on her sweatpants before hauling open the door of the walk-in storage cooler and pushing out a cart full of mangoes. One of the front wheels wobbled, but she was stronger than she looked. She kept the cart from colliding with the door and guided it to the lip of the creature's living environment.

The massive beast shifted eagerly on its feet, and

when the contents of the cart tumbled inside the pen it moved in and snatched a mango in its mouth.

These were not your average grocery-store mangoes. They were a strain of wild mangos, big as melons, known in Africa as jungle chocolate. The mango collapsed in the jaws of the beast, which released the ripe, sweet smell.

"Better, Punkin?" Nancy asked.

The dinosaur blinked contentedly as its teeth made mush of the mango.

It didn't take much to make the apatosaurus happy. All Punkin needed was a comfortable habitat and plenty of mangoes.

"And you need, me, too, don't you, Punkin?" Dr. Nancy Derringer said.

The apatosaurus responded to her voice. It looked at her and blinked slowly while chewing. The bands of black and orange on its neck pulsed as the muscles labored to channel a previous mouthful down the long throat into its dinosaur gullet.

"You're the best person I know, Punkin," Nancy said. "You're such a loyal, gentle soul, you know. Everybody else who comes into my life is just a jerk, loser or weirdo. But I always have you."

Punkin worked the mango down its throat and stretched out for another one. It was an especially ripe one, and the juice gushed out, dripping off its chin.

"I lost another one last night," Nancy continued. "This one was definitely in the jerk category. He didn't care about me at all. All he wanted was you. Parts of you, anyway. You'd never guess what he wanted to do to you, Punkin."

The apatosaurus chomped another wild mango.

The most recent jerk in question was a Hawaiian biochemist. Rory Ahabepela had captivated Nancy with his charms, his youthful vigor, his mellifluous singing voice. He did a perfect Don Ho when they went to karaoke night at the Snuggery. But his interest in her was all an act. He didn't want her. He didn't even want her body. He was only after her apatosaurus.

Before him there was Professor "Burnsie" Burnhard. Burnsie had managed to latch on to Nancy just as his addiction to painkillers began dominating his life, and it quickly became the dominant theme of their relationship. No wonder he was so easy going, Nancy remembered thinking when she discovered his stash of illegal prescriptions. He was sucking down enough narcotics to put a horse into a coma. Burnsie was definitely in the loser category.

Before him was the researcher from Quebec who

interned at the lab. Franz Pell had helped her study the microorganisms in Punkin's digestive tract. It was messy work, collecting and analyzing dinosaur regurgitation, but Franz was a nice guy. Smart, too. They were a couple for a month before he began suggesting that they mix their sex life and his work in the most appalling manner imaginable. Definitely in the weirdo category.

How did she manage to hook up with these guys? She wasn't a stupid or weak woman. She wasn't the kind to prolong a doomed relationship just out of sentiment. Franz the freak? She dumped him on the spot. Burnsie the druggie? She dropped him off in front of a rehab center and programmed her phone to ignore his incoming calls. Rory Ahabepela? As soon as he made his intentions known she got up, told him off in front of a restaurant full of sniggering diners and left him red-faced just as the entrées were arriving.

"You'll never get your hands on Punkin, you murderer," she announced loudly.

But now other faces were streaming before her mind's eye. All losers, jerks and weirdos. Even the ones she didn't have relationships with had mostly turned out to be losers or jerks or weirdos. She recalled men who were inconsiderate lovers, envious teachers, and some who were both. Then there was the biggest prick of them all. Skip King, the man who had funded the expedition to Africa, which had turned out to be a wild-goose chase at best.

She'd been in Phoenix then, with the International Colloquium of Cryptozoologists. It was one of the most well-respected organizations of cryptozoologists anywhere on Earth, but that wasn't saying much. Few serious scientists gave credence to the search for "hidden animals."

Scientists of this discipline were interested in creatures that common zoologists dismissed as mythological or were usually believed to be extinct. Try mentioning at a cocktail party that you're looking for yeti or the Loch Ness monster or the Land that Time Forgot and you'd be the butt of every joke. You would get laughed out of the room. Nancy knew. She'd been there.

But then she was offered high-resolution satellite photos of large mammals in the back country of Gondwanaland, presumably released by a recent African earthquake from a previously hidden habitat. Nancy used all her rainy-day funds to buy the black-market pictures from a satellite operator at the Gaia Satellite Reconnaissance Company. She didn't have enough cash left to purchase airfare to Gondwanaland, let alone enough to outfit an expedition into the wilds to search for the creature in the photo. She sought corporate funding, and ended up partnered with Skip King, the vice president in charge of marketing for the Burger Triumph Corporation.

Skip was not a nice man. Bigoted, sexist, racist, egotistical, duplicitous and unethical. Nancy could have overlooked these faults, even the ass-grabbing, if not for the fact that he planned to bring the African dinosaurs back to the United States not for zoological study, but to grind up into quarter-pound patties and sell as ultra-high-end Bronto Burgers at $5,000.99. Drinks and fries extra.

She had been desperate to put her trust in a man like that. Skip King was so smart and slick, he almost got away with it. In the end, Skip King pushed Punkin too far and Punkin got pissed and swallowed the vice president in charge of Burger Triumph marketing.

A couple of other men were involved in that little affair. They were in the weirdo category, but they weren't necessarily bad men, it turned out. In fact, she recalled both of them rather fondly. She owed one of them a huge favor.

Some day, she'd have to pay off the favor. That wouldn't happen until Punkin had lived out its natural life. Then she would personally, lovingly perform an autopsy on the creature and remove a portion of its bones for a strange little Korean man named Chiun.

Chiun had not been to visit in quite some time. He usually showed up out of the blue, once a year or so, just to check on the health of the apatosaurus. He never spoke much or stayed long, but he always reminded her of their agreement.

She clutched her stomach. After leaving the Hawaiian liar at the bistro, she had come home and drowned her sorrows in two bottles of pinot noir. Her mouth tasted like something terrible.

Maybe she was being morbid and dwelling on negative thoughts. She was thinking ahead to the time when Punkin would die. Who knew how long that would be? Punkin had been healthy for years, but now—unless it was Nancy's imagination—the great beast was looking pale and wobbly.

"You okay, sweetie?"

"*Hrrggooo,*" Punkin said pleasantly, munching on another mango. It was the special noise of contentment the dinosaur made when it was feeling fine and eating well.

"Good to hear," Nancy said, but gagged on the sweet smell of the African mangoes. "Yuck. I think that bunch got a little too ripe. I guess that's why you like them so much."

Nancy retreated to the kitchenette and scrounged around for food. The fridge was empty except for a half gallon of soy milk.

"Who cleaned out the fridge?" she demanded. "I had half a carton of chicken-fried rice in there." She could really use some good, salty, oily fried rice about now. She'd grill the lab staff about it later.

In the cupboard, more food was missing. Popcorn. Tuna pouches. There was nothing but frosted wheat shreds. She grumbled as she dumped them in a bowl and sloshed on the soy milk.

"Yuck," she said. The soy milk and the frosting made the cereal too sweet. Like candy. But her stomach needed something to fill it. She breathed through her nose as she chomped up the shredded wheat.

Harrooo.

That sounded strange. Nancy walked from the little kitchenette carrying her breakfast and found that Punkin was no longer eating, although a few mangoes remained. The dinosaur had its head held high and its serpentine neck was stiff. It groaned again.

The air was thick with the sickly sweetness.

Too sweet. Nancy's heart leaped to her throat. She climbed over the rail and snatched at one of the uneaten mangoes, bashed it open on the steel guard rail and then held it to her nose. The liquid gushed out. Sugary sweetness disguised a rancid, bitter tinge.

She knew what it was. Poison, masked by sugar. They were trying to kill her apatosaurus!

Punkin made a miserable sound of gastric distress, and Nancy ran back to the office. She had to get the whole research team in here as fast as possible for emergency treatment of the gigantic creature.

There was someone standing in the door to her office.

"Rory. You did this, you son of a bitch!"

Rory Ahabepela gave her his simple smile, with his tanned cheeks and sunny smile. "You should have played ball with me, Nancy. Would have made it a lot easier on you."

Her rage clouded her vision, but she was dimly aware of others appearing around her. Many, many men in work clothes. "Easier? To help you kill Punkin?"

"At least you'd be alive to do it," Rory explained.

"What?" Then Nancy felt foolish. Of course. The shredded wheat was poisoned, too. Her body was feeling numb. Her vision was clouding over. "Murderer!"

"Big-game collector," Rory explained, his smile never fading.

Nancy was helpless and she knew it. She was dying on her feet. She turned away from her killer and took a few lurching steps toward Punkin, but as she watched, the neck of the great apatosaurus fell heavily to the ground. Punkin's eyes were wide open and staring at Dr. Nancy Derringer. Its body collapsed, shaking the ground.

"'Bye, Punkin," Nancy said lovingly, and then she too fell in a heap.

Rory Ahabepela tapped the button on his watch timer. "Okay, people, we have sixty minutes to get the animal secured, in the air and lifted to the freezer. Let's get moving."

The workmen hustled forward with chains as a pair of operators powered up the apatosaurus habitat's cranes, specially designed to move the forty-ton specimen. Section by section, the chains were wrapped around the beast, used to lift it a little more off the ground and allow more chains to be pushed under the body. Weeks of rehearsals in the warehouse on Oahu paid off; the dinosaur was securely wrapped in chains when the sounds of the first chopper could be heard overhead.

"Cover it," Rory barked.

The work crew was already on it. They pulled a netting of woven steel links over the top of the suspended creature.

"Clear!" Rory shouted.

The workmen scampered out of the habitat, and the chopper went to work with a massive hook that was lowered through the frosted skylight. The window shattered, raining glass fragments down on the habitat. The chopper moved slowly to the other end of the building, and its big hook caught the steel framework of the roof, peeling it back noisily. From the protection of the overhang in the personnel work areas, Rory saw the heavily overcast night sky revealed.

The chopper released the braided steel cable, and the end of the roof flopped to the ground like a long, limp tongue.

"Good," Rory announced into the radio. "More than adequate. Where's the heavy-lifter?"

The interior of the habitat reverberated with sudden violence. It was as if an explosion started and never stopped. The walls shook. Pieces of the roof collapsed, the air palpitated and something like a hovering blue whale blotted out the stars.

"I am here," the pilot radioed.

"No shit," Rory said, but his words were lost in the

roar. He keyed in the signal to proceed. Green lights blinked on the radios of the entire team. The aircraft—as big as a Boeing 727—disgorged heavy-lift cables one after another. Teams of workmen, hired from skyscraper construction teams, handled the connection of the chains to the cocoon of steel that now wrapped the apatosaurus. Soon there were fourteen cables connecting the dinosaur to the roaring helicopter.

The connection team foreman gave the go signal.

"Extracting now," the pilot said as the slack began to tighten on the cables. "This had better work."

"It'll work!" Rory snapped irritably, but to himself he said, "This had better fucking work."

CAPTAIN TASSEL COULDN'T look. It took all of his concentration just to monitor the controls and keep the big slab of metal in place. This chopper was a monster. And old. And there was a reason only three of the damn things were made in the first place— they didn't work so well. Even with a fresh outfitting of computerized controls it was sluggish and wobbly. The problem was the old engines. The thirty-five-year-old, 6500-horsepower Soloviev D-25VF turbines operated as smoothly as the first restart of a junkyard Desoto.

So here he was, holding a ten-story building in the ugly night sky with the help of four oversize riding-mower engines and a lot of faith.

The aircraft jerked.

"What's happening?" he demanded.

"Slack's in," the operations commander radioed. His name was Rory Something-or-Other—something Hawaiian. And he was the most vicious son of a bitch in history. Tassel hadn't known there was such a thing as a mean Hawaiian. They always seemed so nice and happy.

"About to lift," Rory radioed.

"We're ready."

Now, Tassel thought, is the moment of truth.

Sure, the aircraft was designed to lift as much as forty tons of cargo. But had it ever actually done it? The old Soviet propaganda said yes.

And what about the computer-controlled crane system? Would it be able to lift the cargo evenly, even with fourteen crane cables to coordinate?

And what if they didn't? There was no quick release. And if one of the cables slipped and yanked the chopper off center, would Tassel be able to wrestle it back into level flight before one of the massive props touched the building?

And if one of the massive props touched the buildings, and the whole affair crashed to the ground, then would he really find an endless supply of virgins in Heaven?

The computers were feeding fuel to the four engines as the weight of the cargo was taken up. Then the aircraft sunk a few feet, wobbled and steadied.

"We have it! It's coming out," the operations commander announced. "It's clear!"

Tassel radioed back to the base. "We're clear and heading for the freezer."

Tassel eased the massive aircraft into the sky.

"How is it handling?" his copilot asked, wiping his brow with his sleeve.

"Sluggish. But not as bad as I expected."

"Yeah, well, it gets a lot worse from here."

Tassel didn't want to think about. It was bad enough trying to lift a thirty-ton sack of bones and meat, but that was nothing compared to lifting the same animal inside a ten-ton block of ice.

Theoretically, this flying hunk of low-grade Cold War junk was capable of such a thing.

If you believed the Soviet propaganda.

2

His name was Remo and he was trying to make sense of the directions he had been given.

Story of his life.

These particular directions came from a sleepy clerk at the Moscow International Airport rental-car desk. She traced the route with a yellow highlighter on a flimsy map, which was so old it still referred to Moscow as the capital city of the Union of Soviet Socialist Republics. "This is your deztinashun—see little star?" She highlighted a yellow star on the map.

Remo found the little star not at all helpful, and the step-by-step driving directions on the right-hand side of the page were written to take him a hundred miles out of his way.

Still, he was trying to make use of those directions, now that he was actually in the Russian city of Monino. He was on the correct street, as far as he could tell. The street had seen better days, and the street numbers were missing from most of the buildings. When he was about where he thought the museum should be, he had two choices, one on either side of the street. One was a black, silent hulk of a building that looked big enough to hold a couple of simultaneous World Cup matches. The second one appeared to be a convenience store with so many female employees they wouldn't all fit inside.

"Howdy, ladies," he said as the employees actually emerged into the street to see what they could do for him. Now that's Old World service for you.

"Ha-loh, American," said one of the employees. "What are you looking for tonight?"

"Military aircraft," Remo said, forcing his friendliest smile. "Got any at your place?"

The women went back into their convenience store, and Remo tried the building on the other side of the street. The speaker beside the front door clicked and buzzed, then a tired voice said, in Russian, "Yes?"

"Is Homer home?"

"What?" The speaker switched to uncertain English. "Who is this?"

"This is Remo. I come to see Homer. Is he home?"

"This is not a house."

"I know. It's a museum. Central Museum of the

Air Forces. I came all the way from the United States to see it."

"We're closed."

"Since when?"

"Since 1997. We are getting no more funds. All the visitors go to the new Moscow Aerospace Museum. Monino is too far from Moscow for visitors to come. You go to Moscow, too."

"But I came just to see one special aircraft that you have. I came all this way. I will pay whatever the admission fee is."

The buzzer box clicked off and the door popped open. A tired man in a rumpled old sport jacket and wrinkly gray pajama pants stood there with a light in his eyes. "How much you pay?"

"Five hundred dollars?"

"A thousand."

"Six hundred."

"Nine hundred."

"Seven—oh, forget it. Here. Just take the damn thousand." Remo produced a fat wad of folded U.S. twenty-dollar bills and clapped them into the caretaker's hand. The caretaker fanned them, counted them in a hurry and grew a smile that seemed to spread past his ears to the back of his head.

"Thank you, sir!"

"Lastly. Remo Lastly. Nice to meet you. Can I come in now?"

"Yes. Yes. Come in. Come in. I am Pummel. I will take you through the museum personally."

Remo was ushered into the front hall. The space inside was cavernous and hollow. The air tasted of dust. The only light came from a small, dingy cubicle off the entrance hall, with a tousled cot where Pummel had just been sleeping.

Up ahead, in the blackness, the first cavernous room contained the ominous, silent shapes of Soviet aircraft.

"We have very interesting machines to show, yes. We have Russian spy planes, contrail plows, fighter jets—everything! Come!"

"Thanks," Remo said, "but I'm really just interested in one exhibit."

"Yes?" The caretaker listened as he walked.

"You know. Homer."

The caretaker considered it carefully. "I don't know this Homer. It is Soviet? We do not name our planes Homer."

"Damn." Remo shook his head. "I forgot the designation. It was 'Mi' something."

The caretaker shrugged. "All Soviet aircraft are 'Mi' something. How about a special Mig? Fighter

jet, very fast, shot down *Apollo 21*. You want to see?"
He flipped on the lights. Hundreds of fluorescent
tubes flickered to life, shining stark white light on the
dingy shells of the retired dregs of the communist air
force.

"No, no. It's a helicopter."

"Ah. Good. Lots of helicopters here."

The caretaker snapped off the lights and led Remo
along the wall to another corridor, then into another
cavernous space. The flickering lights came on to reveal a handful of drooping vertical-takeoff craft, several of them stripped for parts.

"Mi-6," the caretaker announced grandly, waving
at a hunk of rusty junk. "First helicopter ever in all
the world to go three hundred kilometers per hour
and winner of international trophy in 1961."

"Very impressive. But not what I'm looking for."

"Mi-8?"

"Never heard of that one."

"It is the most widely used helicopter in the
world!" the caretaker exclaimed. "Ten thousand of
them were put in service in forty countries! Very
easy now to get parts."

Remo examined the hunk of metal that slouched
in the gloom. "Not big enough to be Homer. Got anything bigger?"

"Big? You want big, I give you big. Here is the Mi-10."

"Where?"

"Right here, in front of you!" Thousand dollars or no thousand dollars, the caretaker was beginning to get annoyed with this Remo Lastly.

"Oh. I see. But that's not really so big."

"It could lift fifteen thousand kilograms!"

"Homer's bigger than that."

Pummel nodded, touched his lips with his fingers and nodded again. "Of course! This way."

Pummel used his keys to open the padlock on a pair of double doors and led Remo into an overgrown courtyard.

"Mi-26 Halo," Pummel announced grandly. "Biggest operational helicopter in all the world. It carries ninety soldiers, as much as Lockheed C-130 Hercules. First helicopter to be engineered successfully with eight-blade main rotor. Very important to Soviets and then to Russia. Many different configurations. Mi-26MS for medical evacuations. Mi-26TZ is a flying fuel tanker. Mi-26TM is flying crane."

"Flying crane to lift how much?" Remo asked.

"Twenty thousand kilograms," Pummel announced like a sideshow barker.

"Not enough," Remo declared.

"But it has to be enough. Nothing can lift more than this."

"Homer can. Homer can lift 80,000 pounds. What's through there?" Remo didn't wait for an answer, but strode purposefully toward a padlocked steel door set into a cinder-block wall.

"There is nothing through there." Pummel scampered in front of Remo and stood in his path, but then Remo vanished. When the caretaker spun around, he found Remo had gotten around him. Somehow.

"If there's nothing in there, why's it locked?"

"There is some storage of dangerous parts. Not very interesting."

"How do you know what I find interesting? So far you've been wrong about everything you thought I was interested in. I want to see what's back there."

"I do not have the key."

"I could just climb over the wall," Remo suggested.

"Be my guest," Pummel said.

To the caretaker's dismay, Remo set his fingertips against the rough cinder block and began to scale the sheer face of the wall. What the man found to grip was unknown, but up he went, twenty feet.

"Wait! No! There is razor wire set in the top. It will cut you to pieces."

Remo was kneeling on the sheer side of the wall and holding on with one hand as he pinched at the rolls of rusty razor wire with his fingers. Bundles of rusty wire fell to the ground on either side of Pummel and rolled away like corroded tumbleweeds.

"You are not allowed in there!" Pummel shouted.

But the top of the wall was clear and Remo slipped over soundlessly. Pummel expected—and even hoped—to hear the heavy thud of Remo's body crashing to the ground on the other side of the wall. He would claim the man was an intruder, with some strange purpose of his own. Who knew what the American was up to? He would ask the police. That would solve the problem.

But there was no thud. There was no sound at all. What had become of Remo Lastly?

Then, to his horror, the doorknob on the cinderblock wall turned, and the door opened a fraction of an inch. The heavy chain stretched taut. The massive padlock jiggled. The inch-thick steel door seemed to deform, as if the chain was digging into it—but that was an impossibility.

The steel chain was brand-new, links thick enough to tie down aircraft during heavy windstorms, but it stretched apart as if it were made of taffy and parted.

Remo swung the door open. "It wasn't locked on the other side," he explained.

Pummel didn't know what to do or say, so he followed forlornly after Remo.

The storage room was, in fact, a gigantic plot of hard-packed earth inside the cinder-block wall. A cracked slab of Soviet-era concrete was blackened with ancient mechanical grease and oil.

"Where's Homer?" Remo asked. "He was here. Oh, look. It tells all about him."

Remo strolled to a faded wooden display for the museum visitors to read. Under yellowy protective acrylic was a faded page describing the aircraft that had once been here.

"Mi-12! That's it!" Remo said.

Pummel had no idea how he could read the old sign in the nearly lightless night.

"Lessee. Biggest helicopter in the world. Two outriggers. Each outrigger had two engines in it to power a rotor. Three of them built in the late 1960s by the U.S.S.R. and they never entered active service." Remo made a low whistle of amazement. "Hey, wow, listen to this. The Mi-12 was bigger than a Boeing 727. It was made to carry 120 passengers. Once carried a 36-ton payload to an altitude of more than two kilometers. Now, that's a helicopter!"

"Yes," Pummel agreed, feeling glum and searching in his pants pocket for his old Tokarev handgun.

"So, where is it?"

"Gone."

"Gone where?"

"To another museum." Pummel didn't really expect the American to believe it.

"That's funny," Remo said, "because the Russian government records say it's still here."

"Actually," Pummel said, "I sold it."

"I thought so." He saw the gun. He couldn't help but see the gun. But he didn't seem bothered by the gun. "Who'd you sell it to?"

"That is my secret. Who are you with? CIA?"

"I'll tell you if you tell me."

Pummel sighed. "I don't know who they were."

"Then I don't know who I work for," Remo snapped.

"It doesn't matter," Pummel said. "For now, your disappearance will remain a mystery." And just like that, he shot point-blank at Remo Lastly's chest.

The bullet smacked into the cinder blocks on the far side of the empty yard that had once displayed the massive Russian helicopter and made a tiny puff of dust in the moonlight.

But where was Remo Lastly?

"Here," Remo said as he appeared alongside the caretaker, wadding up the antique Tokarev like a newspaper full of bad news. The old die-hard Soviet soldier regarded his mangled keepsake with shock and awe.

"Who really bought the Homer?"

The caretaker, who was ex-KGB, after all, delivered a sudden blow to the American's abdomen, but the American stepped aside and snapped the caretaker's wrist with a jerk. The caretaker flopped on the ground and lashed at Remo's ankles with a savage kick. He missed, although he could have sworn it was a perfect kick.

"You're a nimble old cuss," Remo commented as he flicked the caretaker's leg with his own expensive Italian shoes and broke the bone cleanly in half. "Not the nimblest or the oldest I've ever met, by a long shot, but pretty slick. You an old Soviet special-forces type or something?"

The caretaker answered by panting through clenched teeth.

"Not answering, huh?"

The old caretaker refused to answer. It was simply a matter of pride. "There are Russian soldiers in the guard shack outside. See how fast they come." And with that he began shouting in Russian—he didn't have too much pride to call for help. He was an old man, after all.

"Wow, listen to that echo," Remo commented.

Pummel's bellows reflected back to him from the four brick walls and met in the middle, then bounced off the opposite walls, multiplying exponentially. The din was maddening.

"Wow!" Remo exclaimed so loud it hurt Pummel's ears. Then the echo gave him a shove in the back, and the next echo made him wince.

"Echo!" Remo bellowed, and the noise was as immense as an overhead airburst.

Pummel clapped his hands over his ears but it was too late. He was overcome with the pain as the echo sucker-punched him in the back of the head.

"Forgot to mention!" Remo shouted, each word like an air horn in the eardrums. It was louder than any revving aircraft engine, louder than anything. "I gave the guards the night off!"

The jumble of words had no meaning to Pummel, who was on his knees, letting the sonic booms of Remo's voice support his body. When the immense echoes finally diminished, Pummel toppled on his side. The ringing still filled his head, but it was only in his head. His ears were as nonfunctional as a Soviet lunar lander.

"Gonna ask you again," Remo said. "Who has Homer?"

Pummel shook his head weakly. He couldn't hear a thing.

Remo took the man by the hand and effortlessly dragged his limp body to the hard-packed earth, where he used a finger on Pummel's left hand to write letters in the earth. The abrasion quickly tore off the flesh and crumbled the bone. When the first finger was worn down to no more than a nub, Remo used another, then propped Pummel up in a sitting position. The old man contemplated the bloody stumps, deeply embedded with oily dirt.

Remo gestured at the message written in blood and gore on the ground: "Who has Homer?"

Pummel somehow got beyond the torture in his hand and the muddled condition of his brain and managed to refuse once again.

"Do your worst," he said.

"Okay," Remo said with a shrug, and did as requested.

That lasted all of fifteen seconds.

"Guess I should have tried that trick in the first place," Remo said.

Pummel was rapidly scribbling the name of the buyer of the Homer on a piece of scrap paper from his pocket. He thrust it at Remo with his good hand, then rolled his eyes, pleading for Remo to release his earlobe.

Remo examined the information on the page, decided it was as complete as he was going to get and said farewell to the murderous little museum caretaker.

"Bye-bye," he said, patting Pummel twice on the forehead. The force was not enough to break the skull, but was sufficient to liquefy the neural networks that kept the old man walking, talking and breathing. All such function ceased.

Remo returned to the stinking little apartment with its miserable little cot, and he used the phone to make a person-to-person call to the United States of America.

It was a Soviet-era phone, but at least it was late Soviet. It did have buttons instead of a dial.

Remo put his finger on the 1 button and held it down.

Somehow, in ways that Remo didn't want to begin to understand, pressing the 1 button from anywhere in the world gave him a direct connection to his home base. To Upstairs. It involved some sort of computer magic that Remo didn't even care to understand. All he cared about was that the phone was answered and answered by the correct person. Mr. Upstairs himself—Harold W. Smith, director of the ultra-awfully-secret agency of the United States known as CURE.

"Hi, Smitty," Remo said.

"Remo," Smith said.

Remo heard the unmistakable sound of another human being breathing in the same office as Harold W. Smith. He still wasn't used to that. "How's Junior Smitty coming along?" Remo asked. "What's his name? Mick? Horton?"

"Mark Howard is doing just fine. Give me your report on the situation in Monino."

"Ugly. Gray. Depressing."

"The air force museum?"

"That description fits the museum, the town, the hookers, all of it."

"The helicopter?" Smith demanded, his voice as sour as a bottle of kosher dill brine and just as pleasant to have spit out at you, even from across the ocean.

"Homer ain't home. The nice man who runs the place supplemented his income by selling it to another nice man in Greece. I will spell the name rather than try to pronounce it."

"Go ahead," Smith said.

"H-i-m-i-n-o-p-o—"

"Hermes Himinoplous of Athens," Mark Howard interjected. "Up-and-coming arms merchant out of Athens. Specializes in small arms, but he's been more ambitious in recent years. Looks like he has contacts in Turkmenistan and Georgia who'll channel him Soviet leftover hardware. He must have found some friends in the Russian military, as well."

"I agree. What sort of surveillance does Mr. Himinoplous rate from the intelligence agencies?" Smith asked.

"Hello?" Remo said. "Remember me?"

"Very little," Mark Howard answered in the background. "Small-arms merchants are a dime a dozen. Looks like the Greeks have a man inside the Himinoplous organization, but the mole's reports don't say anything about wholesaling helicopters. The inside man could be loyal to Himinoplous or he could be in the dark on this one. It's the kind of sale you'd want to keep low profile as much as possible. Even keep it from your own people. Stealing the world's biggest helicopter would be worth bragging about in the taverna."

"Agreed. Where's Himinoplous now?"

"New York City. He's on his honeymoon."

Remo hung up, then stood in the middle of the

horrid little room trying not to breathe the smell of very unwashed linens. The phone rang.

"Dmitri's Yoga Studio. Our slogan—Get Bent."

"Remo, why did you hang up the phone?" Smith asked, irritation creeping into the sourness.

"You were done talking to me, right?"

"Wrong."

"Maybe you should acknowledge my presence. Common courtesy. Do you want me to go bust up the Greek honeymoon?"

"That won't be necessary. Mark has already tracked down Himinoplous's customer. The trail leads to Wyoming, then quits. We'll keep looking for the Mi-12 from this end."

"Smitty, why do we care about a great big helicopter, anyway?"

"Clandestine, large-mass cargo transfers have a tendency to be highly illegal. I'll be happy to explain the implications when you return. Suffice it to say, the very fact that someone invested the resources necessary to secretly repair and take possession of a craft like that is enough to arouse my suspicion."

"I came to the armpit of the world because you have suspicions?" Remo demanded.

"They may turn out to be fully grounded or they may be insubstantial," Smith admitted. "Regardless, your part is done for now. You can come home and forget all about it, if that is what you wish."

"It is what I wish," Remo said as he cradled the phone and left the museum. He was annoyed, but Smith annoyed him constantly. The new man at the office—just a kid, really—annoyed him just as much. He'd be more than happy to forget all about the really big, suspiciously stolen helicopter.

In fact, Remo didn't think of it again for eight years.

3

Once he had been an ordinary man living an ordinary life. Then, out of the blue, he was given the opportunity to become something more. Something better than human. He became Camou-Nin, one of the most highly trained camouflage artists on the planet. Using the traditional martial-arts techniques of the ninja warriors, combined with the latest technological props, the Camou-Nin were the world masters of hiding in plain sight.

Camou-Nin 098 may have been born Herman Oscar Jacobs, but he gave up his identity when he joined the ranks of the Camou-Nin, and now the Camou-Nin were his family, his society and his lifestyle.

Camou-Nin 098 was at one with a maple tree at the moment, lounging in a split in the trunk. His uniform was a synthetic, ultradurable, dual-layer fabric. The inside layer, against his skin, was filled with narrow capillaries that opened when a tiny electric current was applied to the fabric, and performed a sort of high-frequency directional constriction that pushed air through the channels. The openings of the capillaries were in the bottom of the built-in footies. The top layer of the material was an entirely non-porous compound material that persistently absorbed the ambient temperature.

The effect of this was that a human body clothed in the material had no thermal signature in almost any environment—except for the feet, where air was channeled into the underside of the tip of one foot and channeled out the other. In a moment of crisis, the Camou-Nin 098 stealth warrior could stifle the airflow simply by clenching his toes.

This was just one of the engineering marvels incorporated into the design of the Camou-Nin outfit. There was also more standard equipment—the very best available in terms of miniaturization and levels of electromagnetic and radio-frequency emissions that were virtually undetectable by modern spy-detection sensors, as well as audio magnification electronics and eye-blink-controlled video optimization systems.

Add to that the most thorough self-concealment training in the business, including self-camouflage techniques, motionlessness training, breath-stifling skills, as well as lock picking, electronic-security disabling and biometrics-bypass education. The end result was a Camou-Nin man or woman with the ability to infiltrate and penetrate virtually any secure environment.

The Camou-Nin commandos were developed with just one task in mind—the penetration of the security system at the special research laboratory in the little hidden valley in Pennsylvania. They were the brainchild of the HAAC—Health At All Costs—special projects director, after the failure of his normal breaking-and-entering teams.

Camou-Nin 001, 002, 003, 004 and 005 were dispatched after a year of training to the Pennsylvania suburbs with a single mission: obtain a full-tissue-spectrum sample of the apatosaurus—blood, bone, skin, muscle, fat.

The team was dropped off in the parking lot of the Sunny Fields Condominiums and never heard from again.

Camou-Nin Team II was twice the size and made a dispersed insertion. They approached the compound on foot from miles away in every direction. They made it into the grounds, melting through the darkness like silent and skilled vipers after field mice. There was no sign of alarm or security, but one by one their video feeds went black and their audio turned off. It was as if they just stopped existing.

Subsequent Camou-Nin had more success at least in the penetration phase of the operation, if you measured the penetration in yardage. Not that any of them had ever managed to actually reach the building, the actual biocontainment structure on the special-purpose research campus. Let alone sneak inside. Let alone neutralize the human element and steal the thirty-ton biological specimen they had come for.

Always something seemed to go wrong, and eventually the corpses of the Camou-Nin commandos began reappearing. They were shipped overnight to the offices of the company that had funded the Camou-Nin. At least, that was the rumor Camou-Nin 098 had heard.

Frustration at the top levels was said to have been extreme, and resulted in Camou-Nin Team VII, which wasn't so much a team as a terrorist attack that somehow went eerily silent before any of the rocket-launched grenades even started firing. The bodies of Camou-Nin Team VII ended up being arranged on the front lawns of the corporate entity that sponsored the teams. That was a nuisance.

But what was truly meaningful was that, arranged

along with the corpses of Camou-Nin Team VII was the personal assistant to the vice president of new product development. With him was the vice president of new product development himself.

The bodies had been laid out very carefully on the fresh-cut front lawn. Must have taken the killers a long time to do it. They were bent to form letters that read: "WHO'S NEXT?"

Two commando corpses made the *W.* Another two were used for the *H* and the *X.* The apostrophe was the right forearm of the assistant to the vice president. It seemed to have been removed with the precision cutting tools preferred by a purveyor of fine cuts of beef. The vice president himself was used for the question mark—his body for the hook-shaped part, and his severed head for the little dot on the bottom.

The loss was alarming, the message was clear and the company, amazingly enough, continued the Camou-Nin program anyway, but took a new approach to the problem. Clearly, they were not going to insert an armed force to steal away the biological specimen—yet. But maybe someday they would. Meanwhile, they had barracks full of Camou-Nin commandos on the payroll, already trained and ready for action. So the company sent them into action.

Sort of.

"The Camou-Nin commandos were trained first and foremost to be invisible," the new vice president of product procurement explained in his presentation to the president and the board of directors. "Let's send them in as watchers. Surveillance. Their purpose will be to get into the grounds and simply observe. It's what they know how to do."

"Son, you want them to just go in there and keep an eye on the place? What the hell good is that going to do for us?"

"Maybe nothing," the new vice president admitted. "But consider this—we know of at least five other pharmaceutical companies that are actively seeking access to that specimen. Rumors are, they're having the same kind of luck we are. Which is to say, none at all. But one of them might find a way in. Somebody else might figure out what the security at this place is all about and devise a way past it. When that happens, we want to know about it. Or maybe the thing will die. Maybe there will be a fire or earthquake or flood or some other kind of event that will compromise the security around the place. But just maybe, we'll be the first responders to such an event."

"Pshaw. You're talking a lot of what-ifs, son. I

don't see why we ought to sink more money into this little plan at all."

"But we won't be," the VP insisted. "We've got the Camou-Nin commandos just sitting there doing nothing. Why not do something with them?"

The company president saw the financial logic in that. What was missing from the equation was the danger involved. "The Camou-Nin get nixed, who-ever nixed them will come looking for you, too. Just like they did old what's-his-name."

"I'm willing to take the chance that that won't happen. After all, Camou-Nin Team VIII will be dif-ferent. Less threatening."

"HOW ARE WE SUPPOSED to be 'less threatening,' ex-actly?" asked the collective members of Camou-Nin Team VIII when they were assembled for duty.

"Unarmed," the vice president of product pro-curement announced grandly.

This did not sit well with surviving Camou-Nin. Several opted out—opted out of a five-year contract worth a cool million dollars.

Their excuse—can't spend it if you're dead.

Which kind of made sense.

On the other hand, what was waiting for Camou-Nin 098 in the outside world if he quit? He recalled his preenrollment lifestyle disdainfully. He'd been a bum and a loser. He didn't fit in anywhere. In college it was the team, but he didn't make the pros. Then he found the Army, another boys' club where he fit in pretty well—but they kicked him out for his indiscriminate groping of females, enlisted and officers alike. He was desperate to find another boys' club that would take him. He needed that group environment. He was nothing without it. The Camou-Nin had found him, as it turned out, and for a year or so during the training the Camou-Nin were great. Best year of his life. Then the Camou-Nin began actually going out on Camou-Nin missions and not coming home again.

Still, the Camou-Nin were all that Camou-Nin 098 had left. He even thought of himself now by his Camou-Nin designation. The man he was—that loser Herbert Oscar Jacobs—was best forgotten. Call him Ninety-eight.

So Camou-Nin 098 stayed when most of the surviving Camou-Nin left. It was just him and a few pals. Camou-Nin 078, Snate for short, what a joker! Liked to walk around with a couple of lit cigarettes dangling from his nostrils.

Camou-Nin 096 was a sex hound, famous for picking up any female, no matter how ugly or old. It didn't bother ol' Ninety-six when the other guys made fun of his unappealing bedmate. "Fact is, I'm sneaking some stranger into the barrack and you dudes ain't. Something's better than nothing, ain't it?" He saw his numeric designation as a sign of his virility. "Ninety-six is the same thing as 69, see?"

Another one was Camou-Nin 100. "Call me Hunnert, please," he'd say. He was a little dude, just barely tall enough to get into the military. He had a pretty stellar career working for Uncle Sam until one of his regular physicals showed that he was, in fact, a quarter inch too short for what the regulations required. The physician was a by-the-book kind of doctor who wouldn't take bribes or listen to reason, and next thing he knew the well-decorated soldier was booted on a technicality—just in time to pop up on the Camou-Nin radar. Whatever his name was before, he was Hunnert now.

And there was Camou-Nin 088. Another funny guy. Never met a meal he didn't like. He loved casinos and he knew every one of them within driving distance and could describe the pros and cons of their buffets in detail, though he never gambled. "I got my number 'cause when the recruiter found me, he bought me dinner at the local Old Mongol Buffet and I ate and ate the whole time he was talking. Get it? Ate and ate?"

There were a couple others, but it was a sorry handful of Camou-Nin now. Sorry because there were so few of them, and sorry because they essentially had no more balls left. They were in the field unarmed. Unarmed!

But at least they weren't getting killed anymore. The crazy idea had worked. The Camou-Nin were permitted by the unknown powers that protected the place to roam around the woods, keeping silently to the shadows, and just watch. And watch.

It was actually kind of a stupid, boring job, but it was something.

They were all surprised when the nutty scheme worked. They penetrated the grounds of the special-purpose research campus and lived to tell about it. They had been returning night after night, always unarmed, never venturing too close to the building, but keeping close watch on the goings-on in the facility.

But for a long time, nothing at all had happened. The job became downright boring.

Tonight, it went back to being terrifying.

4

Tom Dappling came awake, rolled onto the floor and snatched at the handgun that was hidden under his mattress, then got to his feet and aimed the weapon into every corner of the bedroom.

Empty.

He ran to the computer desk and tapped at the keys, silencing the beeping of the alarm. He looked at the graph of the disturbance that triggered the alarm.

The spikes went all the way to the top. This wasn't another false alarm. There had been a hundred false alarms, but the acoustical disturbances that triggered them were small. This was really, really big.

"Oh, shit," Dappling murmured and hurried to the front door, checking the bolt, even tugging on the security chain to assure himself it was tightly attached. He checked the peephole, then put his ear to the door. He saw and heard nothing.

Only then did he head back to the computer and

slip on the headset, tuning in the voices coming from the eavesdropping device. The tiny laser was mounted on the roof of the apartment building, directed at the skylights of the half-hidden facility down the long hillside. Most of the apartment dwellers had no clue the facility was even there.

Thomas Dappling hadn't understood the job when he took it. He thought it was easy cash. Then he heard the awful rumors from the other residents of the apartment building, and a few whispered questions back at the office gave him enough data to get the whole picture: there had been many watchers before him. They were all dead.

What made the rumors most bizarre was that it had not been the company that killed them. Muck Pharmaceutical was as ruthless as any pharmaceuticals company on the planet, but what reason would there have been for Muck Pharmaceutical to be killing off its own spies?

No. The others had been killed by the competition. Maybe Pharm & Farm LLC. Maybe HAAC. Maybe Meds-4-U. Hell, there had to be a hundred more out there. The little start-ups were just as ruthless as the pill giants with a prize like this. The truth was, whoever got the prize would be catapulted instantly into the top position. The prize was that big.

In the world of drugs and dreams, this was the biggest prize ever.

Which made the life of an insignificant corporate spy valueless.

Dappling had tried to resign his position, only to realize that was no safer an option. His supervisor referred his request to an upper-echelon Muck Pharmaceutical executive whose name wasn't even mentioned on the corporate financial reports. He informed Dappling that he had taken over Dappling's supervision personally, and that he had concerns about Dappling's request for transfer or resignation.

Dappling got the picture. He could quit if he wanted to, but then Muck Pharmaceutical would have to take measures to ensure he would not become a security leak.

"Nobody needs to know our business in Philadelphia," the unnamed executive said sternly.

"You can count on me," Dappling said sincerely. "I won't break the terms of my confidentiality agreement."

"This?" The executive made a derisive sound and lifted the signed form from Dappling's personnel file. "Worthless." The executive demonstrated how worthless it was by wadding it up and tossing it over Dappling's head. The stark little conference room had two chairs and one table and one wastepaper basket, all made of age-dulled brushed aluminum. The wad of paper bounced into the wastepaper basket loudly. Dappling didn't need to look to see it had made it in.

"Nice shot," he said sullenly.

"Thanks. I was in the NBA eight years." The executive waved his hand, where one finger sported a fat, glimmering world-champions ring. "Oops. Now I've gone and revealed my identity to you."

"No, really, I don't know anything about basketball," Dappling said.

"Still, it compromises my position."

"I absolutely promise you I'm not a security risk."

"You promise? You know what good a promise is? About as good as a confidentiality agreement."

In the end, Thomas Dappling deemed the wisest course of action was to stay with Muck Pharmaceutical and retain his position as their corporate spy at the special purpose research campus of the zoological gardens in Philadelphia.

He only prayed that whatever he was watching for would happen, and he could move on to other, safer jobs.

And he was pretty sure he knew what Muck Pharmaceutical was waiting for.

They were waiting for the creature to die—or for someone to kill it.

Many companies had already tried to take it or kill it. They had all been stymied as mysteriously as had the Muck Pharmaceutical corporate spies who came before Dappling—or so he had heard. Just rumors, really.

But the executive who denied Dappling his resignation felt compelled to give the young man the full story.

"Hired us one of the best paramilitary units on the world market," the executive said, toying with his ring, finding enough light to make it glimmer under the dusty fluorescent tubes that flickered in the uncovered ceiling fixture. The gold ring reflected in the executive's mirror-like sunglasses.

Dappling didn't want to hear the story. The more he heard, the more he could never, ever be trusted to leave the company. But the story went relentlessly on.

"Mercenaries. Mostly Americans who were not supposed to be inside the country, if you know what I mean. Uncle Sam gets really ticked off when he spends a quarter-million bucks to train a special-forces solider, only to have the soldier turn on him and do something antisocial. You know, murder."

Dappling did not want to know.

"Anyway, there couldn't have been a tougher bunch of grunts on the planet. We sent them in with all the right equipment. Automatic weapons and body armor. Specially designed troop transport with a flatbed for the specimen, fully armored. They could have staged a coup in Chicago with that much fire-power. We send them out to get us the specimen, and guess what?"

Dappling didn't want to guess.

"I'll tell you what. They were ambushed. Broke through the guard gates and drove up to the lab without any sign of trouble, and then they get attacked. By what, we don't know."

Dappling gulped, and couldn't help saying, "By what?"

"Yeah. What. They got attacked by some kind of a what. We heard it on their communications. We even got a glimpse of the thing. I'll tell you one thing. It wasn't human. It didn't come in an armored vehicle. And from everything we know, it was just one of whatever it was. The only thing we're too sure of is this—it wore an ivory dress."

Dappling's nervous giggle died in his throat. The executive wasn't joking when he added, "With orange embroidery. Of a dragon. And whatever it was that was wearing an ivory dress with orange embroidery, it wiped out our entire mercenary team."

"Killed them?"

"They got off a few shots. That was it. Then their communications went dead. A few hours later, the armored transport flatbed that they were supposed to use to extract the specimen drove itself through the plate glass into the lobby of our headquarters in Arlington, with the mercenary team on board. You wouldn't believe what it took to cover that up."

"I would, I promise."

"Whoever it was that wiped them out didn't use firearms. The only gunshot wounds were from friendly fire. Not knives, either. They were killed by hand. Broken necks. Crushed skulls. Burst hearts. Getting rid of the bodies was a real fiasco.

"The message was pretty clear. They knew the team was coming. They knew how to stop it. They knew where it came from. So that's why we're just sitting up on the hill watching the place. Now you know the whole story."

"I guess I do." Dappling gulped.

"Sorry. Got off on a tangent," the executive said with a wan smile. "What did you want to see me about?"

Dappling seemed to have forgotten himself. He

apologized for wasting the time of the unnamed ex-NBA executive in the mirror sunglasses and he went back to work.

He was more terrified than ever, but he was now more afraid of quitting than of staying. He began to pray every night that something would happen—at the facility, not to him—so that he could end his vigil.

Whoever wiped out the mercenary team must have been responsible for killing the other spies. According to apartment building gossip, the residents of 632 were always single men who stayed for a while, then began getting impatient. Dappling knew that feeling. A stakeout got old fast, and when you were staking out an apparently unmonitored, insecure facility, why not just venture in one night for a closer look?

Was that how the others got killed? They got too curious? Or was it simply a matter of whenever the unseen protector of the facility got around to snuffing them?

One thing was for sure: Thomas Dappling kept to himself. He did not venture out. He did not sneak over the line into the property of the research lab. He did not even go out onto his apartment balcony to take a look down at the grounds.

He just kept the computer up and running, and listened in on the acoustic sensor whenever the alarm went off. Half the time it was nothing. Somebody dumping a bunch of feed mangoes for the creature might make enough noise to trigger the alarm on the PC.

The laser and the sensors picked up recognizable sounds when conditions were perfect, which was almost never, but now he could make out human voices. Commands. Shouting. A clunk of something metal being dropped. This was definitely not the regular staff doing their regular business. Dappling heard the whine of the overhead cranes. That always set off the sound-activated alarm system, but even the crane sounded different. Burdened. Straining.

Dappling was shocked when he realized what he was not hearing—the honking of the creature. That idiot dinosaur—or walrus or whatever it was—was constantly honking and bleating and lowing for any reason. When people came, when people left, when food came, when the food was all gone, when the rain fell… Any minor disturbance was a cause for complaint.

But now it was silent.

Which meant the creature was unconscious or dead.

Dappling prayed as he dialed the hotline number, "Please be dead please be dead."

5

Remo was a dead man, but he didn't let that slow
him down.

His death was old news, anyway. He had been executed in the electric chair, framed without malice
for a murder he did not commit.

Remo Williams had been a police office in
Newark, New Jersey, war veteran and rookie. He
was quite a skillful executioner while working for
Uncle Sam, and the authorities found it easy to believe he had brought a commando's sensibilities to
the police force—where they didn't belong.

There should have been some understanding for
the young man who had served his country well. An
orphan, raised as a ward of the state, who had made
something good of his life. There should have been
some leniency by the courts. Life in prison, at least.
Surely he did not deserve the death penalty.

But Remo Williams got death, in one of the most

efficient, streamlined, book-him, try-him, fry-him cases ever to cascade through the U.S. court system. Remo's assertions of innocence went unheard. His conviction went unappealed. It all happened so fast even he didn't quite believe it.

It all seemed surreal. His stay in the penitentiary was as brief as a trip to summer camp. The priest who showed up the night before his execution date handed him a pill. It would save his life, the priest said. Yeah, whatever, Padre. Still, Remo took the pill, stuck in his mouth and chomped down on it as instructed. He never believed it would work.

He didn't believe it when he woke up, either. Not dead at all.

He didn't believe it when he learned that the whole affair—the frame-up, the trial, the tinkering with the electric chair—had been engineered by his prospective employers. It was their way of recruiting Remo Williams.

Normally, Remo did not respond well to these kinds of strong-arm tactics. But, as the priest explained, the organization that was doing the recruiting had no choice but to engineer things the way it did. It was a supersecret agency within the federal government, known as CURE. The priest—and Remo had guessed this already—was no priest. He was a former CIA Agent Conrad MacCleary, now half of the staff of CURE.

"You could have asked me first," Remo insisted.

"Naw. Wouldn't work," MacCleary said. "If you said no, we'd have had to kill you."

"And if I say no now?" Remo pressed.

"Well," MacCleary admitted, "we'll kill you in that case, too. No hard feelings."

"So you could have asked me first," Remo insisted.

Conrad shrugged. "I guess you're right. Upstairs is sort of a coldhearted son of a bitch, and I guess he didn't think it through. He just assumed you would do your duty to your country when called upon."

"I'd like to meet Mr. Upstairs," Remo said.

Remo's choice—duty or death—didn't amount to much of a choice at all. He took the job with every intention of stabbing Upstairs in the back when the time came and blowing the lid on the whole CURE cover-up.

He still had days when this seemed like the best course of action.

But years had passed, and he still worked for Upstairs. MacCleary was long gone, an honorable death in the line of duty. Upstairs took the news in stoic silence.

Upstairs had a name, if not much in the way of emotion or personality. Upstairs was Harold W. Smith, also from the CIA. He was as old and tough and sour as last year's dried-up lemon still dangling on the tree. He had been calling Remo's shots for years.

He wasn't the only one. Remo's shots were also called by the man hired to train him.

Just as Conrad MacCleary had chosen Remo, having witnessed the man's battlefield exploits, so too did MacCleary chose Chiun. Chiun was a senior citizen, and the current legacy-holder of the Sinanju dynasty of assassins. They were said to be the world's most skilled assassins, and from what MacCleary had heard and witnessed, the reputation was deserved. MacCleary was insistent, and Smith signed off on the hiring of the old Korean martial-arts trainer. MacCleary actually sneaked into North Korea to fetch the old man.

There was little chance that the Master of Sinanju would turn out to be anything more than a village elder with a few karate skills. There was no chance whatsoever that the Master of Sinanju would accept a commission to train a non-Korean, let alone an American. It was against the Sinanju code and, besides, the old man was probably a loyal communist.

But Chiun agreed to come.

If he did come, he might not even survive the journey to New York State.

But he survived.

And, when he came, the man with the lofty title of Master of Sinanju would almost certainly turn out to be far less in terms of skills and ability than Mac-Cleary promised. MacCleary, after all, drank to excess.

But Chiun was everything MacCleary had promised, and far, far more. His skills and abilities turned out to be so impressive that CURE eventually dismissed Remo's other trainers and handed full responsibility to Chiun. When Remo emerged from the training for his first mission for CURE, he was already skilled in methods the CIA never dreamed of, that the KGB would have invaded a country to obtain. He was on his way to learning the art, the way of Sinanju. Remo's early field success as CURE's hired assassin were all Smith had hoped for.

Harold W. Smith was pleased with the success of the one and only member of the CURE enforcement arm, and he fully intended to remove Chiun from the equation when Remo's training was complete, but Smith found that dear, departed Conn MacCleary had opened a real can of worms. CURE had created a two-headed monster in the partnership of Chiun and Remo, and Smith realized gradually as the years passed, that Remo Williams was no longer under his control. His coldly calculated plan for controlling his enforcement arm was in tatters. Remo had become skilled in the ways of Sinanju. If Smith ever required the assassin's execution—well, he was out of luck. Remo wouldn't cooperate.

Smith had counted on having complete control over the life and death of the CURE enforcement arm. He had never counted on Remo becoming his own man.

This was problematic. CURE's very existence depended upon its anonymity, and Smith himself lived with knowledge that the slightest exposure of the organization would require it to immediately be shut down and the evidence of its existence erased. That included himself.

Sewn into the lining of Smith's suit jacket—each and every suit jacket he owned—was a coffin-shaped pill. And it was there for the purpose of erasing Harold W. Smith.

But if the worst happened, and CURE needed to be shut down and erased from existence, Remo would not go down easily. It would require astounding trickery to bring that about.

And if Smith was successful in carrying out this feat, Chiun would know. And Chiun would retaliate.

The retaliation would be savage and public—for what would Chiun care to expose the ridiculous subterfuge of the upstart democratic republic that dominated in North America? He would expose CURE, he would seek vengeance on Smith and then on the one man who held some sway upon CURE: the President of the United States. Chiun would not stop there. He would not be satisfied until he had claimed the lives of all the men who had ever been in that position. Every living ex-President would die. There was little doubt that Chiun would succeed in killing them all.

But that was inconsequential next to the scandal that would erupt with the exposure of CURE. The public outcry would be monstrous. The powerful, fraternal twins that filled the allotment of spaces in the American two-party system would be equally culpable, equally discredited, and they would probably both crumble. The best that could be hoped for would be disastrous and costly political upheaval. The worst would be the disintegration of the federal governmental authority.

Smith knew how strong the established government was, but he knew its linchpin could be pulled by a single old and enraged man, should he feel the urge to do it.

Smith ran the numbers in his head. Then on a calculator. Then on computer. He used all his skills to assess the probabilities, and even using his most conservative estimates, the percentages were staggering.

SMITH COULD NOT even remember the day that his understanding of the situation shifted inexorably. It was on that day that he understood that even attempting to assassinate either of the Masters was so unlikely to succeed, and the repercussions of the failure were so monstrous, that he could no longer consider it. If and when CURE was required to be erased from existence, the safest possible option was to simply erase all the senior staff—there were three of them now—and hope the Masters of Sinanju moved on to other things and kept the knowledge of CURE to themselves.

Harold W. Smith was not inclined to hope for anything, certainly not in terms of security strategy, but it was clear that the entity that was CURE was no longer in his control as he had hoped it would be, back in the early days.

That seemed like a long, long time ago.

TONIGHT—RATHER, this morning—Smith had more-immediate problems to deal with. He had stayed at the office late to debrief Remo Williams face-to-face. It was the best way. Remo could be absent-minded about the facts, and getting a good, comprehensive report out of the man over the phone was virtually impossible. He wanted to satisfy himself that a certain persistently troublesome drug importer in Ohio was no longer importing drugs—and that his demise had been accomplished in a manner that would not grab too much attention.

Remo described a drug-running boat on Lake Erie and the iceberg that appeared out of nowhere to rip the hull open and send it to the murky depths, 150 feet down.

"An iceberg, Remo?" Smith demanded.

"Hell, I don't know. It was something big and sharp enough to put a hole in a cocaine boat. If they ever find it and take a look, they can decide for themselves what did it."

"I take it there were no survivors," Smith asked.

"Smitty, of course there were no survivors."

Remo went down below and went to bed in the private suites Remo and Chiun sometimes occupied at Folcroft. Smith was planning on heading for home when the first indications of trouble came out of Pennsylvania. Mark Howard was still at his desk when they came in.

"It's the special-purpose research campus," Mark Howard announced.

"I see," Smith said as he returned to his seat behind his desk and pressed the hidden button that brought his under-glass monitors to life. He watched the feeds from the zoological gardens in Philadelphia SPRC security system. He took only enough time to convince himself that this was not a systems failure or a false alarm. There was nothing false about it.

Smith was not surprised by what he saw.

In fact, he'd seen this coming for years.

"Mark, please get Master Chiun," Smith said. "At once."

Mark was already heading out the door and he almost jogged out of sight.

Any delay would have risked attracting the anger of Master Chiun. And Master Chiun was going to be very angry indeed when he saw what was happening in Philadelphia.

IT WAS a little after three in the morning, and the high-security wing at Folcroft Sanitarium was especially quiet. The young couple who lived across the hall had recently moved out. Now the only residents of the high-security wing, aside from a few human vegetables, were the Masters of Sinanju. Remo and

Chiun had maintained their unpleasant, sparse suite at Folcroft since Remo's very first days as a CURE recruit. He didn't like it there, but at the moment it was the only home he had, aside from a tin box on wheels somewhere down in South Carolina. The camper in the mostly deserted campground near Myrtle Beach wasn't much of a home, either, not to Remo's way of thinking.

Once he and Chiun had lived in a castle. Castle Sinanju was an old church in Boston renovated for condominiums then purchased by CURE to appease Master Chiun. Remo and Chiun were its sole occupants until the place was burned to the ground by a Mafia arsonist. The arsonist and the crime family who'd hired him were no longer in existence.

Now Remo and Chiun lived at Folcroft or they lived in the camper in South Carolina, but Remo had been unwilling to go back to the camper. He wanted Chiun to be at Folcroft. He was worried about Chiun. Somehow even knowing Chiun and knowing Sinanju, and knowing that Chiun could diagnose his own illnesses and that he would never go to a Folcroft doctor, it still made Remo feel better that he and Chiun were at Folcroft.

Chiun was sick. Chiun didn't look sick, he didn't act sick and he was still one of the two strongest human beings on the planet. There was no evidence of palsy, jaundice, accelerated heart rate, difficulty breathing or even nasal congestion. Still, Remo was convinced that Chiun was sick. The dogs had known it, too.

These particular dogs had been trained to sniff out human disease, even when the disease had not yet begun to do its destructive work. Those dogs could have been of great beneficial to humanity—except that the dogs were also trained to make sure the sickies never became a drain on the profits of their medical-benefits provider. These dogs tore the throats out of a lot of people whose only crime was that they would probably be getting an expensive disease. It was a big insurance scam, in this case perpetrated by the insurance company. Chiun and Remo had put the dogs to sleep.

They weren't bad dogs. They were just trained that way.

And those dogs had known Chiun had some kind of illness.

Remo wished he had kept one of those dogs.

Sometimes he lay awake at night and listened to the loud breathing of Chiun as he slept, until Chiun would abruptly bark at him across the room to quit making so much racket and go to sleep. There was no sign that Chiun was losing his edge. If Remo's wakeful breathing was enough to annoy and wake Chiun, then the man clearly had his faculties.

Still Chiun was very, very old and he had lived through much physical strain, and even a Master of Sinanju could not live forever.

The problem was that Chiun would not admit that he was sick. The dogs who had sniffed out his illness, he claimed, were mistaken. Any signs of weakness or aging that Remo saw were figments of Remo's imagination.

But that's what you would expect Chiun to say, and Remo knew in his gut that it was not true. He knew Chiun was sick; he just didn't know what to do about it.

He worried about it more and more, and sometimes it kept him up nights and sometimes it came to him in his dreams. Sometimes he didn't even know if he was awake or asleep. Like right now, when the worry changed to curiosity. His hearing picked up the clap of leather-soled shoes in the hallway of the private wing of Folcroft Sanitarium. It was pretty late at night for someone to be visiting the vegetables. They had to be coming to the Masters' suite.

Remo could identify the visitor by the cadence of

the footsteps. There was a knock on the door. Remo knew better than to wait for Chiun to rise and answer it. Remo was already at the door, sweeping it open before the knocking was done.

"Hey, Junior," Remo said. "Are you working late or in early?"

"Both," said Mark Howard, assistant director of Folcroft Sanitarium and assistant director of CURE. He looked uneasy. "I need to speak to Master Chiun."

"He's sleeping right now. Would you care to leave your calling card?"

"I must speak directly to Master Chiun," Mark Howard said.

"I am here." Chiun was at the door of his own bedroom, fully dressed, at ease in a green kimono embroidered with golden dragons, his arms tucked in the sleeves, as still as if he had been standing there for an hour in deep meditation.

"Master Chiun," Howard said. "Good morning."

"Good morning, Prince Howard," Chiun said with a slight bowing of his head.

"I am sorry to wake you," Howard said.

"No apology is necessary for the Prince Regent," Chiun said. "How may I be of service?"

"May I speak to you, Master Chiun?"

"We are speaking."

Mark Howard was uneasy. He seemed to remember something important, then with grave deliberation reached up and scratched his throat with one finger three times.

"Three words. A song," Remo said. "'Stairway to Heaven.'"

But Chiun seemed to get the message. He stepped forward urgently, taking Mark Howard by the elbow and leading him out of the suite. "You are overtired and speaking nonsense," Chiun said over his shoulder. "Go back to bed."

Then Chiun and Mark Howard were gone and the door closed behind them. Remo wondered what that was all about. He could have followed them. He could have stayed at a distance and listened to their conversation, but Chiun would have heard him listening.

He tried going back to bed.

MARK HOWARD FELT the old man's fingers like a plumber's wrench on his elbow, tight enough to hold it firmly without exactly breaking it. Mark was fairly levitated down the hall, and carried up the stairs to the executive office of Folcroft Sanitarium. It was a quiet wing at all times, but especially now a full five hours before Harold W. Smith's secretary, old Mrs.

Mikulka, showed up. There were no lights on in the adjoining halls, just the minimal exit-sign lights on the stairwells, until they came to Harold Smith's office.

Smith was at his desk, and the air in the office was warm in a way that Chiun could sense that they had been working here for hours. Bleeding their body heat into the walls, and allowing their electric machinery to taint the air with ozone. Chiun did not care about these things.

"What of it, Emperor?"

Harold W. Smith, director of Folcroft Sanitarium, director of CURE, looked at the old Master and said, "There has been an incident at the special-purpose research campus of the zoological gardens in Philadelphia."

Chiun's ancient hazel eyes glistened with alarm. "It has been some time since the conspirators dared to approach Dr. Derringer."

"They have dared this time, Master Chiun, and they have succeeded."

Chiun's face blanched. "Do not tell me the private garden was violated."

"It was."

"Emperor, what of my dragon?"

Smith shifted uneasily in his seat. "We don't know

yet, Master Chiun. We believe that there has been some sort of break-in at the facility. The security systems would suggest as much. A substantial break-in."

"Emperor, do not mince words. What of my dragon?"

Smith waved his hand helplessly and said, "The dragon is dead."

Chiun's eyes blazed.

"Its keeper is dead, as well. She and the apatosaurus appear to have been poisoned."

"Poison? The tool of the amateur assassin. To what purpose?"

"They wanted the specimen, Master Chiun. They wanted the apatosaurus and they are taking it. It is still happening." Smith gestured at his desktop and depressed a button under the desk with his foot. The screen mounted under the glass top blazed to life, with a number of vivid windows showing ridiculous data and the grainy images of the special-purpose research campus.

Chiun knew the place. He had gone there many times, and it was easy to see at a glance that much was very wrong. He stepped behind the desk, something he very rarely did, and jabbed a finger at an image in the corner, where it showed the collapsed body of a woman with strewed hair, her face hidden against the ground. "It is Dr. Derringer."

"Poisoned," Mark Howard said. "We have to assume she is dead."

Chiun nodded sadly. "She no longer breathes. Her body stiffens already."

Smith touched a button and brought another window to life. It showed the holding pen of the great beast that had been brought back from Africa by Chiun himself, with the help of some others and the interference of many.

Master Chiun was aghast at what he saw. At once he knew that the great creature, like its handler, was dead. It no longer breathed.

"The dragon flies in death!" Chiun gasped. "This is unheard-of in all the tales of dragons that are reliable."

"It does not fly, Master Chiun," Smith said. "It is being airlifted out of the holding pen."

Smith did something on his keyboard that seemed to alter the view of the great indoor holding area, and now Chiun could see that the roof of the structure had been ripped apart. Even in the grainy, dark images he could make out a network of cables ascending from some hidden harness around the belly of the flopping dead beast and pulling it skyward. Smith adjusted something else on his computer contraption, and sound came from hidden speakers. It was a roar, the throbbing of helicopter rotors. They sounded massive. They would have to be in order to lift the beast.

"They murdered it and now they are stealing my dragon," Chiun said.

CHIUN APPEARED silently angry, yes, but even more so intense, when he said, "Will you have a transport plane prepared, Emperor?"

"There is little we can do until we know where to send you."

"Charter a plane. A fast falcon of a plane with well-glued wings. It shall be of the kind that spans a continent on a single fueling and takes horrid See-Ows to their horrid gatherings."

"See-Ows?" Mark Howard asked.

"CEO," Smith explained hurriedly. "Master Chiun, these thieves will surely be gone before you can reach the research campus. I do not know yet if it is best for you to go on this pursuit."

"Best for who?" Chiun asked shortly. "I do not act now in the interests of the Eagle Throne. It is for the House of Sinanju that I go."

"Perhaps it would be best if we wait until we know who has taken the specimen."

"I shall not wait," Chiun informed him. "I depart this place within minutes and shall be in the air by half-past the hour. I will hire aircraft myself, if need be."

Smith nodded seriously and slowly, recognizing Chiun's urgency but hoping to slow the proceedings. "I will get you an aircraft."

"I shall be at the airport in minutes."

Smith's mouth fell the slightest bit open. There was only one airport close enough to reach within minutes. "In Rye? Master Chiun, it is out of the question."

"I will waste no time traveling to another airport."

"I can have a Cessna for you in White Plains by four o'clock," Mark Howard said.

"By four o'clock, I shall be landing in Philadelphia," Chiun said courteously as his hands emerged from the sleeves of his green-and-gold kimono. The little phone in his palm was alight and seemed to be answered at once.

"Good evening," he said in his sing song voice, "this is Mr. Chiun speaking. I would like transport immediately please. A small town in the state of New York. The name is Rye."

"Master Chiun!" Smith hissed. "I will get you an aircraft, but this must be handled with our usual attention to security!"

"That will do fine," Chiun said. "I shall be arriving just minutes ahead of you. Goodbye."

Chiun snapped the little phone closed and explained, "I have a prepaid account with the company. They have a plane available. It is often in use by the See-Ows of the local firm to visit their Chinese factory where they make their electric blending, mixing and toasting devices. They are currently at home and the aircraft is available. My account is substantially prepaid. They always give me excellent service. Shall I drive myself to the airport, as well?"

"Master Chiun, you will have a car to the airport and I will arrange a plane for you, but only on secure terms."

Master Chiun bowed his head and said, "Thank you, Emperor Smith, but that shall be entirely insufficient."

Then the office door was closing, and the place where Master Chiun had been standing was empty.

Mark leaped to his feet. "I'll go!"

For the second time that night, Mark Howard was running down the dark and silent hallways of Folcroft Sanitarium. He shouldered through the doors and clattered down the back stairs, and when he slammed through the doors to the parking lot there was a scream of tires. The lot filled with acrid smoke and the glimmering navy Lincoln careened out of the parking lot, then vanished.

"Criminy," said a voice from the heavens. Remo Williams appeared on the roof, the security light illuminating him against the angry, boiling cloud cover. "That guy was in a hurry."

Mark Howard said nothing.

"In your new car, too, huh, Junior?"

"Yes, Remo."

"Hope he doesn't wreck your Zephyr. Guy drives as bad as Chiun. Know who it was?"

Mark Howard turned to look up at the figure on the distant roof. "Don't be dense."

Remo slithered down the wall like a salamander and appeared at Mark's elbow. "Are you saying that was Chiun?"

Mark Howard stomped back into the building.

"Where's he going in such a hurry?"

Mark Howard would not answer.

"WHAT'S GOING ON, SMITTY?" Remo demanded, and the old man was startled out of his chair.

"Remo!"

"Sorry. Chiun just car-jacked Junior's new Lincoln and now Junior's giving me the silent treatment and I want to know what's going on."

Smith glared at the door. "What did you do to Mark?"

"Ran faster than he did. What is going on?"

"There has been an incident in Philadelphia," Smith said tightly as the door opened and Mark Howard trotted in, out of breath. He and Smith exchanged a worried look.

"What?"

"Chiun took my car," Mark said.

"We know that," Remo snapped. He was feeling his patience wearing thin. "Why? Where'd he go?"

"The airport," Smith said.

"He goes to the airport all the time. Why didn't he call a cab?"

"He was in a hurry," Smith said.

"Hey, Smitty! Over here!" Remo snapped his fingers above his head. "Somebody better tell me what is going on around here."

"He's heading for the airport. He's driving fast. See?" Mark Howard showed Remo the display on his screen. A computer map of Rye showed a tiny green MH jittering along the roads. "GPS on the car."

"What's the '96' down here mean?" Remo asked.

"Miles per hour."

"I was afraid of that." Remo watched the little

green MH take a corner without getting below sixty, then quickly reach the triple digits on a straight stretch of road.

"Nice little car," Remo said. "Wait a second. He's going to the Rye airport. Isn't that against the rules?"

"Of course it is," Smith said through clamped lips.

"Mr. Smith, Mr. Howard? I'm about to start breaking things if I don't get good answers. Really expensive things." Remo put one finger in the middle of the empty glass surface of Smith's desk. "Where's Chiun going and why?"

"He's going to the airport to get on a plane he chartered to take him to Philadelphia. He's in a hurry to get to the special-purpose research campus of the zoological gardens. There's been a break-in. It looks like the specimen has been exterminated and stolen. Get your hand off my desk before you break the glass."

Remo was applying enough pressure to stress the glass but not break it. The extra pressure needed to make the break was infinitesimal, but there was no danger of Remo slipping up—unless he became careless and distracted. And his mind was spinning. "What kind of a specimen? And why would Chiun care?"

"You don't know about the specimen at the SPRC?" Mark Howard asked.

"No."

"Yes," Smith countered. "Remo, you helped put it there."

Remo scowled at Smith.

Smith blurted, "For heaven's sake! The apatosaurus!"

Remo nodded. "Old Jack."

"Punkin," Mark Howard corrected. "They call it Punkin. It looks as if they poisoned the creature and its handler, then made off with the carcass."

"Dr. Nancy? Is she the handler?"

"Nancy Derringer, Ph.D.," Howard confirmed. "We believe she was killed at the scene."

"Why?" Remo demanded, feeling his temperature rise. He hadn't known Nancy very well and he hadn't seen her in years, but she had been the cutest dinosaur scientist he ever knew. He liked her. Why would anybody want to kill her?

"To get to the apatosaurus. They killed it so it would be easier to transport. They took the apatosaurus to be dissected and to have its blood chemistry analyzed. It was undoubtedly agents of one of the pharmaceutical companies that organized the theft. They think there's some sort of life-extending agents at work in the blood of the apatosaurus."

Remo felt all kinds of pieces fall suddenly into

place, including several pieces that had been floating around for months.

"It's the last dragon," Remo said. "Chiun's dragon."

"It is not his and it is not a dragon."

"Wrong, Smitty. Dr. Nancy promised Chiun he could have Old Jack's bones. And it's a dragon for all the reasons that matter to Chiun. Whatever supervitamin the big lizard has got inside that the drug companies want, well, Sinanju discovered it a few thousand years ago."

"I doubt it, Remo," Smith said, his tone scornful.

"Stuff it, Smitty. How'd he find out about it?"

"We alerted him, naturally," Mark Howard said. "Remo, we've been watching the facility for years."

"News to me."

"Chiun did not want you to know," Smith said. "He has been handling the security of the facility himself. There were more than twenty attempts to penetrate the facility. The apatosaurus had to be removed from public view to protect it."

"Protect it from who?"

"The drug companies. They backed off eventually. Chiun made sure of it."

"You should have told me about this."

"Why?"

"Because I'm Reigning Master, that's why."

"Not a good reason to violate Chiun's trust," Smith replied.

"Yeah. You're right." Remo closed his eyes and sighed long and low. "He wants the dragon bones. He wants the cure for whatever it is that's eating away at him. He's been waiting for Old Jack to kick the bucket so he could reverse it."

"What?" Mark blurted. "Are you saying Chiun's ill?"

Remo's eyes looked dark and hollow. "I guess everybody is learning new things tonight."

"How ill?" Mark demanded.

"I don't know. Chiun's not talking. I tried to get him to let me examine him. That didn't go over. I even tried to get him to see the doctors, just to prove me wrong. He wouldn't do that, either."

"He seems hale," Smith commented.

"That's part of the problem," Remo complained. "He can hide his symptoms better than anybody you ever knew. From me, too. He claims he's not sick. I can't prove him wrong."

Remo didn't miss the look between Smith and Howard, then Mark Howard asked, "Remo, are you sure Chiun's really sick?"

"Yes. And why shouldn't he be? He's an old man. Even by Sinanju standards, he's old."

"And what are Sinanju standards of longevity?" Smith asked.

"How long do the Masters live, you mean? Hundred and twenty, maybe. Sometimes older. One guy lived to be 148, but we're not supposed to talk about him."

"And why is that?"

"Closet skeleton." Remo shrugged. "It was a long time ago. But you know why he lived so long? And you didn't hear this from me. It's because he killed a dragon. The last one—until Old Jack showed up."

"Punkin," Mark Howard corrected.

"Dr. Nancy and Chiun had a bargain. She got the dinosaur while it was alive. Chiun got it when it was dead."

"Chiun has no right to the dinosaur," Smith said.

Remo laughed bitterly. "Who does?"

"The scientific community."

"Says who?"

"I say. It is established protocol in the scientific community."

"Dr. Nancy was a part of the scientific community. She made the deal with Chiun."

"It was not a deal she was authorized to make."

"So sue her. Just leave me and Chiun out of it."

"You're not out of it, I am afraid, Remo," Smith

said. "You're charged with the recovery of the apatosaurus carcass. It must be returned to the special-purpose research campus. I have arranged for a special pickup for you to start immediately. Mark, where is Chiun?"

"On board and taxiing for takeoff."

"Then your time is short. Remo, I need you to get to the apatosaurus ahead of Chiun. He must not do whatever it is he is planning to do to it. You will have transport waiting at White Plains. You'll need to move fast."

Remo stared at the old director of Folcroft. Whatever he had been planning to say, what came out was, "I should leave right away."

"Yes," Smith agreed.

"See ya."

Remo Williams was gone.

"That was way too easy," Mark Howard said.

Smith nodded tiredly. "Yes, it was."

6

Jeremy Landis dismissed the hired girl with a few coarse words. She scampered away, eyes down, and of course she said nothing. Landis just wasn't up for her entertainments this evening. He was tense. Truth was, he was worried about the helicopter.

Pharmacodynamics were his thing. He didn't know squat about aeronautical engineering. He'd had to put his trust in hired experts when it came to that damn helicopter. His hired expert was a burly grease monkey named Scott Wrought. He checked Wrought's credentials and background, then paid him an exorbitant salary to assure his loyalty.

But Wrought was almost fired on his first day on the job.

"I'm telling you there's nothing that can do the job," Wrought said. "You're talking about lifting forty tons at a time."

"Thirty."

"Forty. If the dino is frozen solid, he'll condense a huge amount of ice all around him in a big hurry. How much exactly, I don't know. But a lot. Be safe, you figure ten tons."

"I've seen helicopters lifting big air conditioners up onto my buildings," Landis insisted.

"Sure. They manufacture them in five-ton modules. Maybe ten tons tops. That's a long way from forty. Now, maybe we could have one made special."

"Forget it. Can't afford the publicity."

"We should go overland. A truck's the way to go."

"We won't get five miles," Landis snapped. "We have to go by air. We'll figure out a way to link multiple helicopters in series."

Wrought sneered. "No offense, boss, but you're nuts. There ain't four helicopter pilots in the world that could control their aircraft good enough for the job you're talking about. Them copters will be tanglin' rotors before they even reach the dinosaur pen—and when one of them goes down, the line'll drag all of them down."

Landis folded his arms and stewed.

"Unless," Wrought said slowly, "you could get your hands on a Homer."

"Tell me about Homer," Landis said.

"Big Soviet helicopter. They only made three of them, far as I ever heard. Never flew much. They've been junked in some Russkie airfields since before there was disco."

"Yes?" Landis was feeling better already.

"Supposed to have tree-mendous lift."

"How tremendous?"

"According to the Russkies, August, 1969 they lifted just over thirty-six tons and they went up more than a mile high. That's what the Russkies claimed at the time. That's more than forty-four tons in the U.S. of A."

"Perfect!"

"Well, they could do the job. If the Russkies were being straight about it. And if the damn things hadn't been rotting on the ground for so long."

"We'll buy them. We'll fix them up. We'll up-grade everything. Money is no object. You're in charge. Can you make it happen?"

Scott Wrought took off his greasy cap and scratched his scalp and considered it. "When you say money is no object, what do you mean exactly?"

"I mean money is no object. No matter how much it is, it's worth the investment."

In the end, they bought, retrofit and smuggled out a Russian Mi-12 for chump change. Scott Wrought and his engineering team stripped it and restored every inch in a hangar in Tunisia, then sneaked it into the United States, and they spent less than a hundred million bucks on the whole operation.

A bargain.

But test-flying the monstrous helicopter was no easy task. It had a tendency to show up on any radar.

The Mi-12 also turned out to be notoriously difficult to keep stable, despite the millions of dollars in aeronautical flight computers used to keep the twin rotors stable. They had worked on the aircraft for years. Years! But the damn machine still had its share of glitches.

And the entire operation depended on the helicopter running smoothly tonight. Landis's future, his dream of being a trillionaire, his self-worth, all depended on the successful flight of one antique Russian helicopter.

Well, there were some contingency plans in place. Landis never took any step without a contingency plan, just in case something got screwed up.

Landis hated screwups.

But, it was like a wedding. So much was happening that something was bound to go wrong.

And Jeremy Landis was not the kind of bride who would just shrug her shoulders and enjoy her special day.

7

Harold W. Smith was through being surprised. He'd seen it all. The best and the worst of humanity were evident on the computer screens in his office. Nothing shocked him anymore.

Almost nothing.

"We're seeing highest-level activity at several of the big drug companies," Mark Howard noted. "Fizzer LLC has called in all the top brass. Glasgow-Hythair is on full mobilization. Both have activated their mercenary teams."

"Good Lord."

"HAAC has powered up their international communications hub. Dr. Smith, they've activated sleeper cells in eighteen countries. We didn't know twelve of them existed."

Smith pursed his lips. HAAC, or Health At All Costs, had been one of the more aggressive pursuers of the apatosaurus. Chiun had eventually visited their headquarters personally in an attempt to dissuade them, and HAAC had backed off. But they still had nonintrusive moles all over the vicinity.

Smith dialed into the listening and video devices trained on the HAAC agents on the scene. There was no sign of them. There was no reason for them to stick around now. He switched to another apartment in the complex—all the units were rented by corporate spies of one kind or another.

"The Muck Pharmaceutical agent is still on the scene." Tom Dappling was speaking rapidly into his satellite phone. Smith dialed up the conversation. "He's being debriefed. Doesn't sound like he knows much. What about Pharm & Farm LLC?"

"Their shadow people were evacuated." Mark Howard rolled video that was forty-six minutes old. The green thermal-imaging system had a hard time picking out the shapes of the Camou-Nin commandos in their stealth suits. The men were slipping one after the other through the side door of a minivan that hadn't bothered even to come to a halt. In seconds, the van sped up and left the apartment complex, just as the first police arrived from the other direction, washing out the thermal video image.

Smith tugged at the sagging flesh under his chin.

CURE had placed this facility under surveillance

in the 1990s, but then the first biochemical studies of the creature were published and the pharmaceutical companies became seriously interested. CURE ramped up its surveillance of the facility at the bequest of Master Chiun as the specimen became more and more a target of the drug companies.

The sheer size of the creature made it difficult to steal. CURE had always seen the attempts coming, and Chiun had always been there to make sure it didn't. The drug companies got the message eventually. There was somebody big looking after the apatosaurus—somebody not afraid of killing off a few drug-company executives if that was what it took to get the point across. The drug firms kept their watchers on the scene, but they just watched and waited.

There was an uneasy peace at the special-purpose research campus for years.

Tonight, the peace was shattered. Dr. Derringer was the coroner's problem now. But the specimen. Who had taken the specimen?

"Meds-4-U?"

"No sign of Slim all night," Mark Howard said.

Slim was the Meds-4-U mole. He liked to take long walks during the night as a way of keeping an eye on the campus. He had probably been one of the first to notice the trouble—unless he was part of the trouble.

Smith found the audio-video feed from the apartment unit rented by the man they knew only as Slim. The surveillance record was stored among the vast terabytes of data on the basement computers. The mainframes were known as the Folcroft Four, and they housed more international intelligence than most of the Pentagon.

Among the data they housed was twenty thousand hours of surveillance-camera video from the apartment of the man known only as Slim.

Smith played it backward and told the system to return to the last motion detected in the apartment.

"Slim's been gone since six yesterday morning," Smith announced.

"Slim never misses the eleven-o'clock news," Mark Howard pointed out. "He watches the news and goes for a six-hour stroll. Every night like clockwork."

"Until today," Smith agreed. "He knew it was coming. Meds-4-U may be behind the theft."

Mark laughed without humor. "If there's one guy who's capable of stealing a thirty-ton dinosaur, it's Jeremy Landis."

"What about Jeremy Landis?"

"World's richest man. He's a megalomaniac. He runs Meds-4-U like he owns it personally."

"Yes?"

"And there's this. Have you seen this?" Mark opened his briefcase, which was full of hospital paperwork, and pulled out the latest *News Time* magazine. Landis was smiling, easygoing, wearing a cardigan sweater on a penthouse balcony high above some city.

The cover lines posed the question, Will This Man Be The World's First Trillionaire?

8

Once upon a time, Jeremy Landis would have been happy to have enough money for a new car and a house in the Georgia suburbs. One day he found he actually had that much money, but it wasn't enough.

He dreamed of wealth. A million-dollar portfolio. A house in a better suburb. His job as a medical-lab technician wasn't going to give him that. He divorced his money-sucking wife and got his doctorate and married a better wife, and found himself supervising part of the pharmaceutical research labs where he used to be a peon. He upgraded to one of the most expensive Atlanta suburbs and made his wife dress as if she were going to a cocktail party—all day, every day.

It wasn't working out. The wife moaned and bitched about his dress code, so she was history. The house wasn't quite right. It was nice, but not nice enough. Not as nice as the nicest houses he had seen.

It took the salary of a vice president and chief of

research technicians to afford a house like that, and there were three scientists in the lab with seniority over Jeremy Landis. He shopped his résumé but got no better chances for advancement. He was stuck in a dead-end job at Plassibaugh Pharmaceutical Research, a washout before he was even twenty-seven years old.

But a man with true ambition makes his own opportunities, and such a man was Jeremy Landis.

It helped that he was not well liked by the other three research supervisors, or by the current chief of research. They naturally excluded him. They'd go out after work without him. They had all left together one night, leaving Landis at his desk, alone in the executive wing, when he planted his evidence. He drove an hour south of Atlanta, bought a disposable phone at a gas station and used it to call the three most paranoid members of the board of directors. He disguised his voice. He burned the phone.

The next day was his day off. His phone rang at eleven in the morning. He rushed into the lab, full of concern. The executive offices had the atmosphere of a funeral.

"We have a crisis," said the chairman of the board of directors, bringing Landis into the boardroom.

The rest of the board was there or soon to arrive. The big table was piled with paper and specimen vials.

"Tell me what you see."

Landis perused the paperwork that was thrust in front of him. He pretended to scour the results, then stopped to look up, aghast. They asked him what he made of it.

"Somebody has been doing very sloppy research—or they are falsifying their results," he told them.

The next stack of pages came to him. He found the same problems in the reporting. And the next set. The last set of numbers was clean.

"What makes you think the last report is not the report that was falsified?" challenged one of the directors, a professor of medicine from a local university.

Landis pointed to the anomalous results. "Here. On this date the profile of the results changed. All of a sudden, the efficacy of the trials goes up. It happens all at once. Something changed. It should have been reported, at the very least. I hope these didn't come from this lab."

Somberly, it was explained to Landis that the reports did indeed come from the lab. Of the four simultaneous trials, only Landis's staff showed no anomalous results. Landis pretended to be horrified.

"It appears from the lab samples that were being tested as of this morning that a higher level of antiprostaglandins was being put into the test dosages."

Landis used his best horrified face. He was a method actor, totally, but a good one. He was laughing on the inside when he gasped out loud, "Oh, God, Dr. Foxglove is going to be devastated!"

One board member looked to another board member. "I'm afraid Dr. Foxglove is implicated."

Landis looked convincingly shocked.

"We're trying to find a way out of this mess," the chairman added.

A way out. That was a joke. There was only one way out. Contractually, they were obliged to report the fraud to the pharmaceutical giant that had commissioned the research. Their insurance also required it. But that wasn't how it would work. That would ruin it for everybody.

The three scientists and the vice president and chief of research technicians, Dr. Foxglove, were ushered into a quick and furious meeting with the board. They protested their innocence, naturally. The board showed them the evidence.

"Planted!" Foxglove insisted.

Then the board offered them a deal. They would leave the lab at once and never return, but would keep getting their paycheck for a year or until they found other jobs.

"But we are not guilty of this fraud!" Foxglove howled.

"The other option is a full-scale investigation," the chairman offered. "Think an audit of the evidence will support your claims, Doctor?"

There it was. They could go by the book, report the fraud, triggering an independent audit by the pharmaceutical company that hired them, as well as an investigation by their own insurance agency. Nobody, innocent or guilty, would come out without a seriously tarnished reputation. The lab would get a black eye that would cost it millions in future lost business. It would have to cut its rates to get any work at all. Every scientist associated with the lab would be sullied. Deserved or not, they would all be cast as fraudsters.

In the world of high-stakes pharmaceuticals, every competitor and politician with a grudge exploited every weakness, and no drug company could afford to tolerate the tiniest smudge of perceived impropriety.

"It's simple, Hermann," said Dr. Plassibaugh, the lab president, and the man who had founded the company twenty years before. "You walk away and keep your careers, or you stay and bring us all to our knees."

Dr. Foxglove looked stricken. "Darren, I've been your right-hand man from the beginning. I helped you build this place."

"Then don't bring it all down," Plassibaugh said.

"But I'm innocent. We all are. This is a setup."

"Ten years ago, we could have proved that and walked away from this mess. Not now. You know that."

"You have to believe I would not have done this."

"Dr. Plassibaugh may very well believe that," said the chairman of the board of directors. "We do not. Leaving you men on the job untested is not an option. You're one of the finest pharmacodynamics researchers on the planet, Dr. Foxglove. If we all agree to keep this quiet, then that will continue to be the case."

Dr. Foxglove looked at his three companions, then nodded seriously. Landis, ignored by everyone else, could see the wheels spinning. Foxglove had already decided on his course of action. Foxglove was a bleeding heart. If it were only his career at stake, he would have called for full public disclosure and an investigation, but he would never have jeopardized the careers of his three younger co-workers. Landis knew this. Plassibaugh knew it, too. In fact, Foxglove had already moved on to other things. His mind was busily considering who it was that could have stabbed him in the back.

When Foxglove nailed him to his chair with a sudden accusatory look, Landis felt his composure slipping for the first time. Foxglove saw Landis's momentary loss of control. That was all Foxglove needed to confirm his suspicions.

But Foxglove said nothing. Just gave Landis a pleading-puppy-dog look.

Foxglove and the three scientists left. Landis was given supervisory responsibilities for the entire lab, and his underlings were told that the missing supervisors were on a special consultation assignment for the company. Landis got his promotion, his huge raise. That was part of the plan. Landis, after all, had to be motivated to stay quiet just like everyone else. As the junior scientist, as the only one not implicated in the fraud, his reputation would have suffered the least if it all went public. His silence must be purchased.

It all worked out beautifully. Landis kept cool, even when Foxglove phoned him at home demanding an explanation. "Was it all for a corner office, Jer?"

Landis denied he had anything to do with it, denied it again and again until Foxglove finally left him alone.

It all worked out exceptionally well. What no one ever discovered was that the recent reports were not faked—but the older reports were. The clinical trials had been showing the drug was doing what it was supposed to do, successfully and consistently. Jeremy's faked numbers gave the appearance that the drug was doing a poor job originally, only to have the success rate shoot up when his faked numbers ran out.

Now, under his supervision, and under added clinical scrutiny from hired auditors, Jeremy's results were almost, but not quite, as good as the faked results. The research proceeded on schedule. The pharmaceutical company was pleased with the results—drug companies were always happy to get good news. The dismissed scientists found new jobs, all except Dr. Foxglove. He took early retirement. Landis discovered Dr. Plassibaugh was still socializing with his old friend. Landis knew what that meant, well enough. Foxglove was revealing his suspicions to his old friend.

Landis had been vice president and chief of research technician for a full eighteen months, and that was long enough. The money was already starting to be not enough. His newest house had palled almost immediately but appreciated in value.

Time to move on. One of these days, Landis was going to reach a comfortable level, but there was no reason he had to stagnate now. He was twenty-nine years old. He still had a few good years left in him.

But where would he go next?

He was pushing up against the ceiling at Plassibaugh Pharmaceutical Research. Dr. Plassibaugh was years away from retiring as president, and if he had communicated any of his fears to the board of directors, they would pass him over for the president's role even if Plassibaugh were to keel over dead one day.

That was probably the reason that the independent clinical auditors remained on-station at the lab, always watching, always scrutinizing. Landis was getting tired of being under the microscope anyway.

But what would he do next?

Start his own clinical lab? That was an expensive proposition. He had the credentials but not the years of experience needed to secure good, solid funding.

Go to work for one of the big pharmaceutical firms? That's where the real money and power were to be had in the drug world—and Landis could score a good position with one of the firms, no doubt. But good meant middle management. It would take him years of brownnosing to climb the ladder.

That wasn't the life for Jeremy Landis. He wasn't a patient man. He wanted to reach the top and he wanted to get there soon. What good would it do to have all that power and cash when he was over the hill and in his forties?

The answer dropped in his lap. He had to break into Dr. Plassibaugh's private office safe in order for it to actually drop into his lap, but that was the easy part. The hard part was murdering Dr. Plassibaugh.

The old fart never seemed to stop struggling. His pillow was one of those lightweight foam models, and Plassibaugh could breathe right through it, no matter how hard Landis pushed it against his face. Finally, after what seemed like five minutes, the old man was limp and unconscious. Landis poured a potent potassium-bromide solution down the man's throat and had to stroke his neck—disgusting!—to get him to swallow the stuff. He planted the bottle. Made it look like a suicide. Waited around to make sure the dose was sufficient.

It was.

The board had heard the accusations expounded by Foxglove and communicated to them by Plassibaugh, and the morning after Plassibaugh's death they looked on Landis with frank suspicions. If Landis was the monster the accusations painted him, then he could be capable of murder, as well as sabotage, to further himself. If he had framed the four scientists to become vice president, it seemed logical that he would have committed murder to be president.

Jeremy Landis confused them all with his choking admission on the morning after Plassibaugh died. "The truth is, I was ready to resign my position and go into private research."

He could see the uncertainty on the faces of the hastily gathered board members. One of them mentioned that he was now the senior scientist at the lab.

"I hope you're not considering me to take Dr. Plassibaugh's place!" Landis said. "I've had enough of administration."

They thought he was making noises. They thought he would show his true colors soon enough, and then they would know he was vying for the top position in the lab. But Landis suggested Dr. Foxglove for the job. "In my heart, I think he is an honest man," Landis said. "He's the one who has what it takes to run PPR. I guess I'm just a white-coat at heart."

Nobody was more confused by all this than Foxglove himself. Even he seemed to have changed his assessment of Jeremy Landis.

Until he moved into Plassibaugh's office. Landis was already packing his things when Foxglove called him in for a talk.

The safe was standing open.

"Independent research?" Foxglove demanded. "Using Darren Plassibaugh's research?"

This time, Landis was mentally prepared. His mask of denial never wavered. He claimed ignorance until Dr. Foxglove gave up the interrogation, but by then Landis had learned that Foxglove didn't know the nature of Plassibaugh's research.

That saved Foxglove's life. If he'd known the focus of the research, Landis would have had to kill him.

When Landis launched his own drug company a year later to market the heart medication he had invented, Foxglove held his tongue. He knew it was Plassibaugh's research. He knew Landis had stolen it, but he couldn't prove anything.

For the longest three years of his life, Landis worked on securing his next position of power. First he duplicated Plassibaugh's old research documents on his home computer, then paid good money for preliminary testing on the new pharmaceutical. The results were incredible. Landis had known they would be.

Armed with his test results, he was able to attract corporate backing on favorable terms, then got the new drug into more trials and finally submitted it for approval from the Food and Drug Administration. It took forever.

Then the rumor circulated that the FDA was going to approve Jeremy Landis's new painkiller. That's when he heard from Dr. Foxglove again.

"There's a reason Plassibaugh never tried to market it, Jeremy," Foxglove said. "It's dangerous."

"Are you speaking of my patented molecule, acetylsalicylic meperchloride?" Landis demanded.

"Yes. Plassibaugh did extensive animal testing. It damages blood cells over time."

"You're wrong. It's metabolized easily, which is one of the reasons it's so safe."

"But every dose damages blood cells minutely, and the damage is passed on when the cell reproduces."

Landis chuckled. "Are you claiming Aceteride changes DNA?"

"No. I doubt it. Plassibaugh thought the chemical was cytoplasmiphilic and tries to get to the cytoplasm. Don't ask me how. Whatever the mechanism, it abrades the membrane and the flaw is passed on to the daughter cells. It took half a lifetime for the hemophilia-type symptoms to appear in the test animals, then all at once you've got rats with plummeting platelet levels. It's uncontrollable, no matter what clotting-factor therapies he tried."

"A fairy tale."

"Plassibaugh watched one hundred test vermin transform from healthy to critically thrombocytopenic in a matter of weeks."

"Absurd."

"He tried controlling it with coagulants and synthesized fibrinogen. The therapy didn't work because the platelets just weren't there. Only a blood transfusion could get the platelet levels back up, but then the new blood began to degrade rapidly. Jeremy, every test animal developed the syndrome, and Plassibaugh couldn't reverse even a single case."

"The FDA seems to think my drug, on the other hand, is safe," Landis said.

"You'll need twenty-year human trials to replicate the results Plassibaugh found in his lab studies. That's why it's so dangerous. Don't you see how many people will end up dead? Landis, are you still there?"

"I'm thinking."

Landis was thinking that old Doc Foxglove sounded serious. Passionate, even. Old Doc Foxglove was a notorious bleeding heart. So to speak. Foxglove was not going to let Landis move ahead with his patented Aceteride without raising a humongous stink about it. That would delay commercialization of Aceteride, and Landis had already spent three long years getting to this point. That was too long already. Landis had sworn to dedicate himself to making a major move up every four years or less. Never again would he waste a ridiculous number of years on any one goal. It still galled him to think about the seven years he wasted in higher education, with nothing more to show for it than a run-of-the-mill M.D.

He wasn't going to go through that again. He wasn't going to allow the old fart in Atlanta to get in his way.

"I have to think about this, Foxglove," he said.

"Good. I'm sure you'll come to the right decision. But I think I'll call you back tomorrow, just to see how you're coming along."

Landis bought another disposable phone and called an acquaintance in Atlanta. He had never met the man face-to-face.

"I'm the one who's been sending you Christmas presents for the last three years," Landis explained.

"You wanna tell me why you been doing that?" Clement Muskier asked.

"It's a way of showing you what I'm all about."

"Why you want to do that?"

"Just in case I ever needed to hire you."

"Damn suspicious, sending a man ten grand every damn year just 'cause you might want to give him a job offer some day."

Landis explained, "Look, Clement, a cop never would have put out that much money over that much time just to try to sting you, right? I think you know I'm not a cop. And you pretty well know I'm willing to pay some good cash. Now, you want to trust me to not be a cop and to send you more cash?"

"I guess I do."

The next morning, Dr. Foxglove called Landis in his Virginia office at nine o'clock on the dot.

"You in the office?"

"Yes. Why?" Foxglove asked.

"Just wondering how everybody is doing."

"Everybody is fine. How's your thinking, Jeremy?"

"Explain it to me again—all about the clinical trials Plassibaugh conducted," Landis asked.

"Why?"

"Humor me."

So Dr. Foxglove started going through the whole long story again. He told about the animal testing on lab vermin. He detailed the apparent success of the drug, and then the awful, swift and irreversible side effects that appeared in one hundred percent of the test animals.

"You're talking about the animals that were getting daily doses throughout their lives. What about short-term use?"

"Plassibaugh's animals all developed platelet loss. It just took longer in those that received the short-term therapy with the drug."

"Lots of drugs have serious side effects."

"This drug is one hundred percent lethal, Jeremy. It's not a drug at all. It's a slow-acting poison."

"It's a pretty effective nonnarcotic analgesic."

"So's aspirin! Please tell me you'll put a stop to this! Because if you don't, I swear to God I will."

Landis heard the crash of glass, then Dr. Foxglove seemed to be gargling. There was a heavy thump. In his last breath, Foxglove gasped, "You did this, you son of a—"

Silence. A moment later, people were shouting and screaming. Landis hung up.

The FBI was knocking on his door three hours later. Landis's phone number was right there on the phone display. Can you tell us please, what you and Dr. Foxglove were discussing when he was shot?

"We were old friends," Landis told the FBI when they stopped by his office. "He was happy for me. He heard rumors the FDA was about to clear Aceteride and he was very excited for me and gave me a call. I told him I was expecting the clearance to be announced any day. He called me the next day. You should have heard him. He was about to explode. I swear he was more excited than I was. The next thing I knew, I heard glass breaking. I heard him make this terrible sound and then people started screaming and nobody would pick up the phone. After a while I just hung up. I was in shock. I didn't know what to do. Then I got the call from my friends at the FDA, and I hardly even heard them when they told me the approval was granted for Aceteride."

The FBI believed him. They asked if he knew if Foxglove had any enemies.

"Who'd want to hurt Dr. Foxglove? Nicest man in the world. He was like the grandfather I never knew."

The FBI went away.

Aceteride went on the market. Sales were brisk.

Jeremy Landis had reached his next three-year milestone. He paid off his backers and then owned

Meds-4-U Pharmaceuticals outright. He became very rich. He recruited maverick drug researchers—the bad boys of pharmaceutics. He brought three more patented drugs to the market within three years, and hired a thousand field reps to push them onto every doctor in the country.

His team of lawyers and private lobbyists worked night and day to get Aceteride approved for over-the-counter sales. That's where the real money was. Ten million doses at twenty bucks per prescribed dose was chump change compared to a hundred million doses sold off the rack for ten dollars each.

The FDA dragged its feet.

But Landis achieved his next three-year milestone. Sales were through the roof, and his personal worth topped five hundred million dollars.

Three years later, and he was a billionaire. His next three-year goal was to have ten times that much.

Countless young upstart scientists tried emulating Jeremy Landis's success and failed, and Landis bought out patent rights by the boxful. Most of them weren't worth the paper they were printed on, but one out of every thousand patents was a gold mine waiting to be opened. Landis was very good at finding the pearls among the swine, and his entrenched sales force was very good at getting it into the hands of the nation's medical practitioners.

Sales swelled and Jeremy Landis was worth in excess of ten billion dollars. Milestone reached.

He could see the future and the future was his. He was going to be a tycoon. Like JDR with oil or BG with software. He was going to be the richest man in the world. The richest man of the whole twenty-first century.

Meds-4-U went public. It was one of the biggest public stock offerings ever, and Landis played the game perfectly. He bought and sold and bought his own stock, skirting the fringes of legality but increasing his worth exponentially. Three years later, he had a personal worth of fifty billion dollars. Milestone reached.

Richer Than Gates! exhorted the cover of a respected news magazine.

"What next, Mr. Landis?" he was asked on a rare television interview.

"There are still people richer than me, aren't there?" Landis asked.

"Two or three," the commentator admitted.

"In three years, there won't be," Landis said.

Three years later, there weren't. Milestone reached. Landis was the richest man on the planet, and that discouraged him greatly.

"Now what?" he asked his hired girl, Cilly. Cilly raised her eyebrows questioningly and said nothing. She hadn't been hired to speak. It seemed every time he hired a girl, no matter what she promised, she sooner or later started talking. Landis hated that. Now he would only employ mutes as his hired girls. At the salary he offered, they were standing in line to have their vocal cords surgically snipped. Cilly was in her freshman year at Tennessee State University in Nashville, on an engineering scholarship of all things, but she didn't hesitate for an instant when offered the job as Landis's hired girl. She was surgically muted on Saturday and showed up for her new job on Tuesday.

That was the kind of service you could buy when you were the richest man on planet Earth. Now Landis furnished each of his three homes with a hired girl. Unlike his lousy wives, he could also dictate his hired girls' dress code without argument. Cilly, for example, wasn't allowed to wear a stitch of clothing until her contract was up.

"I mean, what mountains are left to climb?"

Cilly smiled her silly smile and rubbed her fingers together, indicating money.

"Cilly, I'm the biggest billionaire of all time. I'm the best, baddest billionaire, with a capital fucking *B*."

Cilly shook her head and shook her finger.

"No? No what?"

Cilly lay back and drew on her own bare stomach. A big *B*. Then she drew an *X* through the *B*.

"No *B?* What's that mean? No *B?*"

Cilly smiled and drew a big, silly *T*. It went across the tops of her big boobs, and then descended between them. She added a lowercase *r* next her navel.

Jeremy Landis felt his breath taken away. He sat down hard on the floor cushions. His mind was awhirl. His forehead was sweating. Now Cilly was crawling on top of him and pleasing him—and he had never been so aroused in his life.

"Cilly," he gasped. "You're a fucking genius!"

Cilly rode him through climax after climax, but he was so thrilled that he just kept right on going. When he flagged, she straddled him and used their moisture to draw the letters on her body again.

"Yes, show me!" he whispered.

She finished the big *B*.

"*B* for 'billionaire,'" Landis said, speaking like a stupid child.

She teased him by leaving it there for a moment.

"Come on," he begged. "Do it!"

She suddenly slashed her fingers across the glistening *B*, scratching herself with her scarlet finger-nails.

Then she dipped her fingers again and drew the huge *T*, which crossed from one shoulder to the next, then descended down from her collarbone to her pelvis. When she playfully added the little *r*, it was highly erotic.

"Trillionaire!" Landis squeaked. It was the first time he had dared utter the word.

He was instantly ready for more of Cilly's silly delights.

9

Was it even possible for one man to amass a fortune that big?

He tried to imagine it. One trillion dollars.

It was a third of the budget of the United States federal government.

So what? A billion dollars was the budget of your average African nation. Ten billion dollars was the budget of Iceland or Guatemala. Landis had made that much money already. He was simply taking the next step.

But a trillion dollars was staggering. Unthinkable. Impossible. How could one man have that much money?

But the truth was, he was already well on his way. He was the richest man in the world. He was worth a tenth of a trillion already. All he had to do was increase it tenfold, which he'd done it before.

But he wasn't fooling himself for a second. Most

of his hundred billion came from one-time-only stock sell-offs and growth spurts. Those were once-in-a-lifetime windfalls. You couldn't expect more than a couple of those to fall into your lap.

Turning a hundred billion into a trillion dollars was going to take planning.

He left Cilly passed out in cushions and went to his workstation to crunch the numbers.

He was going to have to be realistic here. He wasn't going to make a trillion dollars in three years. Even six or nine seemed unrealistic.

He gave himself twelve years.

His first step was to assemble the vast resources and technology needed to launch the product. There were other trillion-dollar products in the world. Oil, of course. But Landis understood instinctively that this would have to be a more personal product. Not something that people needed to live, like gas for their car and power for their plants. His product would have to be something people loved, worshiped, thought about constantly, craved all day every day. Like cigarettes. Only less unhealthy. In fact, a product like cigarettes couldn't have been launched successfully in today's world. His product should be the opposite of unhealthy. It would need to generate its own hype and its own goodwill, if it was to grow to be a trillion-dollar product.

Since he managed to bank from twenty to fifty percent of company sales, his trillion dollars in personal wealth would come in the next phase. He'd be in his fifties by then, but he'd still be young enough to enjoy his wealth.

Now, how was he actually going to make the money?

A tricky problem.

The dilemma was simply one of scale. Even if he sold his product across the country, around the world, it would have to be exceedingly expensive for sales to reach into the thirteen digits. Let's say, hypothetically, he could come up with a product that two out of every three human beings in the United States would be willing to pay for, at say one thousand dollars per year. Two thirds of Americans had the income to afford a product like that, no problem. It was about as expensive as smoking, right? What if you extrapolated that figure to the rest of the world's moneyed population?

Time to think demographics. U.S. population would be about 315 million, next census. Canada 32 million. Japan 130 million. Australia, New Zealand, Singapore maybe 20 million moneyed human beings—people who made enough to afford a thousand-dollar-a-year habit. He was up to about 500 million people. Now add Western Europe, Hong

Kong and the hundreds of millions of individuals in the expanding middle-class populations in countries that were still called Third World—China, India, Indonesia, the whole Middle East, South Africa, Russia, Southeast Asia...he was well over a billion already. A billion potential customers. A billion human beings who could theoretically afford, if properly motivated, a thousand-dollar-a-year habit.

All he needed to do was come up with the next tobacco—then monopolize the market.

Jeremy Landis was getting giddy. The numbers were falling into place with amazing ease.

Okay, let's say for the sake of argument that he was able to create a customer base that consisted of one third of the moneyed population, or approximately 350 million. Whatever the product was, let's say it cost a grand a year. No good. That would gross 350 billion dollars annually.

Okay, say you hooked two-thirds of the more than one billion possible customers. Now things were looking up. Let's just say the cost was not one thousand dollars but, oh. Fifteen hundred.

Hey. Good. Now his company was grossing: $1,125,000,000,000 annually.

And if the product actually cost the company something on the order of three hundred dollars to manufacture and ship, there was plenty left over for the Meds-4-U spreadsheet and plenty for Landis to take his forty percent cut of the gross.

At that point his paycheck would total 420 billion dollars annually.

Not too shabby. Three years times 420 billion dollars makes 1.260 trillion bucks. Plenty of room for error.

He'd make his goal no problem.

He would be the world's first trillionaire.

Now, that was settled. It was as good as done. Just one question left to answer.

What would 750 million human beings pay fifteen hundred dollars a year to have?

Jeremy Landis smiled.

He already knew the answer.

10

Dappling had lived in utter terror for years spying on the special-purpose research campus of the zoological gardens in Philadelphia. He was just one of countless such spies living in the vicinity. Every unit in his apartment complex was taken up either by SPRC researchers or by pharmaceutical company spies. It had become almost like a small community.

It wasn't friendly at first. Attempts were made on Dappling's life the first week he moved in. Dappling retaliated against the Fizzer LLC guys up the hall. Yanked out some fingernails, only to find out later it was the Onohla Organic Supplements toughs with the patio apartment who had been shooting at him. Dappling stripped the three of them to their altogether, tied them up and sent them rolling down the hill. One of them had the guts to return to the apartment complex, this time with four big tough dudes.

They were hell-bent, crew-cut Marines, and they were the first ones to have an example made of them.

Dappling witnessed it personally. He saw the Onohla Organic Supplements mercenaries get all dressed up in black special-forces gear and go sneaking into the campus grounds in the middle of the night. They acted professional and fearless, but there had been a few who tried this same thing, more than once. They vanished. They just disappeared.

The Onohla Organic Supplements crew did not disappear. They emerged from the campus in pieces. One of the heads and two arms showed up in Dappling's living room the next morning. The Fizzer guys down the hall found a whole torso and a shin on their kitchen table. Throughout the apartment building, pharmaceutical spies were waking up to find body parts inside their units—and not a single security alarm had been activated.

The message was clear. Whoever was protecting the zoo campus was getting fed up with all the incursions. They were getting tired of killing the intruders and disposing of their bodies. They were going to start taking the violence to the intruders—and would-be intruders.

Amazingly, Onohla Organic Supplements didn't give up. Maybe they never actually heard about the fate of their first team. None of the resident spy households ever publicly admitted to receiving their own ghastly breakfast delivery. Dappling only learned about it gradually through garbage-bin gossip, where all the dirty little spy-community secrets were whispered and news exchanged.

The new Onohla Organic Supplements team was a carbon copy of the first, but there were eight of them this time. Dappling didn't think it would make a difference. Just more bodies.

Dappling watched the team go in on a Monday at one in the morning. He retreated to the roof with his stun gun. Let them come and bring whatever they wanted to his apartment. Whatever it was would find him not home.

He was the last one to arrive. The boys from Fizzer huddled against the low brick ledge. Pharm & Farm LLC had recently sent out a new-generation, unarmed version of the Camou-Nin, and those guys were standing in the shadows of the exhaust vent trying to be unseen—but the wide whites of their eyes gave them away.

Dappling took a position next to his neighbor, the industrial spy from Meds-4-U.

"I was about to come down and knock on your door myself," the man said.

"I appreciate that, Slim," Dappling said. "I had myself convinced to stay and face down the—whatever. Or whoever. That lasted about twenty seconds."

Slim chuckled, and his teeth chattered a little as he crouched low on the wall and peered into his night-vision binoculars. Slim, last name unknown, had always seemed the most confident and fearless of them all. Why not? Meds-4-U was the most powerful corporation on the planet. They could hire the best. Whatever Slim's background, he would be the best money could buy—and even Slim was scared.

"I'm estimating seventeen souls have gone missing in the campus since Punkin came," Slim muttered. The man was talking nervously. Giving away too much information. This was not industrial espionage!

The Fizzer boys exchanged glances. "We count twenty-four during our time here," said the tall one.

There was a bitter scoff from the shadows. "I got news for you," said the most senior of the Camou-Nin. "We've lost twenty-six guys. Just us."

"Really?" asked one of the younger Camou-Nin.

"Overheard them talking about it at HQ one time," the senior Camou-Nin muttered.

Then Tom Dappling felt all eyes turning to him. He was the patriarch of the little community of pharmaceutical-industry spies. They knew he had been here for years, longer than all the rest of them. He was a kind of hero for having survived so long. They actually looked up to him—even the Fizzer boys, whom he had once beaten the tar out of.

Being the old man of the apartment building, he'd know better than any of them how many had been lost on the wooded grounds of the special-purpose research campus of the zoological gardens in Philadelphia.

"Sixty-one," he admitted morosely.

Noises of somber alarm.

Then Slim said, "Hush up."

Then they all felt it. The ground seemed to reverberate. The trees were rattling. Something crunched on the gravel surface of the roof and rolled to a stop at the feet of the Camou-Nin unarmed warriors. Another object bounced down alongside Dappling, and Slim and two of the Fizzer boys were actually hit in the head with the flying objects.

"It's raining heads!" the Fizzer leader exclaimed, barely able to keep from shouting.

Dappling covered his own head, even when the Fizzer boys were standing there examining the decapitated heads.

"That's not all of them!" he hissed.

They got wise and covered themselves. Head number seven landed with its eyes rolling and its teeth chattering at them, as if it had gone through some sort of a nervous excitation at the moment of its death.

Head number eight never came.

"I tell you what, a head doesn't have a nervous reflex like that except for within the first twenty seconds of being decapitated from a living body," Dappling hissed later. It was almost dawn. They had all agreed to go downstairs, together, at dawn. "Whatever attacked them out there sliced their heads off and tossed them up to us instantly."

"Pretty fast killin'," Slim admitted.

"What kind of animal can kill that fast?" whined the big fat Camou-Nin.

His rail-thin friend smiled unhappily. "Eight-eight, here, he thinks it's a dinosaur running loose down there."

Dappling kicked at one of the dead heads, spinning it to show the cut of the neck. "Look at that slice. It's perfect. A roast-beef slicer couldn't cut that straight. Even the bone is perfectly cleaved."

"Laser cutter?" Slim suggested.

"Could be. No burn marks, but if it were really powerful and cut so fast it didn't char the flesh—I guess it might work."

Head number eight never appeared. Neither did the bodies of the decapitated Onohla Organic Supplements mercenaries. But soon enough the news was on the front page of every paper in America. The police had been tipped off to mass murder at the offices of Onohla Organic Supplements. They found the executive offices strewn with everyone from top management. There was also the body of an unidentified soldier, as well as the decapitated bodies of seven more soldiers. No dog tags to identify the soldiers. The heads were never found—the community of spies had burned them in a garbage can and scattered the ashes in the shrubbery.

Rumors spread that the heads had been ground up into Onohla Organic Supplements. The heads were in the calcium supplements. Everything else had been cooked off and used to fortify Onohla's Amino Acid Power Pack. That was the rumor, anyway. The truth was that Onohla had ceased production and was closing its doors. Nobody was left to run the place; nobody seemed interested in stepping into the management void.

Slim assured them that the mass of metal and the nearby high-voltage wiring meant the big garbage bin was the one place on the apartment building's exterior that none of their bugs could work. It was their

unofficial neutral zone, where they passed a few un-
guarded words. When they met at the garbage bin,
it seemed they could stop being enemies and spies
for a minute, and just be guys who lived in the same
apartment building. They shared jokes and barbs,
and they exchanged gossip.

Dappling remembered the terrible day he heard
the news about the Camou-Nin. It came from Slim
himself, just a few months after the rain of heads.

"The Camou-Nin have been ordered to go into the
grounds," Slim whispered as he bent over his kitchen
garbage pail and tied the white garbage bag. "Their
bosses think they'll be okay since they're going in
unarmed."

Dappling was stunned. "I'd rather flee and take
my chances on my own," he said.

"I think they're gonna go through with it!" Slim
exclaimed, and tossed his bag into the big outside
bin.

They rendezvoused on the roof again that night,
Dappling and Slim and the four Fizzer guys, plus the
new arrivals from Guangdong Vitamin Factory Five,
American Operations Limited and a few other in-
troverted spy squads and sullen loners.

With trepidation, they watched the Camou-Nin
leave their apartment, behaving normally at first.

They gave a goodbye wave to their colleagues on the roof, then slipped into the shadows.

It was a long, long night.

At four-thirty in the morning they heard whistling out front. It was the Camou-Nin! They had survived a night on the campus! They pretended to be coming back from a late-night outing and gave their comrades on the roof a surreptitious thumbs-up.

The Chinese were not amused. "You lied. All the talk was lies to scare us! Was it some sort of an initiation in frat house. What fools!" The agents from the American offices of Guangdong Vitamin Factory Five stalked off the roof in a huff, tried to make their own penetration of the campus the next night and were later found dismantled on the front ground and strewed across the company offices in Newark.

"They went in armed," the fat Camou-Nin pointed out nervously during an impromptu gossip exchange at the garbage bin. All the spies were taking out their garbage much more often these days. "Or maybe they got too close. You know, we went in unarmed, just looking around, and we didn't get too close to the place."

"Or maybe you got lucky," added one of the morons from Fizzer, barging between them with his own limp white sack. "You guys going back in there?"

"Better believe it," said Camou-Nin 088.

The Fizzer jerk pantomimed a duck-and-cover.

But the Camou-Nin began making regular patrols of the outskirts of the campus, never penetrating too far. And they continued to survive. Slim from Meds-4-U, who did his own patrolling in the middle of the night, had hinted that he also penetrated the campus slightly.

Dappling never asked outright. These guys were on the other side. This was spy-versus-spy. They could be friendly to one another when their paths happened to intersect at the garbage bin, but they couldn't be expected to cooperate.

But when the end came suddenly and almost anticlimactically, Dappling was a little bit sorry to leave his neighbors. He and the Camou-Nin had even shared quick six-pack out by the garbage at five in the morning and said their goodbyes. The Fizzer jerks he wouldn't really miss. The other spy rabble he hadn't even bothered to get to know. They all came and left or vanished too rapidly to be worth the emotional investment.

The only other guy he was going to miss was Slim, but Slim seemed to have vanished.

"Must have gone in too deep," muttered the fat Camou-Nin, Eight-eight, as he poured a beer on the ground in remembrance of Slim.

"I don't think so," said Camou-Nin 100, the one called Hunnert.

"Where, then?" Eight-eight demanded.

Hunnert looked at Dappling, who smirked. They were on the same wavelength.

"Somebody got the specimen," Hunnert suggested. "Doesn't look like it was us. Doesn't look like it was our buddy here from Muck got the specimen. Sure wasn't them losers from Fizzer. Had to be somebody."

Eight-eight was downcast. "He wouldn't have left without saying goodbye, though, would he?"

Some people just didn't have the personality to be good industrial spies.

Tom Dappling clapped the Camou-Nin on the back, then went in to pack his things. There was no need to stay. Muck had called him back to HQ for debriefing, and then he'd be able to move on to a less hazardous duty. He was elated, not knowing Death was about to pay him a visit.

He stuffed dirty laundry in his Samsonite, unaware that Death was silently opening the double-locked glass doors to his apartment.

He never heard the sounds of approaching footsteps, because the footsteps made no sound.

When he turned and faced Death at last, he said, "Hey!"

Death said nothing.

"Who are you, old-timer? You can't just go walking into people's apartments without knocking, you know."

Then Dappling realized he was already thinking like a civilian.

Dappling spun around and snatched the handgun from under his bed pillow. Death had not moved.

"Only one person's ever broken into my apartment without setting off the security system, bub."

"I am not bub. I am the Master of Sinanju, and I grant you more life than you deserve. When this gift is used up, I will grant you death, and it shall be swift or it shall be excruciating. This is the choice you have now."

"I didn't think so," Dappling said.

"Someone has stolen my dragon. I wish to retrieve it. You were one of the foolish ones who coveted the dragon. What know you of the thieves?"

Dappling wasn't making sense of it. He thought the little old man was trying to distract him with nonsense, but distract him from what? The old man stood in the door, and this miserable little cubicle had no window to the outside. So nobody was going to be sneaking up on him.

"How'd you do it? Get through the alarm, I mean? Have help?"

"Help? It is insolent even to ask such a thing. None of your copper wires and silicon circuits can hinder a Master of Sinanju. Do they not teach you of the capabilities of the Sinanju in the schools where you learn your ridiculous skulking techniques?"

Dappling was feeling too good about the way his life was going to be confounded. "What did you use? Some sort of an electrical-disruption emitter?"

"I do not use tools! If you ask how I came through your pathetic glass walls, I can explain easily. Behold, the Knives of Eternity!"

The little old man withdrew one hand from his brilliant scarlet robe and displayed them for Dappling.

"Nice manicure job, Grandpa. You saying you cut glass with your fingernails?"

"They cut glass most effectively. They cut through metal, as well. See?" The old man slipped close, snicked at the handgun and was back in his place before Dappling could react. The front end of his handgun bounced heavily on the carpet.

"They cut through flesh and bone just as well. You have seen my handiwork before."

Dappling gaped. "You decapitated the Onohla Organic commandos!"

"Exactly."

Dappling wouldn't have believed it if he hadn't just seen the man slice through forged steel with nothing but his fingernails. The cut was so neat it had not deformed the barrel mouth.

The damn thing would still fire. It just had less of a barrel to guide the trajectory. But at this distance, aim wasn't a problem.

Dappling fired. Somehow he missed, and blew a hole in the wall directly behind the little old man.

He fired again. And again. Then the little man pinched the end of the weapon and closed the barrel. Dappling couldn't fire it again without it blowing up in his face.

"How many of you are there?" he demanded. He was stalling for time.

The little man sniffed. "Just one. Have you convinced yourself of your helplessness? Will you answer questions now, and die swiftly? Or suffer excruciating pain, then die?"

"Why do I have to die at all?"

"You sought to steal my dragon," said the little man. "No one steals from Sinanju. No one may even attempt the act and escape punishment."

Dragon? There were dragons on the old man's Asian-looking robe. "Wait—the specimen?"

"That was kept below in the enclosed garden. It

was stolen, but not by you and your employers, I think. So who did the deed?"

"I don't know! Could be anybody!"

"Who?"

Dappling made a break for it. The little old man with the wrinkled face looked as if he weighed in at maybe eighty pounds. Surely Dappling could muscle his way through.

But he couldn't. He went into the wall and he never even saw the blow that sent him there. When he slumped to the floor he muttered, "I think it was Meds-4-U. Slim was their agent. He's been missing since yesterday. Unless you killed him." Dappling coughed up blood. Things had broken inside when he hit the wall. He'd hit it hard.

"I did not kill this Slim yesterday. Would that I was here then. What other evidence is there?"

"None." Cough.

Dappling looked up and found himself alone. The old Asian was gone.

Bleeding internally. He had to get to the hospital fast.

He tried crawling to the phone, but the blood was pouring out of him fast. His vision faded quickly, and he settled on the carpet for some much needed rest.

MASTER CHIUN LEFT the despicable would-be dragon stealer to bleed out his last moments and went in search of other such conspirators. This building of ugly little dwellings was packed full of them. Each unit was home to spies and watchers from another organization that coveted what belonged to Chiun—the dragon called Punkin.

Chiun felt angry within himself that he had allowed this situation to fester unchecked for so long. He was too softhearted and too agreeable for his own good! He had allowed these weak emotions to override his common sense, and see what had happened as a result!

But Emperor Smith had practically pleaded and begged of Chiun not to take the drastic steps that Chiun thought wise: moving the dragon and its handler to some hidden location, where it could live the rest of its natural life unmolested by those who sought its precious bones.

Smith was at times a madman, full of extravagant and foolish ideas. But his gold was good, and Chiun was nothing if not agreeable and accommodating. He had allowed himself to be swayed by the Emperor's assurances that the dragon was safe where it was, in the little valley built for it and for Dr. Nancy Derringer, its owner.

But surely, Chiun had suggested humbly to the

Eagle Throne Emperor, it was wise to remove the pesky, obvious spies who stood sentinel upon the hill above? Again, unbelievably, the Emperor stayed the hand of Master Chiun. This emperor, for reasons Chiun could never understand, kept secret the very fact that he held the country's reins of power and insisted always that the assassins in his employ remain low in profile and clandestine in deed. Harold the Mad informed Chiun that the mass extermination of the spies might cause some kind of an uproar, but Chiun argued that the uproar would be beneficial to convincing others to keep their distance. In the end, Chiun agreed to stay his hand against the spies, unless they came into the grounds around the dragon garden armed. Unarmed men did not worry Chiun.

So he had let them watch the dragon garden from a distance. The shadow huggers with their ridiculous black clothing would enter, too, just so long as they were without weapons. Men of this ilk were harmless without weapons. Smith would dispatch Chiun back to the grounds occasionally, when one of them or another would make yet another attempt to reach the dragon garden with arms.

These spies failed each time. Their employers, the wealthy potion blenders and pill dispensers, were persistent and greedy and corrupt beyond imagination, and they would send more waves of warriors. Chiun simply adopted a policy of returning these hired thugs to their employers personally, and typically would dismantle them for easy transport. This was a most effective method of sending a communiqué. The message was understood and the armed incursions halted.

For many years, the grounds around the dragon garden were at peace, and the dragon lived on inside its shelter with the good Dr. Nancy, who never knew about the dozens of assassinations committed for their safety.

Dr. Nancy was the one to blame for these troubles, Chiun thought. She had tested the dragon with her vials and chemicals, and written about the dragon in her journals. The other scientists had gone into an uproar when they read of her experiments, for in the particles of the creature's blood was evidence of the old, old secret.

The gift of life. Sinanju had known this truth for millennia—that there was some precious substance in the bones of the dragon that extended one's life. Dr. Nancy had seen this particle and written about it.

Of course—it was what scientists do. Chiun should not have been surprised. He should have expected it from the beginning, and acted to prevent it.

He should have claimed the dragon from the very beginning. He knew it at the time, but again, he had allowed his compassion to supersede logic! When would he ever learn to harden his heart?

The foolishness of this softhearted old man may have sealed his doom. The last dragon had been taken away from him. If he did not find it again, then there would be nothing to save him from the inevitable destruction of age and disease.

So find it he must do, at all costs.

He had questioned many of the spies in the building already. Let the outcry come when the remains were discovered. Smith would know how to deal with it, and let it be his penance for conniving Chiun into allowing this foolish situation to exist and lead to the theft.

Smith's anger was of no consequence now.

But Chiun learned very little, until the last man gave him the clue pointing to the one from the company called Meds-4-U.

It was time to visit his old friends, the shadow bumblers in the black clothing.

They were arguing inside their apartment even now, and he found the words of such interest that he refrained from entering at once. He heard them speaking of a new destination.

They had been ordered to go after the dragon and steal it for themselves. They were apparently angry about this turn of events. There were other tasks at hand. But the other tasks must wait.

The dragon came first, and it seemed as if the employers of the shadow bunglers knew where the dragon was.

Which was fortuitous for Chiun.

11

The old school bus served faithfully for twenty-eight years in the Creighton School District in Phoenix, Arizona, until it was old and tired and sent to be scrapped—only to be whisked away from the brink of destruction by kindly old Papa Alfred Theodore Zed. They painted it sky-blue with big yellow sunrises on each side.

Papa Theo drove that blue bus out of Arizona at top speed. His faithful followers were very clear about what they would do to him if they ever saw him again. It would be worse than what the police would do to him, and that was bad enough. He cursed his luck. Never again would he believe some bubble-headed teenage choir girl when she told him she was on the Pill.

Papa Theo left behind his flock and his charges of indecent liberties with a minor, but he didn't leave his bus. The bus was his home for a while, and he disguised it by scraping off the name Papa Theo

Ministry and filling it in with more sky-blue. He swore he would one day soon paint a new name on the side of that bus.

He changed his professional name to Papa Zed and found a new flock in a new town. They were a different breed of folks, these mountain people of upstate Pennsylvania, and if anything more gullible than the hicks in Arizona. Papa Zed Ministries was born, and he promptly painted the name on the side of the bus in big, black letters with spray paint and stencils from the hardware store.

Papa Theo, aka Papa Zed, never could explain why people seemed to heed his words, but dammit they did. He had some sort of charisma and confidence that went straight into the heads of people—some people—and stuck there. Those people would keep coming to him and keep being more and more entranced by his words until he could tell them just about whatever he wanted and they would believe it. Now, sometimes his influence would slip. Like when he made one of their daughters pregnant. But he wasn't going to let that mistake happen again.

Papa Zed was a smart man. A genius, even. But he wasn't smart enough to escape the lies of the velvet-tongued trickster that was himself. Eventually, he fell into the same pit that had trapped the thousands who had come before him—he began to believe his own words.

The more he believed, the more confident he became, and the more his followers believed. Oh, sure, some called him a nut and left the congregation, but that only reinforced the commitment of those who stayed.

The years went by. The congregation in the old barn in the Catskills became less social and more devoted to their Papa, and one day Papa told them of his new revelation about achieving eternal life.

Not in Heaven, but right here on Earth.

Papa Zed had never bothered to let on that he had been an M.D. in Bismarck once upon a time. He left North Dakota—and medical practice—for more or less the same reason he left Phoenix. He never let on to the country bumpkins that he read lots of scientific and medical journals. He liked them believing that his medical skills were somehow a divine gift rather than the result of years of medical practice.

So when he told his congregation about the discovery in the field of molecular biology, he did not explain to them that it was a recently isolated erythroid-specific type of pathway protoenzyme that had been extracted from rare samples of bone tissue and bone marrow. He said it was a miracle elixir, intended by God to be consumed only by the children of Papa Zed.

12

The specimen from which the marrow was harvested was unique. In fact, it was the only known specimen of its kind, making large-scale testing impossible. But the few test results that were conducted indicated that the new pathway enzymes in question acted as blank-slate healing agents. They adapted their makeup based on the blueprint DNA of the organism and strived to restore the body to match that blueprint through regenerative processes. The absolute neutrality of the enzymes meant that they were infinitely adaptable to the chemistry of the organism in which they acted.

What this meant was that the organism would try to heal the body in any way it could find until the body perfectly matched its DNA blueprint. Since the DNA blueprint was for an adult, it would also rapidly adjust the tissues of the host to match the DNA blueprint. If an aged organism were to host the enzyme, the enzyme would seek to "heal" the damage of time.

Poor Dr. Derringer. What a dolt. She had no clue what she was getting herself into when she published her test results. The firestorm of attention caught her entirely off guard. Of course there had been no human testing; she tested only on lab mice. Of course there would be no further testing; there was only one source of the enzyme and the specimen was not to be harmed.

She went on national television and stated in no uncertain terms that she had been describing an interesting side effect in her paper. There was nothing to indicate the effect was applicable to other mammals. This was not a miracle cure for aging and all diseases. It was simply a noteworthy development that occurred from a tissue-sample test of a one-of-a-kind biological specimen.

The commentator seemed to be in somber agreement with her conclusion, but when she had spoken her mind he asked, "And when do you think the drug will be available to the average man in the street?"

Dr. Derringer was appalled when the scientific community demanded that her sponsors force her to euthanize the creature to make its tissues available for the good of mankind.

Instead, Dr. Derringer and her blubbery, unimpressive-looking "dinosaur" went into seclusion in their facility in Pennsylvania, and the outside world largely forgot they even existed.

There were demands from medical organizations and pharmaceutical companies for increased access to the creature—which meant more bone samples.

Many claimed that no one could have ownership of such a unique specimen. Those who claimed this—mostly medical organizations and pharmaceutical companies—called for the formation of a global advisory conference on the inherently nonproprietary status of unique, naturally occurring biological specimens. Dr. Derringer declined to give testimony to the conference. The conference went ahead without her and decided unilaterally that all unique biological specimens that were not artificially developed and that could benefit mankind could not be owned, claimed or harbored by any one entity. Essentially, it said the apatosaurus belonged to the world.

The federal government of the United States didn't comment on the decision. Several lawsuits that tried to enforce the international decision in U.S. courts became stalled in fantastic bureaucratic delays that no one seemed capable of sorting through, even though the defendant wasn't actively involved in defending itself. The people who actually had possession of the specimen didn't even acknowledge that there was legal action being taken against them.

Eventually, they were right. The lawsuits collapsed, despite hundred-million-dollar investments in legal resources.

Others tried to simply barge into the facility and take what they saw as their fair share of the specimen, then cried foul when they were forcibly prevented from doing so. The papers even hinted that others were making attempts to steal the specimen.

But they did not succeed. The apatosaurus—or mutant whalephant or whatever you cared to believe it was—lived its life in solitude, watched over by its loyal and dedicated caretakers, year after year.

The reports on its health were in the public record, and they showed the creature had an amazingly stable metabolic profile. It showed no signs of disease. There was no evidence of degeneration of skin cells.

Papa Zed got hold of those reports just so he could confirm what he suspected lots of people knew but nobody wanted anybody else to notice: the number of replicatively senescent cells in the apatosaurus had not changed—ever. Its skin, blood, muscle and bone cells continued to divide just as fast as they ever had. There could be no more incontrovertible evidence that Punkin was not aging.

Papa Zed knew that the old claims about the enzymes in the dinosaur were true. And lots of drug companies knew it was true. This fresh revelation should have ignited a public firestorm. Instead, there was more silence.

Papa Zed got the picture. He was a latecomer in a game that had been going on behind the scenes for years now. There was a gigantic struggle going on around the apatosaurus. Lots of very powerful people wanted the specimen.

Papa Zed realized he wanted it, too.

And he knew how to get it.

PAPA ZED TOLD his people about the gift that God was going to bestow upon them if they were worthy.

"First we will lay claim to the beast that God has promised us!"

The congregation was enthusiastic. They had a cause! There were lots of volunteers to go down into the southern part of the state to serve as watchers. He chose five pairs of watchers, who would live in their cars and guard for the day the apatosaurus left its home.

The watchers were there for six months and nothing happened. Then Papa Zed got the call he had been hoping to get.

He ran into the yard and clanged the old dinner bell that aroused the congregation. Others had to be alerted by phone. They flocked to the barn and Papa Zed exhorted them.

"The beast is in flight! The watchers have reported it! Go now, my children, and watch the skies!"

The enthusiastic followers ran to their cars and tore out of the barnyard, and they dispersed across the state within hours.

The watchers down below were already pursuing the flying beast, and they remained in contact with old lady Marilyn Sidivy, who had a devil of a good time taking one phone call after another and marking positions on her laminated map of the state of Pennsylvania.

The beast was dangling from a big helicopter, which ran without lights.

"The children of Papa Zed must drive without lights, as well!" proclaimed Papa Zed. "Else they shall be seen by the beast thieves, and the beast thieves shall seek to elude them!"

"Thy will be done," Mrs. Sidivy said, and began relaying the message to the watchers.

They were spreading out on county highways,

doing their best to keep up with the lumbering helicopter. It was thunderously loud, making it easy to follow by sound, but its trajectory was obviously planned to keep it away from human habitation and roads as much as possible. The watchers lost it, then picked it up, then found it again. The rest of the congregation were in cars racing to the scene but they were still a good forty-five minutes away. They were keeping touch with Mrs. Sidivy via cell phones. More than forty of them, each labeled with a professional-grade label maker with the name of the congregant member or members on the other end.

"Oh, dear," Mrs. Sidivy said. "Brother Oscar and Sister Sally were pulled over by the police. Sister Sally says the policeman says Brother Oscar was going fifty miles over the speed limit and he was driving without his lights on. Oh, dear! Sister Sally says Brother Oscar does not have a driver's license! She thinks the policeman will arrest Brother Oscar."

Papa Zed examined the location of Brother Oscar's car on the map. He was in the best position to pick up the helicopter.

"Papa Zed can't afford to lose the eyes of Brother Oscar that can pierce the darkness of night!" Papa Zed cried. "Brother Oscar is given dispensation to violate human laws to continue doing the work of the Lord!"

"Thy will be done," Mrs. Sidivy replied, then said to her caller, "Listen, sis, Papa Z says you're a-okay to give the slip to Johnny Po-po."

Papa Zed and old Mrs. Sidivy held their breath together until they got the callback from Sister Sally. "We made it, Sister Mar, and we hear the beast!" Sister Sally had always been a quiet, mousy young lady but she seemed to have a wild streak to her. "Here it comes! Praise be to Papa Z the beast is flying right over our blessed heads! Yahoo!"

The sound coming out of the little telephone was quite a mixture of screaming teen and pounding helicopter blades, interrupted by the strident chirp of a police siren.

"Dangit!" Sister Sally screeched. "Leave us alone, pig!"

"Get out of the car with your hands in the air," crackled a voice over a megaphone.

"Oh, dear," Mrs. Sidivy murmured.

The helicopter sound was already receding. "Don't let them lose the flying beast," Papa Zed ordered.

"Thy will be done. Pull out all the stops, Sister."

"Now you're talking! Eat buckshot, porky!"

There was a blast. There was another blast.

"That would be Brother Oscar's twelve-gauge," said Mrs. Sidivy.

"Thy will is fucking done, Papa Zed!" Sister Sally exclaimed.

"Oh, dear!" Mrs. Sidivy reddened. "Watch your mouth-drool, girl."

Papa Zed was wiping his brow, amazed at his own power. He had just ordered one of his flock to gun down a police officer—and his will had been done without hesitation.

Mrs. Sidivy was alerting all her units converging on that part of the state to tune into the emergency bands. She said that there might be trouble coming to lay its nasty hands on Brother Oscar and Sister Sally. Sure enough, the phone wouldn't stop ringing. Mrs. Sidivy was only one human being, after all, and she needed help. She grabbed the landline phone just long enough to call home, and then Lord God almighty ten minutes later in came the Sidivy daughters. Wearing nighties, of all things, tucked into their blue jeans, and wearing the messed-up look of girls who'd just been dragged from bed. They were Mrs. Sidivy's pride and joy—high-school graduates, both of them, and the older girl, Barbara, was apparently somewhat of a rising star in the cashier pool at the local Tarjé Discount Superstore.

They each gave Papa Zed a shy and yet flirtatious smile.

"You leave Papa Zed be and help me out with the phones, ladies," Mrs. Sidivy said. "Stephanie and Barbara are very good girls, Papa Zed," she explained over her shoulder. "Just so full of such spunk and life."

Papa Zed smiled and nodded benevolently. Oh, criminy, old lady Sidivy had planned this as a way to get Papa Zed interested in her damn daughters! The nighties they wore as tops were revealing, silky things, so brand-new that the younger girl still dangled a Tarjé tag from her collar. The jeans were new, too, rising so low in front they were practically pornographic and so tight on the behind they looked painful.

Mrs. Sidivy got the girls to work with quick orders. They began fielding cell phone calls. There was only one chair, so they did a lot of bending at the waist. Papa Zed stammered about getting them chairs and removed himself into the back room. Normally, he would have welcomed the display, but tonight of all nights he could do without the distraction. And they were a true distraction. He wasn't going to be able to keep his eyes off of them. At least a couple of chairs would keep them from bending quite as much.

They thanked him extravagantly for the folding chairs.

"You shouldn't have put yourself to all that effort!" Mrs. Sidivy insisted.

Actually, the communications table was set up in the rear of the church-barn, and Papa Zed had strolled about eight feet to get the chairs. It really wasn't that much of an effort. The girls each had to give him a cheek-smooch in thanks for his efforts. They pressed up on either side of him, their silky polyester fronts pressing into his rib cage on either side, and he just couldn't help cupping them each on their behind.

But he was a man of great strength and personal fortitude. He sent the girls back to their seats. They were giving their momma little victory smiles when they joined her at the worktable.

"Let's focus on the task at hand, ladies," Papa Zed said.

"Thy will be done," the girl replied. But did they have to turn and look at him when they said it?

Then events began moving fast and furious, and it was easy to put thoughts of the Sidivy daughters out of his head.

Stephanie reported breathlessly, "Brother Howie says he hears lots of excitement in the police bands in Munster. They found a policeman shot dead and they have the license plate on the car the policeman had pulled over and it's Brother Oscar's car!"

"Oh, dear!" Mrs. Sidivy speed-dialed Sister Sally and Brother Oscar. "It's Papa Zed C3I, Sister Sally.

You got a whole county full of the law coming after you. They got your wagon tags. Better ditch the wheels."

They could hear Sally cry to her Oscar, "It's a police chase, Oscar, and they're chasing us!"

"That's quiet little Sally Horner?" Stephanie Sidivy asked.

"That child has let loose tonight," Mrs. Sidivy said. "Like I never would have thought possible."

"Sometimes the humblest demeanor can hide a wild child just waiting to spring out," Papa Zed observed thoughtfully. "Course, once it is let out, it's hard to get it stuffed back inside."

Dead silence except for the voices coming from the open cell phones. Papa Zed didn't notice it until he realized Mrs. Sidivy was exchanging concerned, somber looks with her daughters.

"We see them!" cried Sister Sally. "They're coming after us, but they're way behind."

"Turn south or you'll start getting into Gettysburg. They'll probably have more police coming to cut you off from that direction. You got about ten miles to the state line."

"They have pigs waiting there, too. Let's go north into the mountains. We'll take them into the hills!"

"They'll box you in for sure," Mrs. Sidivy said.

"Your only hope is getting into Maryland and hope they're not ready for you there."

"We can dodge them longer in the hills," Sister Sally said.

"But there'll be no way out. Them hills ain't that big and you'll have every cop from Harrisburg joining up in the chase!"

"Momma," Barbara said, "the hills is a good idea."

"What in blazes do you mean? You want Sister Sally and Brother Oscar locked up in prison?"

"Of course not, Momma," Barbara said, and gave her mother a swift kick to the shins. "But it will attract police attention."

Mrs. Sidivy got the picture. She turned on Papa Zed. "They wish to put their own freedom in grievous risk for the sake of Papa Zed and all his flock."

"A selfless sacrifice," Papa Zed said, nodding his affirmation.

Mrs. Sidivy barked into the phone, "This is Papa Zed Command, Control, Communications and Intelligence, Sally. It's into the hills for you and Brother Oscar."

Sally whooped deliriously.

"Brother Oscar and Sister Sally are good and brave and selfless people, aren't they, Papa Zed?" Stephanie asked, with innocent, teary eyes.

"They most certainly have shown their devotion to the flock. We must pray they make it to freedom."

"Thy will be done but I fear they haven't an ice cube's chance in hell, Papa Zed," Mrs. Sidivy said with false sorrow. She barked into the phone, "This is Papa Zed C3I, Sally. It's into the hills for you and Brother Oscar."

"But if they do, by a miracle, make it back to us, think of the adoration we will bestow upon them!" Papa Zed said, just to get the three women further agitated. He chuckled soundlessly when he saw the concerned faces.

"Oh, great, Barb," Steph whispered. "Now you gone and made the little miss into some kind of hero."

"Shh!" Barb hissed. Then she turned to look anxiously at Papa Zed. He beamed.

If Papa Zed had one physical flaw, aside from tremendous girth and triple chin, it was his hearing. He was half-deaf, he claimed. A lie that served him well in all walks of his life.

"Get the call out to everybody, girls," Mrs. Sidivy ordered. "Lay low and obey the traffic laws for the time being. Another twenty minutes and every cop this side of Altoona will be occupied with Brother Oscar's shenanigans."

"This is Brother Canduity," shouted a voice from

an open cell phone on the table. Stephanie, the younger sister and the one without a promising career in the Tarjé cashier pool, scrambled until she found the right one.

"You got Papa Zed C3I. Go ahead now, over," Stephanie said.

"You don't need to say 'over,' darling," Mrs. Sidivy said. "It's a phone, not a CB."

Stephanie ignored her mother and turned on the speaker. "Not a damn thing out here!" Brother Canduity shouted.

"Calm yourself, Brother C," Stephanie said warningly, then turned to Papa Zed. "He hasn't spotted the flying beast."

"The beast thieves should be almost directly over him by now," Papa Zed announced loudly for Brother Canduity to hear.

"Naw, there ain't nothing out here but frigging cows every damn direction. They're just standing there looking at me!"

Sister Stephanie Sidivy took control of the situation. "Canduity you get ahold of yourself and stop the car right now, right where you are. I say so, Brother Canduity, and you go ahead and do what I say. Turn off the car. Forget about the cows and just listen. Tell me what you hear."

Stephanie waited. Her momma and sister and Papa Zed were watching her intensely. Young Stephanie never buckled under pressure, and in fact she knew how to keep others performing well under pressure.

Stephanie turned to smile upon her beloved Papa Zed. "Brother Canduity has heard the helicopter of the beast thieves. It's northwest of his position."

"Good work, Stephie!" Papa Zed blurted.

Stephanie, who hadn't been called Stephie since grade school, tried to hide her gasp of delight. Mrs. Sidivy beamed at her, then beamed at Papa Zed, and Papa Zed beamed at Mrs. Sidivy and then he beamed at Barbara Sidivy. Barbara Sidivy did not beam. All she could manage was a sick smile.

"Stephanie," Barbara sniped, "you have a tag showing on your pajamas. I don't think Papa Zed is gonna be impressed to know you spent $13.99 for your camisole."

Papa Zed came between them to stand behind Mrs. Sidivy and leaned over, examining her laminated map. "Where are the beast thieves, then?"

"Strange enough, Papa Zed, they're headed toward a populated area. Why, they're headed for Whershee. Whatever for, I wonder?"

"Seems a strange place to take the beast," Papa

Zed reflected. "But they've gone out of their way to stay away from towns big and small up until now. They're going to Whershee, they must have a good reason."

13

The Camou-Nin emerged with their baggage. They were moving out and the sun wasn't even starting to glow below the horizon. The Ditzy Donuts panel truck was waiting for them, as expected. There were two drivers. One was in a white uniform and was sweating profusely.

Camou-Nin 098 nodded at the driver. "Who's your friend?"

"Trainee."

"Huh."

Camou-Nin 098 thought the trainee too old to even get a driver's license in most states, let alone get high-security driving work, but let the company do whatever it wanted. They could all go to hell. The company had just shafted the Camou-Nin big-time.

"They're gonna do the show without us," Camou-Nin 078 said dejectedly as the shadow warriors, disguised as regular civilians, piled their gear in the back of the doughnut truck and closed themselves inside.

"They can't do that, Snate," Eight-eight protested. "They got the show already in production. They done all the effects shots already. They told me all they're waiting on is us to do the live-action shots, and then the show's ready to go on the air. See, it's all set up. And you can't tell me they'd throw all that good money away on a show that's already done, right?"

The truck pulled out onto the road and headed for their next destination—wherever that was.

"Eight-eight, you moron, don't you see? Yeah, they got the show all ready to go and all they need is the live-action shots, but what the hell do they care who does the live-action shots?"

"They can't do it with the Camou-Nin," Eight-eight insisted.

"But they get to decide who's Camou-Nin. They created Camou-Nin, not us. We're just hired to play the damn part. They were selling Camou-Nin toys for twenty years. What do they care if it's you and me on the damn *Camou-Nin Adventures* cable show?"

There was a dismal silence in the rear.

Camou-Nin 098 spoke at last. "Listen, Cams, we got a serious problem."

They all looked at him in the dim light from the

two rear windows. Ninety-eight was the designated leader of the small band of warriors, but he had earned a position of trust among his men that came from being intelligent and perfectly honest with them. They respected him, and they respected his wisdom.

"The problem as I see it is this," Ninety-eight said. "We got promised this *Camou-Nin Adventures* show, right, but we only get the show if we get the dino. Right? Read your paperwork. That's the deal. Don't matter what they told you, Eight-eight. Maybe they're inclined to give us the show anyway, even if we don't get the dino. But why would they bother?"

"Because we're Camou-Nin," Eight-eight whimpered.

"Camou-Nin action figures haven't been selling as good as they ought to be for a long time," Ninety-eight declared. "I read it in the business part of the newspaper. There's a big toy convention in New York, and there was people laughing at the sales people who came from HAAC Toys 'cause they had all these new figures and nobody wants them anymore. They had figures of us. Me. Snate. Eight-eight. All of us."

"We're action figures?" Eight-eight said excitedly.

"Don't get all excited. It ain't good news, necessarily. Like I said, Camou-Nin action-figures sales are in the toilet. They're banking on us to make or break the whole line of Camou-Nin franchise. That's what they called it—a franchise. But the guy who wrote about it said HAAC Toys has no business bringing the Camou-Nin to the toy exhibition 'cause it's over. Really over. The TV show? It's over before it even starts.

"And you know what? The suits at HAAC know it. They're ready to pull the plug on everything that has to do with Camou-Nin. Only one thing is keeping it going—the dino. If they get the dino, and they can tell the whole world how it was real Camou-Nin that got them the dino, then the Camou-Nin are gold. They'll sell millions. The show will be a hit. Everybody will be interested in the Camou-Nin. Otherwise, they pull the plug."

"Oh, shit," Snate said.

"So here's what it all boils down to—it's all or nothing. It's good that we get to have another chance to get that dino and we got to really get it, because if we don't, it's back to being a security guard at the mall."

The sweating driver wondered if the man in the passenger seat had gone to sleep, or better yet, died spontaneously. The Chinaman looked old enough that spontaneous death seemed reasonable. The strength of the old man did not seem reasonable. The way the old man could create a universe of pain just by grasping a man's wrist was also unreasonable, but horribly true.

When the driver glanced over, he could see the old man was alive and awake, and he appeared to be listening to something.

"They speak of going to take back the dragon that does not rightfully belong to them," Chiun announced in a quiet singsong voice. "You will take them to the dragon?"

"I'm just supposed to drive. I don't know where—I swear to God I don't. They'll phone with instructions, they said."

"Who will phone?"

"HAAC special-projects director or one of his people."

Chiun would be patient. When the phone finally rang, the driver fully understood that he would say nothing and react normally. The call came from the special-projects director's special assistant.

"They told me to go west," the driver reported when he hung up the phone.

"Where is this Whershee?" Chiun demanded.

"You never been to Whershee?"

"I have been many places in this land of cultural desolation. Few are worth remembering."

"This place I think you would remember," the driver dared to state. "Do you like chocolate?"

"I do not like chocolate. I would just as soon ingest poison from a blowfish as feed upon such poisons as candy. What has this to do with Whershee?"

"The answer is in the glove box," the driver said.

Chiun opened the glove box and extracted a flat, paper-wrapped bar of chocolate with a dark brown wrapper that said, in big block letters, WHERSHEE. The smell assaulted him.

"Repulsive." He lowered the window an inch and slipped the candy out. It disappeared in the darkness.

"That was my breakfast."

"Then I have saved you from further self-destructive behavior. You are welcome."

14

Bill Zonka hunkered down behind his desk with the sports section and a cardboard container of egg *foo yung*. He searched in the gravy with his bare fingers until he pulled up a stingy omelette dripping with black gravy and wolfed it down in two bites without tearing his eyes away from the roundup of the day's soccer riot. When the phone buzzed, he wiped his hands on his sleeveless white T-shirt. The stains it left were hardly noticeable among the older brown stains.

He grabbed the phone. "Yeah?"

"Are they there yet?"

"No, they ain't here yet. I'll call you when they're here."

"They're supposed to be there by now."

Zonka sighed heavily, shrugged his shoulders and raised one hand. "Whacha want me to do?"

"Well, I talked to them a few minutes ago. They're

very, very close. They should be there any second. Are you prepared?"

Bill rolled his eyes to the ceiling. "I been prepared all day."

Bill Zonka hung up the phone and fished another egg *foo yung* out of the black gravy and continued to read.

Outside of his office the factory floor was dark and silent until the roof began to open up with a screeching of agonized bending metal. Hinges that had not opened in twenty years cried out as if in pain. But open they did, their rust crumbling among the vats of bubbling foodstuffs below. Some of the hinges were so corroded and rusted by the passage of time they couldn't take the strain and just snapped explosively. Those that remained intact continued to screech and wail, and as the rattling aluminum frame of the roof parted it let in the thunder of a massive machine that was somehow floating above the roof.

The interior of the factory resounded at once with the air-raid-like sirens of an intrusion alarm system that didn't know how to compensate for the opening of the roof. The alarm had come long after the roof had been closed for good. At the same time, the phone in Bill Zonka's office twirped excitedly. That would be the alarm company, reacting to the sudden alert.

Bill Zonka was determined to finish reading about the soccer riot. He loved soccer riots. Wouldn't you know, one of the best ones had to come on a night he couldn't be in front of the TV watching the footage. He wiped another gravy stain across his T-shirt, folded the paper and pushed himself to his feet—which made him a scant six inches taller than he had been when he was sitting on his desk chair.

He yanked at the phone. "Yeah. False alarm. No, some machinery in the plant set it off. No, don't send anybody, I'll take care of it, it's fine. I said don't send anybody." He slammed down the phone and trudged out to the factory floor.

The sleeveless T-shirt was itchy where it was crusted, and he lifted it up to scratch those places as he observed the operation in his factory. Technically, he was not supposed to be on the factory floor in a sleeveless shirt. He had a file full of citations from the health inspector that spelled out specifically that factory manager William Zonka was to wear a sleeved shirt on the factory floor at all times. Well, sometimes he did and sometimes he didn't.

The doors hit their stops but continued to rattle under the reverberations from the massive rotors.

Sticking his hands in his pockets, Bill Zonka had to admit that it was an impressive machine. The helicopter was about as big as a 747. Imagine a 747 in the air but sitting still right above your damn factory with a damn dead dinosaur hanging underneath on some cables. The noise was tremendous. Bill Zonka wondered what the hell they were waiting for.

Then he remembered what they were waiting for.

"Ah, shit," he said, and brought his meaty fist down on the green industrial switch on the door next to his office.

In the middle of the plant blazed a circle of light. In the midst of the illumination a vast tank of swirling white clouds was being agitated by the downdraft. The circle of light made a target for the operations crew in the belly of the big chopper. They looked like little bugs standing up there, a couple hundred feet above him.

The helicopter pilot and the operations crew began the immensely dangerous operation of lowering the thirty-ton dinosaur on its steel cables. The winch motors inside the belly bay of the Mi-12 Homer helicopter strained and creaked and whined like overstressed electrical transformers. The cables had to be kept equidistant to keep the apatosaurus stable during its descent to the factory floor.

They were all computer controlled, but the computers seemed to be having a hard time dealing with the load. First one corner of the flopping beast dangled on a slack piece of cable, only to be taken up again, then the other side would go loose. The apatosaurus carcass descended at less than one foot per second, and in about two minutes it was at the end of its cable.

Down on the factory floor, Bill Zonka twiddled his hands in his pockets and chuckled. "Oops, ha-ha," he said. The carcass of the dinosaur was still a good six feet above the swirling white fog in the massive vat. "I guess somebody don't know how to use a tape measure. Wonder what those assholes are going to do now?"

CAPTAIN TASSEL, the helicopter pilot, barked on the radio, "Tell me you're effing kidding me."

"I wish I was kidding you. The cables aren't long enough."

If anybody was more highly stressed at this moment, it was the copilot and the little dweeb wasn't even doing any of the flying—he was just sitting there watching the monitors.

"Well, who screwed up?" the copilot asked. "Somebody better find out who screwed up."

"Now is not exactly the time to discuss it," Rory Ahabepela said from the cargo bay. "Let's solve the problem."

"Are we absolutely certain that the winches are fully extended?" Tassel demanded.

Rory's chief engineer had already answered this question two times. "The winches are fully extended—there's no cable left. She's as far down as she's going to get."

"Well, how could somebody even make a mistake like this? It's stupid," the copilot cried miserably.

"What's our clearance?" Tassel asked.

The copilot looked terrified. "You're not thinking of bringing the whole damn thing down on top of the roof?"

"It looks like our only choice," the pilot said.

The copilot was in a panic. "You're not going to bring the chopper down. You're just not. There's maybe ten feet of clearance. We go down any farther and we're going to start hitting the tops of the doors."

"I don't care if we hit the doors. The rotors are well out of the danger zone."

"I got news for you," the copilot wailed. "There is nothing about anything we're doing tonight that is out of the danger zone. Every inch that you get closer to that roof is an inch closer to disaster."

"How much clearance?" Tassel demanded.

The copilot was shaking his head miserably as he leaned into the displays.

"We're fluctuating between fifteen and nineteen feet."

"We have room to spare," Tassel insisted. "We need to go down only twelve feet. That will get the specimen into the chamber."

"And we'll be practically sitting on top of the damn building," the copilot insisted. "We can't do this. We'll crash."

"We don't do this, then what happens?" the pilot demanded.

The copilot visibly gulped. He knew what would happen if they failed in their mission. This was one of those all-or-nothing sort of career choices. Do the job right and get rich. Fail and be dead.

Without waiting for the copilot to make up his mind, the pilot began the tricky maneuver of guiding a small airborne skyscraper lower in the sky, one cautious foot at a time.

DOWN BELOW, Bill Zonka laughed out loud. "Holy shit." He scrambled into his office knowing that things were going to start flying around in the factory again. He didn't exactly want to be there when it happened. He stood against the wall and peered out through his office window, not quite believing what he was seeing. "Got some balls. Gotta give it to 'em."

The dangling apatosaurus had shaken loose from its netting during the rough trip over. The tail dangled off one end, and the limp, heavy head on its elongated neck was dangling partially out the other end. They swayed and stirred up the clouds of cold vapor clinging over the surface of the liquid in the vat. The extreme cold of the vapor must have done something to the head, because when it swung momentarily free of the mists Bill Zonka was alarmed to see that the eyes of the prehistoric creature had popped open.

"Oh God, thing ain't dead, thing ain't dead."

He hid himself behind the wall, not daring to look out the window of his office, as if the thing would reanimate, escape the steel mesh netting, jump to the ground and come after him. He stood there quaking in his shoes and his stained T-shirt. Finally, he got the nerve to look out the window again. The massive neck and head of the apatosaurus were still swinging, the eyes were still open, but they had absorbed a covering of ice from the cold radiating from the liquid in the vat.

The eyes were dull and blank. It was dead. Of

course it was dead. The eyes had opened from some sort of a reaction of the cold on the nerves.

And down came the gigantic roaring helicopter, inch by agonizing inch, until the dinosaur's head disappeared into the vat, and then the tip of the tail and then the body itself touched the mist and vanished into the vat. And just as Bill Zonka was feeling a little bit more like his old ballsy self, just as he was reaching for the door, the interior of the factory vanished from sight.

"What the hell, man?" Bill Zonka said aloud. "What the hell?"

Outside of his window there was nothing but white. They had warned him about the boil-off, but he hadn't really been paying attention. How was some mist gonna hurt him?

The weight of that creature was tremendous and its residual body heat had reacted with the vat of liquid nitrogen, transforming the surface nitrogen instantly into clouds of nitrogen steam and blanketing the factory with a fog like something out of a cheap horror movie.

Bill Zonka sat at his desk and drummed his fingers and watched the agitated whiteness that covered his window, feeling strangely isolated. All he could see was white, and all he could hear was the huge roar of the helicopter, which must have been hovering mere inches over the top of the factory.

Bill Zonka had wished to God he had never volunteered for this whole endeavor. He thought it would be easy. He thought he would have nothing to do except maintain the special equipment, clear the factory out on the right night and then sit there and let it happen. In fact, that was all he was doing. But it was scary as hell. How long was this going to take?

The answer—a long goddamn time. You could freeze a human body stiff in that vat of liquid nitrogen, which was 321 degrees below zero Fahrenheit, in about a minute. The big goofy-looking thing they called an apatosaurus, which some people said was actually a dinosaur, of all things—although it didn't look like any sort of dinosaur Bill Zonka ever heard of—that thing was thirty tons. That cooled a lot slower.

The holding tank was specially designed to be narrower at the bottom than it was at the top so when they lowered the apatosaurus, it would naturally be compacted into a tight little ball. Even the massively low temperatures in the tank would take a lot of time to penetrate deep and made a stiff block out of the warm, soft dino. The fact was that even the liquid nitrogen vats would not freeze solid a thirty-ton carcass. Even when it was rock solid on the outside, it would still be raw, warm meat at its very core.

That's okay. They just needed it cold enough to preserve the thing until they could get it into the special biolab where they would chop it up and figure out if it really did contain the wonder drug that would let human beings live forever. The freezing was absolutely essential. This was the one and only specimen of its kind. There would never be another.

It would be a real shame if it was allowed to spoil.

The freeze tank, so Zonka had been told, was a miracle of engineering. Something about it being an open liquid nitrogen vat. From what Zonka understood, the refrigeration systems were immensely powerful—they had to be to compensate for the big nitrogen evaporation losses that occurred from having it in an open tank. Millions of dollars were spent on just the pumps. Apparently, it took real special pumps for liquid that was almost as cold as the planet Pluto.

Bill Zonka could feel the cold. He could see the frost on the inside of his office window getting thicker. He could go write his name in it up to the first knuckle. He looked at the thermostat on the wall, but it was buried. At that moment, for the first time, Bill Zonka started to fear for his life.

If he stayed in here much longer he was going to freeze to death. He was getting out of his office now. He knew he would risk a little bit of frostbite walking around through the factory, filled with nitrogen clouds, but he couldn't stay here. Simple as that. He grabbed the door handle and screamed when his hand froze instantly to the stainless-steel surface of the doorknob. He yanked his hand back but it wouldn't come off. He could feel his own flesh freezing already. How cold was it out there? This wasn't just the outer surface of his skin, but the very fingers themselves were turning to ice instantly and the pain was excruciating.

He fumbled in his pocket with his other hand until he found his lighter, thumbed it up to full flame height and flicked it. He put the flame under the doorknob to heat it up, but if it was working it wasn't working fast enough. He applied the flame directly to his thumb just underneath the flesh where it met the metal, and after a moment was relieved to see the thumb pop free. He applied the frame directly to each of his fingers until they detached from the metal.

It must have burned and he could smell cooking flesh, but he couldn't feel anything in his hand at all. It seemed as if it had frozen solid virtually to the wrist, and that was where the pain started now. He didn't know what to do. So he just hopped around the office and screamed for a while.

The building was being jolted and bounced by the helicopter. Eventually, the combination of the cold and the violence shattered the window of the office. Glass fragments spattered at Bill Zonka, nicking his flesh in a hundred places, just before the frigid mist drifted in to add to his torment.

CAPTAIN TASSEL WAS by this time resting his wheels on the very surface of the roof of the factory. He had tried for many long minutes to avoid contact with the building, but it was a lost cause. He allowed the helicopter to settle slightly, until the roof doors were crushed and the chopper rested on the roof itself. This gave stability to the aircraft, and they would be safe as long as he kept most of the massive weight of the aircraft from actually settling on the roof itself. The roof doors were a total loss. The roof would need major repairs, as would the underside of the helicopter. But the pilot was pretty sure that these were all secondary considerations to his employers. The fact was, he got the job done, even solving someone else's failure to measure the length of the cables.

On the cockpit screens, Tassel saw the white mist thin and drift away.

"How does she look in real life?" he radioed to the crew commander, Rory Ahabepela.

"Beautiful," Rory answered.

BILL ZONKA LAY behind the desk with his face buried in his hands. Now the ceiling panels were freezing and becoming so brittle they shattered and fell, sharp as tiny razor blades that nicked his flesh. Zonka crawled on crystal splinters until he was completely under the desk, where he had protection from most of the debris. Everything was sharp. He was nicked and cut all over his burned body. Jeez, but it just hurt so much all over. And the helicopter was still just sitting there, blowing its big wind into the factory and keeping everything stirred up. Weren't they about finished?

RORY AHABEPELA WATCHED the operations from the open belly of the Mi-12. He was using his regular field glasses. The thermal night-vision glasses had freaked out trying to adjust to all the heating and cooling.

He watched as the liquid nitrogen was pumped from the vat into underground holding tanks, but the clouds of boil-off continued lingering in the factory.

Then the water sprinklers opened. The liquid was actually a solution with more salt than Dead Sea water and just as sterile, and the water was already cooled to well below the freezing temperature of pure water. It made the transition from liquid to solid as it came in contact with the hard-frozen carcass. The thin layers of salty ice built up rapidly.

The ghostly, glistening ball of ice that was the world's only dinosaur swelled with every passing moment as the salt ice thickened all around it. It was like a jewel, reflecting and seeming to magnify any shaft of light that bounced off of it.

You couldn't go flying around with the world's biggest reflector hanging from your aircraft and try to keep it secret.

And they wouldn't have to.

Hidden plumbing opened and a thick, brown torrent of steaming liquid poured into the vat, hundreds of gallons a second, filling it up in a matter of seconds, sputtering and steaming against the ice block until the carcass was buried under the stuff.

Now the tricky part. The coating was hot. Only a thin layer was needed on the dinosaur—and if the dino was in the hot stuff too long it would begin to melt. The hot liquid had to be removed from the vat quickly. A crude but effective solution had been found.

"Blow the tanks," Rory ordered over his radio.

Tassel watched with apprehension and excitement on his cockpit monitor. Even his copilot had stopped whining to view the spectacle.

What if the explosion was too weak to break open the vat? What if it was too strong and ended up blowing the dinosaur to pieces? Nobody seemed to have a lot of confidence in the amount of explosive being used.

There were twin flashes of fire.

For a second, it seemed as if nothing had changed in the factory.

Then the walls of the steel vat seemed to open like the petals of a flower.

IF THEY'D TOLD him once, they had told him a thousand times. Be careful of the boil-off. It'll be cold! It could really hurt ya!

Somehow, Bill Zonka never believed them. He'd used liquid nitrogen more than once, and yeah it was a little cold when it blew on you but it never hurt you. Now he was lobster-red and he'd be lucky if he didn't need a skin graft—and probably stitches, too. He had a bunch of bleeding gashes along with countless little pricks and nicks.

How long was this gonna take?

There was a deep thump that shook the floor.

What was that?

Then the gonglike sound of falling chunks of heavy metal.

Oh, yeah. The outer coating. Don't be around when the coating goes in, 'cause it's gonna come right back out again. You be sure and be out of the plant when that happens.

If they'd told him once, they had told him a thousand times.

Already, the hot dark liquid had battered down the door and flooded into the office.

His skin screamed, burned again from head to toe. He had to get out! But the stuff was thick as oatmeal and the cloying smell suffocated him. When he tried to crawl onto the desk, it seemed to cling to him and pull him back down. He could barely hold his head out of the liquid.

And the liquid was beginning to solidify.

THE MI-12 ROSE gently under the leaden blanket of cloud cover, and Captain Tassel thought he was starting to get the hang of this ungainly monster of a helicopter. The winches whined and extracted the apatosaurus from the open roof, but it no longer looked like any kind of a dinosaur, alive or dead. It was enveloped in a thick, smooth covering of rich darkness. The light seemed absorbed by its darkness. Even knowing it was there, it was difficult to see.

They moved slowly away from the factory, cruising in darkness.

Tassel felt relieved, but he knew that ahead of them lay the most dangerous part of the whole undertaking—flying this beast into the mountains where it would never be found.

15

Remo's aircraft never did end up landing at the private airport in the Pittsburgh suburbs, and Smith called to explain something about a strange reading on the air-traffic patterns that was most likely the disguised radar ping of the giant helicopter that had absconded with the apatosaurus.

The explanation really didn't matter. What mattered was, Remo Williams was going to Whershee, Pennsylvania. By the time he had deplaned and grabbed the waiting car, the trail of the mysterious aircraft had left Whershee again—vanished.

Remo's only option was to nose around the site where the helicopter had taken the apatosaurus. With any luck, the big, dead dino would be there somewhere. Maybe they accidentally dropped him at the chocolate factory.

REMO HAD LIKED chocolate when he was a kid, of course. The nuns at the orphanage in New Jersey had never understood what good chocolate could possibly do for growing boys, so Remo actually didn't get candy very often. When he was an adult, with his own disposable income, he bought a candy bar now and then and thought he was getting a rare treat. Then he entered the military, and he had all the repulsive, heat-stabilized chocolate bars he could ever hope for, and he got sick of them in a hurry.

Actually, learning to dislike chocolate in the military was a blessing in disguise, because now, of course, he couldn't have any. Chocolate was one of the many, many foods that were not on the Sinanju diet plan.

"Hello?" Remo said, strolling into the wrecked interior of the old factory. This was not just any chocolate factory, this was the chocolate factory that started it all. The plaque on the front of the brick structure claimed this building was a Registered Historic Place. This was the very factory where Wilder T. Whershee created the first chocolate bar and gave birth to the modern candy industry, as well as a century of the escalating Type 2 Diabetes epidemic.

The factory had been modernized since the 1890s, but a lot of the shiny steel machines had been wrecked very recently.

In fact, one of the machines had burst and spilled tons of chocolate all over the factory. It was still warm and liquid below the surface. Remo had to walk lightly to avoid breaking the cool outer shell.

The police had not yet arrived, but there was somebody else in the plant. Remo followed the sound of distressed breathing.

"Burns burns burns."

"Hi, Mr. Burns. I'm Remo."

"This stuff burns. Get me out, please."

There was a man sealed up inside a shell of thick chocolate. Remo tapped the surface, and the brown shell split apart and slid off of the top half of the prisoner's body. The man's T-shirt came off with the chocolate, which also depilated his chest, arms and back with a ripping sound. The man's flesh was lobster-red. The subsurface chocolate was still steaming hot and liquid, and the man hastily withdrew his legs from it.

"What the heck happened here?" Remo asked.

The panting, red-skinned man said, "Machine broke. It spilled on me. Call hospital."

"In a second. How come your roof is open?"

"The roof is open?"

"Must be where they brought the dinosaur in."

"I don't know what you're talking about."

"Bulldookey. What did they do to the dinosaur?"

"What dinosaur?"

Remo stood on the desk and grasped the man by the

ankle and dipped his entire head into the hot, melted chocolate in the spot where he had been standing.

"Burns!" the man gasped when Remo released him.

"You said that." Remo lowered his head into the chocolate again.

The man came up sputtering, "I'll kill you, you piece of dog shit!"

"No matter how many times I do this, you're still not getting any sweeter."

Four dips later, and the fight had gone out of the man as the layer of hardening chocolate became nearly an inch thick. He was having trouble expelling the gruel-thick goo. Remo helped by shaking him vigorously.

"What did they do to the dinosaur?" he asked again.

"Froze it. In dry ice."

"And then what?"

"Coated in this stuff," the man answered.

"Why'd they coat a frozen dinosaur in chocolate?"

Abruptly, a horrible thought occurred to Remo. The big, meaty dinosaur had originally been brought to the United States in an operation funded by one of the biggest fast-food franchises in the country, with the intent of grinding it up and selling it as the world's most exclusive and expensive hamburgers. Skip King, man with that plan, was no longer among the living. But was it possible that some other lunatic had come along and decided to make the apatosaurus into the world's hugest chocolate truffle?

"It ain't chocolate."

Remo breathed in the odor. It was thick with sugar and solidified fats, but there was some other substance mixed in. When he compressed a sliver of the stuff between his fingers, he felt the grittiness like the powder from broken porcelain.

"What is it?"

"I don't know."

The man did know a few seconds later, when Remo let him breathe again.

"Stealth paint. They coated the dino with it. Like the stuff they put on the outside of the B-1 bomber, only it's suspended in a thermal plasticized b-lactoglobulin film. You know. Like chocolate. It's what we know, so it's what we used."

Remo found a non-chocolate-coated phone in the front offices of the Whershee Chocolate Company. "The head elf couldn't tell me where the dino was taken from here," he reported. "There's no sign of Chiun, either. You know where he is?"

"We do not," Smith said. "But I think we have a lead on the current location of the dinosaur."

"What you've told us fits in with what've just observed, Remo," said Mark Howard. "There was a very faint anomalous radar signature we received from commercial air-traffic control, but it vanished. Now it has reappeared again. We're trying to get a lock on it using a thermal-imaging satellite. The coating was probably designed to keep the thing from radiating frigid temperatures. If the coating is deteriorating, we might be able to sense it."

"You're looking for a cold spot?" Remo asked. He didn't really care. What he cared about at the moment was finding the Master of Sinanju Emeritus.

"If there are any supercold icebergs floating over the East Coast, we'll see them," Mark Howard said.

16

"Mama, I feel so cheated," Barbara hissed into her mother's ear as they waited for something else to happen. "That little tart just up and laid claim to him!"

"You know how bold Stephanie is," Mrs. Sidivy said. "You should have been just as bold."

"But that's not my way, Mama," Barbara cried.

"And you don't know what, if anything, is resolved here tonight," Mrs. Sidivy said, patting her daughter's arm tenderly.

"Mama!" Barbara said. "What do you think?" She rolled her eyes to the back, where Papa Zed and Sister Stephanie were practically grinding against one another as they examined maps of the surrounding counties on the bulletin board. "And here I am dressed in my lingerie and I feel like a perfect fool!" She opened her arms to display the flimsy lavender camisole top that was the symbol of her foolishness and gasped when she realized one of her boobs had slipped out of the satiny fabric. She lifted it back inside.

"Things happen for a reason. It might be, Barbara, that you're not meant to be the wife of a messiah. It doesn't mean Stephanie is a better person, just because the living god wants her instead of you."

"Well, of course it does, Mama."

"You'll find the one who's right for you, Barbara. Maybe Brother Canduity."

Barbara's lower lip curled.

"Hush, all!" Mrs. Sidivy applied a finger to one ear as she pushed a purple cell phone against the other. "What now? Hold on, sweetheart, I'm gonna let Papa Zed hear it for himself."

Mrs. Sidivy pushed the phone to her bosom and said, "Papa Zed, I just don't know whether to believe Brother Chent or not. He's saying outlandish things." She thumbed on the speaker. "Go ahead, Brother Chent."

Brother Chent was already shouting his explanation, "—dipped it in chocolate!"

"Dipped what in chocolate?" Papa Zed asked.

"Praise be it's you, Papa Zed. They dipped the beast! They opened the top of the old Whershee plant and that big old helicopter just sank it right on down.

And there was all this steam and then they pulled it out and it's a big hunk of steaming chocolate!"

"You drunk, Chent?" demanded Stephanie Sidivy. This was some kind of no-nonsense, take-control young lady, and people responded to her at once.

"No, ma'am, Sister Stephanie, I haven't touched a drop all night and I know what I saw. I can't believe it myself. Now it's starting to move away and the damn thing is near to invisible."

The glowering Barbara Sidivy seemed to have had enough of her little sister's assumption of power and used this opportunity to assert herself. "Brother Chent, I think you are a damn liar and you need to apologize to Papa Zed for lying to him."

"Quiet, Barb," Steph snapped. Barb and Mrs. Sidivy were both taken aback, but Steph was moving ahead confidently. "What do you mean, 'invisible,' Brother Chent?"

"It's all dark now. No shine coming off the lizard skin of the beast. When it goes against the clouds, it's just a dark place. It's gonna be a lot harder to follow now."

"They have cloaked the beast in darkness, Papa Zed," Sister Stephanie exclaimed.

"But you unveiled the cunning stunt with élan, Sister Stephie."

Stephanie's shining eyes showed she appreciated his comments on all levels. "I merely put my faith in the words of Brother Chent. He's got good eyes even if he is slow to think."

"Route the children of Zed, Mrs. Sidivy," Papa Zed said.

"Thy will be done." Mrs. Sidivy was awash in conflicting emotions. She felt her scheme had worked. She had paired up one of her own daughters with the holy and benevolent Papa Zed himself. She would have preferred that it was Barbara, though. Stephanie was such a strong one she was sure to make her place in the world, with or without Papa Zed. And Mrs. Sidivy knew her own place as the most important woman in the family had just been usurped.

"They're coming this way," Mrs. Sidivy said as she marked the new position of the flying beast. "Northeast out of Whershee and into the mountains. Our people going down south are gonna intersect with the beast. Thy will is done, Papa Zed."

"STOP AT ONCE," Chiun said.

The driver was slow to respond and Chiun pinched his wrist. The driver pulled to the side of the road, screaming.

There were questions and exclamations from the shadow bumblers in the rear of the truck. Chiun slipped out of the cab and moved like a black panther over the surface of the road to get himself away from the lights and the sounds of the vehicle.

Then he ran faster than a panther runs, even faster than a cheetah runs. The thing he pursued was miles ahead of him, and dark as the night. It was another car, careening down the road at speeds that violated the posted limit. Chiun had spotted the car by the glow of the dash lights.

He might have dismissed the car as the suicidal play of narcotized adolescents had there not been another such vehicle that crossed the highway farther ahead. Now the second car drifted, and was forced to put on its brakes momentarily to make the turn without rolling on its roof, then it turned onto the same dirt road and followed the first dark car.

It still could very well be the shenanigans of inebriated young people, but when Chiun stopped and listened, he could hear the sound of a great flying machine, miles and miles away. The darkened cars were chasing it.

Chiun chased after it, too.

"PRAISE BE to Papa Zed, the beast is coming down right to us!" Brother Chent erupted into his cell phone.

"It's crashing?" Papa Zed asked.

Mrs. Sidivy repeated the suggestion to Brother Chent.

"No, Sister, it's landing. Coming right down in a big field of grass about two miles from the gravel road. I'm getting out and going ahead on foot."

Barbara Sidivy was trying to reach Brother Canduity. "Papa Zed C3I calling Brother Canduity. Come on in now."

No answer.

"You got the right phone, missy?" Mrs. Sidivy demanded.

"It's the right phone," Barbara said, but she checked the label on the mouthpiece just in case. B. Canduity. The display told her the line was open and had been open since the connection was established at the start of the evening's events.

"Canduity, you come in now," Barb said sternly, but she didn't sound as stern as she wanted to sound. "Canduity, you pick up the phone right this second." Even that sounded more naggy than commanding. Dangit.

Then she heard the man talking. Barbara pulled the phone away from her head and colored red.

"What's the matter?" Papa Zed asked.

"He's mad. He's using profanity. Sounds like he encountered some cows." She turned on the speaker, wincing as she did so. "See, he hates cows."

It was Canduity, all right, and he was releasing a river of cussing that even Papa Zed was impressed with. Canduity was always a squirrelly kind of guy, and you would never have thought he had it in him. But it was all there. The basic four-letter expletives, some creative combinations and some outlandish combination phrases that brought to mind images of pure depravity.

"He really hates cows," Barbara said apologetically.

"Get that boy back on solid ground and get him doing Papa Zed's work," Stephanie ordered.

Barbara had had enough. "Listen here, little missy—"

"I'll listen later. Right now I'm doing Papa Zed's work and I thought that's why you tagged along. You got better things to do, then get out of the way."

Stephanie had always been a little bossy and when she was mad she got obstinate, but never this bossy—absolutely calm and in charge. She took the phone out of Barbara's fingers without asking.

"Brother Canduity, you shut up and listen."

And Brother Canduity shut up. "Who is this?"

"This is Sister Stephanie and you better shut your pie-hole and listen. You ready to do that? 'Cause all this carrying on is making you worse than useless to Papa Zed and all his children."

A much humbled Brother Canduity reported his location. "I'm on foot, chasing after Brother Chent. The helicopter is coming down across the field from where I am. I'm trying to catch up but there's cows and they keep coming at me and they're running from the noise and they're out of control."

"Get ahold of yourself," Stephanie ordered.

"Steph, the man has fears," Barbara said. "Cut him some slack."

"There's no time for fears. Here. You talk to him, but just keep him under control. And put your dang boob away."

Barbara cried in embarrassment and hoisted herself back inside the camisole. Barbara felt like such an idiot! Her earlier confidence had completely evaporated, while little Stephanie was completely at home in herself, in her skin, in her role as leader, and in her identical, but scarlet, camisole.

"Mama," Stephanie said, "give me Brother Chent."

"Yes, ma'am," said Mrs. Sidivy, and then she looked at her daughter, deeply embarrassed. She had never said "Yes, ma'am" to her own daughter and she had never thought she would. She had never dreamed her little baby girl Stephanie was—whatever she was right now.

Another thing Sister Stephanie did not have time for now was her mother's epiphany. "Brother Chent, you see the landing site? What's there? Nothing? How close are you? There must be a hidden door. Look for a hidden door in the ground. It should start opening up. They're not just gonna deposit the beast in a pasture."

She listened and said over her shoulder, "Papa Zed, it looks like they're going to just drop the thing in the pasture."

"That would be a miracle of good fortune, Stephie sweetie." Nobody had ever called her Stephie sweetie.

"But I kind of doubt that it's gonna be that easy for us, sweet Papa." Nobody ever called Papa Zed sweet Papa, but he didn't take offence. "Does Canduity see anything?"

Barbara's eyes were down on the table and she was speaking softly into her phone, but she relayed the question. "There's the three helicopters up high that's accompanying the big flying beast helicopter and there's another helicopter. A long way off. Lots of flashing lights."

Stephanie nodded. "I think this is not the end of

the line for the flying beast. I think they're just laying low while the traffic clears. What about you, sweet Papa?"

"Makes perfect sense, Stephie. Let's hang tight until they get going again."

17

The command center was two floors down from Jeremy Landis's penthouse suite. It had the muted appointments and soft lighting of a jeweler who sells million-dollar diamonds to very rich old ladies.

Scott Wrought looked entirely out of place, but he still managed to stride around the room as if he owned it. He'd grown his gut another eight inches during his years with Landis, and you could have braided the hair coming out of the top of his shirt. He ran the operation from the twenty-seventh floor, but still got down to the hangar on a regular basis and he always had grease under his fingernails. Even now.

Landis read the body language in the room. Wrought supervised four communications experts and technicians, and they were all on the edge of their seats.

"Thought you were going to stay out of here tonight," Wrought barked.

"What's gone wrong?"

"Relax. We solved the problem."

"What problem?"

"Winch cables. They ended up being short."

Jeremy Landis gaped. "How could that happen? We thought through every aspect of the job a thousand times."

"Not sure. But it's okay. We compensated."

"How?" Landis cried.

Wrought made a rye grimace. "The freeze tanks were repositioned recently at the factory. It looks like that idiot plant manager okayed a new configuration to the production line."

Landis slapped his forehead. He hated this. He hated being at the mercy of other people's incompetence. You just never knew when somebody would do something immensely stupid.

In the good old days his schemes had been his and his alone. He was in control. He did the dirty work. If there were mistakes made, he'd be the one to make them—and he never made mistakes.

But nobody was as careful as he was. Even Scott Wrought had been responsible for an error or two.

Landis moaned audibly. He felt so helpless!

"Don't worry about it. We compensated."

"But what else is going to go wrong?" Landis demanded. "What if we can't compensate again?"

Wrought shook his head. "Look. We're already headed home."

On the screens were three video feeds showing the lumbering giant helicopter flying dark, hundreds of feet below the camouflage of the three survey helicopters. The three choppers, flying in a close formation, concealed the Mi-12 on radar.

A red light blinked to life on every screen, accompanied by a sickening beep. Landis's stomach suddenly felt as if it were full of churning earthworms.

"Nothing to worry about," Wrought said calmly. "We've planned for this. Just another aircraft."

"What's another plane doing there?" Landis demanded. "Shoot it down!"

"Firing weapons is only a last resort. We go just like we planned. Come to a stop. There's a place. Bring her low. Wait for it."

The lumbering Russian helicopter sank into a hilly grazing field in utter blackness. On the thermal monitor, Landis saw terrified cattle fleeing.

Wrought listened in on his headphones. "It's a state police helicopter. Headed for some kind of manhunt in the hills north of Chambersburg. He's calling our guys. He wants to know what we're up to."

"He's spotted the Homer?" Landis fretted.

"Doubt it. They're giving him the cover story. He's checking our registration."

There was a long moment of silence. The cover story was perfect. The three camouflage helicopters were part of a small aerial-survey company that Landis now owned. It was a legitimate business and did legitimate work, and all the paperwork was perfect. The entire reason for the survey company's existence was that it could play this part in tonight's undertaking. Landis had been confident it would work perfectly.

But now, as it all came down he was not sure. Why had he relegated himself to being just a bystander in all this! He needed something to do or he was going to go nuts.

"Something's wrong," Landis declared. "It's taking too long."

"Everything's fine." Wrought nodded and pressed his ear. "They told us to go on with what we're doing."

The cops left the vicinity as the survey choppers went through the motions of taking laser readers of the terrain. Wrought held on for ten minutes, watching for any sign of other nosy aircraft—like maybe the state police helicopter turning around and coming back in their direction.

Then he gave the all-clear.

CHIUN'S SANDALS barely touched the matted tips of the pasture grass, and he flew overland like some sort of marauding phantom. He easily avoided the grazing cattle and their scattered droppings.

There were others in pursuit of Chiun's dragon. They were the ones from the cars that drove recklessly fast and without headlights. They were on foot, as well now, and Chiun had no trouble passing by one of them with such speed and silence the man never saw the Master of Sinanju in the overcast darkness. In fact, the man was completely engaged with his telephone and with the scraping of his soiled feet on the grass.

There was another man far ahead. He was in the pasture. In the pasture, connected by chains dangling from the belly of a very large helicopter, was a mass of a dark substance that must be Chiun's dragon. It was covered with a dark shell, but the shell was cracked and wisps of cold seeped from the cracks.

Whatever the man sought to do Chiun could not guess, but it enraged him that yet another claimant was there for his dragon.

But the pain came then, and Chiun felt his legs become leaden and move clumsily beneath him and he slowed until he was running no faster than an ordinary man. Then the sound of the oversize helicopter became louder and Chiun watched the chains grow taut. He angrily commanded his legs to work and channeled the pain into movement, but the movement was not enough. The dragon was hoisted off of the pasture, and was already out of his reach when he reached it.

Chiun danced with fury beneath it and ignored the rainfall of dirty, salty water spattering him from the melting block.

"No man may steal a dragon from Sinanju and live to tell the tale!" he shrieked in Korean. "You shall pay the ultimate price!"

But the helicopter ignored Master Chiun as if he were of no importance whatsoever.

Chiun silenced his rage and pursed his lips tightly—and then heard the cries of another man. He could see the man who had reached the dragon. The man had adhered himself to the side of the dragon, and was being taken away with it.

The second man, whose shoes were fouled, stood some distance away watching his friend vanish into the dark skies of the overcast night without ever seeing the little Korean Master.

"Sister Barbara," he said into his cell phone. "Brother Chent is flying with the beast itself."

18

"Chent's phone is still on," Sister Stephanie announced. "Brother Chent?" she said into her phone.

The sound coming over the speaker was a maelstrom of wind and the engines of the helicopter.

"Brother Chent, can you hear me?"

"Sister Stephanie? That you?"

"Chent! You did it. You're flying with the beast!"

"Yes, that's right, but I'm not going to last long. I'm a dead man already, Sister Stephanie. Fact is, I'm freezing to death."

Stephanie put her hand to her face.

"I looped my arm in the chain. That wasn't my brightest idea in history. The chain got tight when the helicopter took off, and now I'm trapped on the side of the frozen Beast. My arm's dead already, but I don't think the chain is gonna cut it. It's just holding me here against the ice and I'm freezing real fast."

His speech was already slowing down as his face became stiff.

"You hang on there, Brother Chent," Mrs. Sidivy said urgently. "They'll come down from the sky soon enough."

"Who's that there? Sister Missus Sidivy? You don't understand. The back part of my body where I'm touching the ice is frozen already. Listen."

There was a staccato tapping sound.

"That's my ass. Froze solid."

"Maybe they'll land soon, Brother Chent. When they do, the chain'll come loose and we'll get you to the hospital to thaw you out."

"Don't see that happening," Brother Chent said, slurring his words. "Fingers are freezing. Any second now."

"Don't give in, Brother Chent," Mrs. Sidivy warned him.

"Thy will be done, Papa Z—"

His voice trailed off and he never finished the name.

Mrs. Sidivy called his name again and again. They could hear the wind and the throaty roar of the rotors. The line stayed connected.

"Brave man froze solid with the phone in his hand," Papa Zed said. "He's still holding on to it."

"A stalwart man indeed, if ever there was," Mrs. Sidivy said through her tears.

"And loyal to the very end to our savior Papa Zed," Barbara added graciously.

"Yes. That's the Lord's honest truth. Put your breast away, honey."

"Yes, ma'am. I better see how Brother Canduity is faring."

"I'M NOT GOING to give up on Chent. He might still be alive," Brother Canduity stated.

"He'll live forever in our hearts, honey," Sister Barbara said. "Head northeast by the fastest route available."

Canduity wiped his nose on the shoulder of his jacket and finally made it out of the pasture. There was a nervous knot of lowing cattle nearby. Canduity flipped them off and jumped into his car. He couldn't get away fast enough.

For half a second, he wondered if he should take Brother Chent's car instead of his own. After all, Chent wasn't going to need it anymore.

But, actually, Chent's Chevy Caprice was even older than Canduity's Gallant. And it would be seen as an act of disrespect to take the guy's car before he was even really, for certain, dead.

Canduity pulled away without turning on his headlights, and behind him, Brother Chent's 1994 Chevrolet pulled away, too.

SISTER BARBARA GAVE Stephanie a helpless kind of smile. They were on the road to being friends again. "Brother Canduity is swearing again. Think you can shout some sense into him?"

"Sure. But once you're hitched, you gotta learn to make him listen on your own."

"All right. You can give me pointers."

But this time, even Stephanie's best bullying failed to calm down poor, freaked-out Brother Canduity. After all, this time he wasn't freaking out about cows.

This time, it was the ghost of the very recently departed Brother Chent who was pursuing him through the back roads of west-central Pennsylvania.

SMITH TURNED the pages of the magazine, absorbing the tone of the article more than the information. He already knew all about Jeremy Landis. He made it his business to know the world's most powerful men.

There was a cliché that power corrupts and absolute power corrupts absolutely.

Smith believed at the very core of his being that this was true. And in his experience, it was safest to assume that it was true in every case. The only exception he knew of was himself—but, without the slightest sense of superiority, he would tell you he was exceptional. He had an exceptionally practical mind—arising from a total lack of imagination—and strong sense of patriotism. Maybe there were others as incorruptible as Smith—but he doubted it.

He had always assumed that all rich men were corrupt. If their rise to power wasn't fueled by some form of corruption, then they would be corrupted when they got there.

Dr. Jeremy Landis was corrupt long before he reached the top. His springboard to superstar wealth had been his development of the highly profitable pain medication—and there was nothing in his background to suggest he was capable of pharmacological innovation. He had an M.D. and a background in research, but all his work was mundane and derivative.

Somehow Landis had acquired someone else's drug research and claimed it as his own, and now physicians were prescribing Aceteride a thousand times a day in fifty nations.

Finding and exploiting other people's work was what Landis did best. His specialty was buying drug-research data from companies that didn't have the money to continue developing their drugs. He seemed to hoard pharmaceutical patents. He personally owned the rights, then leased them to Meds-4-U.

Meds-4-U was powerless without Landis. Meds-4-U without Landis was an empty shell.

Landis knew what to do with the patents, as well. He had a bloodhound's nose for sniffing out drugs that held real promise. His success rate with unproved drugs was the envy of the industry. Even the patents he did not personally identify as holding promise had turned into moneymakers, because so many of them were identified by other labs as holding promise. Landis was always glad to license these patents; he never sold them.

Landis is now the wealthiest man alive, a staggering achievement for a man his age. What next for the drug king? Landis is not a man to broadcast his intentions. He claims to have no immediate plans to change course.

"We're going to see huge advances in medicine in this century. There's no frontier that holds as much promise as the health-care sciences. The money is what it is. Maybe I'll make a trillion dollars before I die. It's not out of the question, if I live a long life and remain successful. It doesn't really matter."

It's hard to tell sometimes when Landis is being serious. This is a man notorious for misleading journalists. Even Landis must know that the cyclic nature of the pharmaceuticals business means his business is destined to stop growing at its current pace. Most of his current wealth came from Meds-4-U stock sales, not continued income. Even if the business kept raking in cash as it does now, it would take Landis two centuries to reach the trillion-dollar mark.

Landis is the first to admit that Meds-4-U's growth has been sustained longer than he ever expected.

"I've got a financial cushion in case of a downturn," Landis tells *News Time* magazine.

Indeed, this is a man who spends little of his personal fortune. He is known to own less than four automobiles. So what would he do if he did make a trillion dollars?

"You got me," Landis says. "I wouldn't know what to do with a trillion dollars if I had it."

Harold W. Smith was reading between the lines. *News Time* was trying to have fun with the light banter—and still come up with an attention-grabbing cover line. But the tone was not light at all.

It was an in-depth profile, written recently. Smith counted the number of times Landis referred to the pioneering field of medicine and the number of times Landis talked about helping people to live longer, live healthier. At one point, *News Time* asked Landis point-blank, "Do you have a new miracle drug under development, Mr. Landis?"

Landis carefully steered the conversation when he replied, "I have a thousand of them! Just as beneficial and safe as Aceteride."

Smith dropped the magazine and tapped it with one finger.

"What do you think?" Mark Howard asked. "Is Landis the guy who stole the apatosaurus?"

"Yes. But I came to that conclusion before reading the article. But there's something more. I have the distinct feeling the journalist who wrote this article knows more than he's saying. He and Landis were doing a real dance around each other. What's significant is that they played up the back-and-forth in print. Landis could have had the article killed if he didn't want it published."

"The reporter's heard about all the drug firms' interest in the apatosaurus chemistry, which is not exactly a big secret," Mark said.

"I think this reporter knows there is a lot more going on than just the drug companies' public interest in the apatosaurus. I think he knows there are substantial resources going into the effort. He knows it's bound to break open soon and he's got an idea who'll be the man leading the charge."

Mark glared at the open magazine. "I guess if we had been paying closer attention, we might have figured it out ourselves."

"We'll run a self-evaluation later, after we've dealt with the crisis," Smith said. "Right now, let's figure out where Punkin—the carcass, I mean—is headed."

19

There was bad news coming into the old mountain barn in upstate Pennsylvania.

"We're going out in a blaze of glory!" Sister Sally radioed. She couldn't have been more thrilled.

"Talk her out of it, Papa Zed," Mrs. Sidivy begged. "She's gone crazy, and Brother Oscar does whatever she says. Tell her to just surrender."

Papa Zed was thinking how much less trouble it would be if, well, the crazy kids were not arrested. Then he wouldn't have to worry about their telling all to the authorities. But he had to make a good show at least of trying to keep them from doing anything downright suicidal. As luck would have it, Sister Sally had dropped the phone on the front seat of the car and never picked it up again.

The more convinced Papa Zed was that he wasn't being heard by Sister Sally or her devoted Oscar, the more demanding he became. "Sister Sally, my will is to be done. You do as I say, for your own good. Sally? You there?"

Sally was there, all right, standing in the open door of the car and apparently trapped by the police. Papa Zed heard more demands from a distant megaphone.

"Give me that thing," Sally barked at Oscar. "You want to see me throw down my weapons, Porky?"

"Don't do it, Sally," Papa Zed pleaded, knowing he was not being heard on the other end.

"How about this?" Sally shouted, and then Papa Zed heard Oscar's shotgun go off. Then again. And then, it sounded as if World War III were happening on the other end of the line.

Papa Zed put the phone down, trying to look deeply troubled instead of mildly elated. Mrs. Sidivy took the phone and listened in. "I hear the police talking. They said to call the coroner. Oh, Papa Zed, Sister Sally and Brother Oscar are dead."

Mrs. Sidivy laid her face in her hands.

"Oscar was a dedicated man. And Sally," Papa Zed eulogized, "she was a girl with all the keen fervor of Heaven in her belly. I grieve that I shall never experience her passionate devotion more fully."

Papa Zed went back into his tiny little alcove, apparently to grieve.

Stephanie and Barbara looked at one another behind their mother's back and silently high-fived.

THE STAFF at Papa Zed Ministries Command, Control, Communications and Intelligence—C3I—took a minute to deal with all that had happened.

A minute was about all they had, because the flying beast that would deliver them all was flying right into their own stretch of hill country.

When Stephanie finished consoling Papa Zed, she returned to find Barbara was alone at the command card table. She could hear the all too familiar sniffles and wails of her mother sobbing in the ladies' room.

Barbara was carefully lining up the tumble of cell phones, arranging them in alphabetical order.

She picked up a phone that said Brother Arnold, then studied the top row of phones. No room for another *A*.

"Oh, dear," Barbara said aloud.

"You sound like Mom."

Barbara looked at her and gave a wan smile as she began reconfiguring the layout.

"You and Papa Zed?" Barbara asked.

"Yes. But we're still sisters, right? Not sisters in the ministry but real sisters, the Sidivy girls, best girlfriends, Barb and Steph, right?"

"We are, Steph. I promise."

"Good. Garage the gazonga, will you, Barb?"

"In a second." Barbara completed the new configuration of the top row of cell phones before heaving the vexing breast back into the camisole. A clunky gray cell phone made moaning sounds.

"Canduity?"

"Yeah. Your future might be all wrapped up nice and neat, Steph, but I got a husband on the hoof who's seeing things."

"Barbara," Stephanie said, "just 'cause I got a man tonight doesn't mean you need to make the leap. And I'm not saying that to be like a taunt. I'm saying it because I don't want you to make a mistake on the spur of the moment."

"But you see, Steph, that's the way it is. Things are falling into place tonight. They did for you. You know, this afternoon, when we were buying these nighties for tonight, and I was thinking, tonight I'm going to get my life mate. See, I wasn't thinking, tonight I get me Papa Zed. See the difference? I didn't see the difference until a short time ago when Mama said you and Papa Zed were meant to be and I thought, how can that be? I was meant to be with Papa Zed. I knew it. But then I thought, what did I really know? What I really know is what I said. I'm meant to find my life mate tonight." She nodded at the cell phone from which came another terrified whimper.

"But why Canduity?" Stephanie said. "You got all these brothers to choose from." Stephanie waved at the forty cell phones. "Canduity is very nice, but he's a bit, you know, insane, in a sweet kind of way. And I'm not trying to be putting him down."

"I know you're trying to help me make the best decision," Barbara said. Stephanie had never seen her older sister so thoughtful in all her life. "I guess I'm not convinced it is Canduity. Maybe it's not."

"Maybe you'll know when the congregation comes together again. The night's not over yet. Maybe you'll be with all the brothers and suddenly you'll look at one of them and he'll look at you and you'll both just know."

"Maybe," Barbara said cheerily.

"Maybe you should put a sweatshirt on over that rambunctious rack," Steph said lightly. Barbara's breast had emerged yet again.

"Or maybe I won't!" Barbara said.

They laughed.

From the cell phone, the demon-haunted Brother Canduity whimpered like a fearful hound dog.

20

Rory Ahabepela didn't like the look of things down there.

The dinosaur itself was just fine. But the dinosaur wasn't alone. There was a man on the ice block—a man with a cell phone.

"We're not reporting it to command," Rory insisted. "You know what kind of trouble that'll stir up?"

"But what does it mean?" Captain Tassel demanded. "He couldn't have jumped on at the factory. He's outside the ice and outside the stealth coating. That means he must have caught up when we set down in the pasture. That means somebody is tracking us."

"You're jumping to a lot of conclusions."

"If they weren't tracking us before, they sure the hell are now. His cell phone display is lit up, and I think he's got a connection."

"He's dead as a bluegill in a pond in winter."

"He called before he died."

Rory cursed Tassel and snapped off his radio. He knew the pilot was right. His support crew nervously waited Rory's next step. Rory snatched an assault rifle off the wall, and lay down at the bay doors and commenced firing.

"NOW WHO'S BEING SHOT?" Mrs. Sidivy asked. Quick pops came from one of the cell phones, but she had to lean her head over and do a back-and-forth ear scan to zero in on the correct phone.

"Good Lord, Papa Zed, they're shooting at poor Brother Chent. But why would they do that?"

Papa Zed said, "The beast thieves must have spotted Chent sacrificed on the body of the beast. They see his phone, I bet. They don't want it leading followers to the stolen beast."

A few more shots were accompanied by a crackle of ice, then the roar of the helicopter began to quickly recede.

"They knocked the phone out of his hand," Stephanie said.

"I BLEW off his whole damn hand," Rory radioed Tassel. "That solves that problem."

The frozen arm broke off close to the elbow and fell. Swollen before it froze, the forearm was heavy near the elbow and it fell with the frozen hand raised, holding fast to the cell phone.

It came down in a dank depression where the groundwater collected and the leaves of the nearby bushes piled up to keep it damp. The arm penetrated the leafy blanket and sank in the mud halfway.

THERE WAS a *thwok*.

And the sound of the helicopter decreased slowly.

The phone had fallen all the way to the ground and it still worked.

"Lot of good it does us," Stephanie said.

"THAT DOES NOT SOLVE the problem," Tassel said. "Notice we still have a body frozen onto the side of the specimen. If you don't report it and I don't report it, then one of the guys at the landing site will report it and then command will want to know why you or me didn't report it."

Just because Tassel was right didn't mean he wasn't a huge asshole, Rory thought.

"WE CAN HEAR the helicopter. They're still shooting," Brother Leonard reported. "Don't seem to be shooting at us, though. We're way ahead of them. What are they shooting at?"

"That's a big unknown, Brother Len," Mrs. Sidivy replied, getting her spunk back after her recuperative sob in the toilet. She even managed to lie without a moment's qualm. It was for the good of the whole flock, Papa Zed said, his will be done, that the deaths of three of their congregation be announced later on.

"Maintain your clearance, Sister Helen," Stephanie said on another line. "Should pass over in another five minutes. Stay dark, then haul ass after it. Haul ass for Papa Zed, his will be done."

Papa Zed thought all was going better than he could have dreamed. They were bringing the biological specimen right into his waiting arms. Their course would take them to within thirty miles of where he was sitting right now. His flock was being positioned throughout the mountain area. That Mrs. Sidivy, she was a born organizer.

Mrs. Sidivy's girl Stephanie, she was born for something else.

There had been all kinds of good fortune coming Papa Zed's way tonight.

THE GUNFIRE PECKED at the ice. One leg snapped off. The arm caught in the chain seemed to break off of its own accord. More rounds cracked into the body.

"You damage the dino, there's gonna be hell to pay," Tassel radioed.

Rory snapped his radio off and continued firing until he couldn't see any more pieces of Brother Chent.

"I think you got all of it," his spotter said.

"You think?"

"Well, you got most of it, for sure."

MRS. ELLEN SANDIRO-TUCKER refused to put the dinner tray out in the hall.

"Okay, I'll do it." Keith Tucker put on the white hotel bathrobe, the one with the big red heart stitched on the breast that said His in curly script. Ellen pulled the sheet over her body when Keith opened the door and looked up and down the hallway. Finding it empty, he slid the tray out. Then he locked and bolted the door.

"I survived!" he said. "Whew!"

"Don't make fun," Ellen said. "You'd have fears, too, if you saw what I saw."

"I'm sorry, honey. But we're nowhere near that place."

Ellen sighed and scooted back against the scarlet velvet headboard of the king-size, heart-shaped bed. "The place doesn't matter. It's the karma of the thing.

Me and Jimmy stayed in the resort every night of our vacation. The one night we decide to leave, Jimmy gets murdered."

"But we're in the Poconos. In the middle of America. It's the honeymoon capital of the East Coast. It's perfectly safe here."

"Keith, you promised."

"You're right. No more talking about it. Besides, I don't want to leave the room anyway. We can have the most fun just staying in here, the two of us."

Ellen giggled and relaxed. The images of her former husband's grisly murder were easier to dismiss now that she had her new husband. "We haven't baptized the hot tub yet," she suggested.

"Great idea."

"Be there in a second." She retired to the bathroom to powder her nose while Keith started the timer on the heart-shaped, pink hot tub. He poured more champagne and set the glasses next to the pool, then stretched out in the warm water.

He was joined in the hot tub a moment later by the torso of Brother Chent, frozen rock-solid and crashing through the roof of the hotel like a plummeting meteor. It crashed through Keith Tucker in much the same way. It crashed into the second-floor honeymoon suit and another hot tub, where the young wife had just enough time to open her eyes and see what was coming over her bridegroom's shoulder.

Her bridegroom never knew what hit him.

The foursome continued downward, into an economy-class room on the first floor.

When you went economy class you got the heart-shaped bed but not the heart-shaped hot tub. The crashing bodies ended up in a bloody, broken heap at the foot of the heart-shaped bed. The couple on the bed was spared physical injury—but it was years before their sex life got back to normal. It was a minor emotional trauma.

They got off easy compared to Mrs. Ellen Sandiro-Tucker.

21

Brother Canduity did everything in his power to shake the tail, but Satan's Chevy Caprice could not be shaken. Canduity became more unnerved the more desperate his actions became—the Caprice would follow him into any reckless action without slowing, without hesitation. No living human being would have dared perform some of those stunts.

Finally Canduity tried something really desperate. He was driving down a county back road, full speed, no lights, when he came to a wide gravel turnaround and spun the wheel. The Gallant could not take the G-forces. Hell, a Hummer wouldn't have handled those G-forces.

Canduity's car rolled over, and Canduity knew it had been a foolish act. But the Lord and Papa Zed were with him in his moment of foolishness and they helped the Mitsubishi land upright. Tires didn't even blow.

The spectral Caprice sailed by him, and Canduity

stood on the gas and tore away from there, then cut down a crossroad into the darkness and pulled into a cornfield and waited.

He could see the road through the damaged corn, and he rolled down his window to listen for the sound of the Caprice. He heard nothing.

Then he saw something moving. It was the Caprice, rolling along at better than forty miles per hour without a sound. The engine was not on and there was nobody in the driver's seat—nothing but a pair of gnarled and shrunken corpse hands!

Brother Canduity felt better after that. He pulled onto the road and waved at the driverless Caprice and drove off.

WHEN THE QUASANNA River filled with sediment, it became useless for shipping. That killed Quasanna Shipping Company and the little town of Quasanna, as well. The building was still good, all these years later. All that it needed was a retractable roof, which was powered by the newly installed generator. The thunder of the big helicopter seemed to shake the old houses and stores of the ghost-town homes. They stared out at the monster with dead eyes. They saw nothing.

There was almost nothing to see. All was darkness, despite the wall of noise. There were no warning lights or reflectors or little red indicator lights. Just something big and black in the blackness.

Then something hit the earth and the ground did shake.

The black hovering giant flew away and the retractable roof clattered closed and the dead little town of Quasanna was in blessed silence once again.

The doors of the old dead houses creaked open. Figures emerged into the darkness, silent as ghosts—except for Brother Morris, who had forgotten to put his cell phone on vibrate.

"THE SPECIMEN IS delivered to Quasanna," Wrought reported over his microphone mouthpiece.

Jeremy Landis felt his body go limp with relief and he flopped in a vacant operator's chair. The wait had been interminable.

"I told you, let me handle this. Go back to your girlfriend," Wrought said.

"That would be even worse," Landis said. "I can't believe we made it all this way."

"Completely glitch-free operation," Wrought said, grinning. "We'll have it barged and on the water in fifteen minutes."

On the screen behind him, the shipping panels

were being raised to reveal shallow-draft barge custom-designed for the one and only purpose of hauling the frozen apatosaurus on the shallow Quasanna River. The warehouse crane was being lowered to hook onto the eyehook that was frozen into the dinosaur's harness of high-tensile steel chain.

Landis checked his watch. "We're right on schedule."

"We're ahead of schedule," Wrought corrected him. "We'll be in the PDL lab early."

"The lab's ready," Landis said. "It's been ready for months."

The cavern was on privately owned land in a mountain ravine, right on the Quasanna River. It had been used by bootleggers once upon a time. Now it was the home to the Ponce de Leon Biochemical Laboratory. One day it would be famous, but for now it was one of the best-kept secrets in the pharmaceutical world.

It was in that laboratory, under the sleeping mountains, that Landis's researches would distill the first true potion of eternal youth.

His eyes were arrested by movement on the screen in front of him. It was one of many screens in the command center. The digital label said "Quasanna, street."

"Wrought, what are your men doing outside of the facility?"

"What facility?"

"In Quasanna." That was the moment when one of the people on the screen attacked the padlocked front door of the facility with a chain saw, and Landis realized the people on the screen were not part of his Quasanna crew at all.

Well, there was bound to be at least one glitch, right?

THERE WERE shotgun blasts and deer-rifle cracks and the rumble and roar of power tools.

Rory Ahabepela muscled his way into the front of his confused men and aimed into the darkness. There were lots of warm green bodies glowing on his glasses.

Rory failed to notice somebody voicing a 1-2-3 count, then the intruders snapped open their flares and Rory's glasses turned to a blinding green mess. He pushed the glasses onto his forehead and blinked into the blackness, still seeing green sunbursts. He never saw the hedge trimmers that were used to saw open his throat.

THE THERMAL DISPLAYS at the command center were just as useless. Wrought hastily switched them to standard video pickup.

It was mayhem in Quasanna. Rory the Hawaiian was lying in the middle of it all with his neck sliced open. His men were dead and dying all around him. In the middle of the madness was Landis's prize of prizes—the frozen lump of the apatosaurus. The coating had come off in chunks, and Landis could see the long curved neck of the apatosaurus and the head, hung down close to its feet as if saddened.

"They can't take that dinosaur! It's my dinosaur!" Wrought was talking on the radio to somebody.

"What the hell are they doing?" Landis demanded. "Wrought, tell me those people aren't praying around my dinosaur."

PAPA ZED GAVE his blessing to the dead of his flock. Just three or four, which wasn't bad considering they had just wiped out a whole platoon of armed men. Then Papa Zed raised his arms and joined his hands with Mrs. Sidivy on one side and his betrothed, the scrumptious Stephanie Sidivy, on the other side, and the congregation of Papa Zed prayed together for the wonderful bounty that had been delivered to them.

Papa Zed couldn't quite believe he had actually pulled off this stunt.

They didn't pray for long. The doors were opened wide, and the street outside was filled with the beeping of Papa Zed's sky-blue school bus. It was music to his ears. He had come a long way in that school bus, and it was only fitting that he and the school bus would be together in this moment of his highest triumph.

The rear emergency door of the school bus was swung wide as it pulled to a halt just outside the front entrance of the big, vacant warehouse. The rear emergency door was about thirty-six inches wide.

Altogether, the congregation examined the rear door, then turned their heads as one to take in the sight of the dripping, forty-ton mass of ice and apatosaurus.

Papa Zed held out one hand like a surgeon.

Into his hand was deposited a bright yellow circular saw with a cord that extended into the darkness. Papa Zed tested the power switch. The saw blade sparkled and spun. The saw sang a song like the wails of angels.

"Let us commence to cut, my children."

The congregation raised their chain saws and hedge clippers and replied in unison, "Thy will be done."

LANDIS GRABBED the hair over each ear. "Somebody stop them!"

Then somebody did.

THE REAR END of the school bus was whisked away from the open door, and the sound seemed delayed by seconds. When the sound finally came it was a crash that never seemed to end. There was a different machine where the bus had been—a bulldozer, big enough for quarry work and completely black. The blade turned and approached until it was snug against the door. There was no way out except into the rushing darkness of the Quasanna River.

When the grenades came bouncing in, Papa Zed's flock was cut to ribbons.

The lucky few who were protected by the block of ice fled into the river.

"TELL ME those are my men," Landis said.

"Those are not your men."

"Who, then?"

"I have no idea."

"Where are my fucking men, then?"

"ETA ten minutes."

"That'll be too late!"

22

The dozer wedged one end of its blade into the front entrance and then backed up, dragging the corrugated aluminum front of the building right off and pulling into the plot of weeds next to the collapsing remains of the Quasanna Goods & Groceries store.

The flatbed reversed into town and skidded over the remaining frame studs, halting with the bed parked just inches from the dripping block of ice.

The intruders, all in black clothing and black goggles, got to work without a word, lowering the crane, hooking the dino, lifting it onto the flatbed, covering the ice block with a tarpaulin. It was amazingly efficient work.

Then the leader of the intruders stopped and rubbed his temple, as if he had a headache. One of the other intruders fished in his pocket and pulled out a bottle of headache tablets. The leader opened the bottle, popped two of the pills, then held up the bottle like an actor in a bad commercial.

The two intruders smiled into the security camera.

It was a bottle of Gadicin, the new analgesic that had cut heavily into Meds-4-U's profits in the past two years.

Made by Fizzer LLC.

BROTHER CANDUITY HAD never known such a mixture of emotions. He was deliriously happy and utterly terrified. Papa Zed and all his children had taken possession of the beast! They were dismantling it now. Their enemies were smote. Soon, Brother Canduity would be among them.

But then he would have to face down the lingering specter of Brother Chent, which still tailed him in Chent's old Chevy Caprice.

But with the supporting faith of Papa Zed, he could face the thing he feared second-most in the entire world.

He was three miles from the old ghost town when he was nearly run off the road by a flatbed semi that was going far too fast for the mountain road.

When he reached Quasanna, the place was far too quiet.

He found Papa Zed and all the brothers and sisters lying dead in the warehouse. Papa Zed himself was face up with half his chest removed. Sister Stephanie Sidivy was at his side. Sister Barbara Sidivy was lying there with her legs cut away, but her top half was undamaged and one pendulous breast was lying exposed. Brother Canduity had gotten the idea somehow that she was sweet on him. She was nice, but kind of a cow.

The sight of all his dead friends and neighbors couldn't seem to find purchase in his thoughts until it occurred to him that he was going to be all alone after all when he faced down Brother Chent's Chevy Caprice.

There it was, rolling silently into town. It was heading directly for him. The engine was silent and there were no lights. It was coming for him. Canduity leaped out of the path of the Caprice and heard the front end crunch to a halt against the corner of the demolished warehouse.

And all was silent.

The car was empty. There was not even a pair of hands on the steering wheel.

Then Brother Canduity knew the wonderful truth. Brother Chent had not been pursuing Canduity at all. He had simply been following Canduity back to be with his people when they were all called to Heaven together. Brother Canduity could feel Brother Chent's sudden peace and happiness. He was back with his people.

"As for me, I always thought you were sort of a nutcase, Papa Zed," Canduity admitted aloud. "So, I think I'll resign from the congregation. See you all."

He jumped in his car and drove away, thinking, Whew!

23

He waited in silence. He knew that any sound would set off the extremely sensitive alarm system—so he made no sound. He used the time to meditate.

He was on a ten-inch-wide steel beam that was 145 feet above the concrete floor, give or take. The building used to be a fish-processing plant. It had processed and frozen fish on a very large scale. Outside were more silent feeder plants that processed fish bones into antacid tablets and mashed fish entrails into pet food. That hadn't happened here in recent history. The complex was at a standstill and appeared deserted. Even the fish smell was muted. A slate-colored Lake Erie slapped at a concrete retaining wall.

For a deserted factory it was pretty busy. When Remo Williams arrived at daybreak, three men had been skulking around the roof and fiddling with the nozzles of compressed-gas tanks. Two of them used rappel lines to shimmy down the outside of the building. The third man was still on the roof. Probably baking in the morning sun. He wasn't making a sound except for his rambunctious breathing.

Remo let himself into the building silently and looked for a place to wait—only to find that there were five more individuals inside the building already.

"I don't know who they are," Remo said when he reached Mark Howard on the gas station telephone a half mile up the road. "All I know is they don't look like they belong there. I'm just reporting in like you asked me. Don't I always do what I'm asked?"

The real reason Remo called CURE was to get an update on Chiun.

"No word," Harold Smith said. "Let's wait and see what the other parties are up to."

"You sure? I could kill some time by assassinating them."

"Let's hold off," Smith said sourly. "Remo, if Chiun shows up, you are not to allow him to take possession of the specimen. I hope that's understood."

"We've been over this and over this," Remo said, and he hung up the phone with superhuman speed—so fast, in fact, that he never heard Smith demand that he not hang up the phone.

The fact was, Remo Williams had every intention of giving the dragon bones to Master Chiun if there was any chance they would save the old man's life. Smith could sue him. Smith could fire him. Smith could hold him in breach of contract.

Smitty could go to hell, and his little prince, too.

Remo went to join the party, climbing a wall and slipping through an open window slit ten yards off the ground. The man who was hiding on the roof never knew he was there. The men in the ninja costumes inside the place never knew he was there—and they were watching.

Remo Williams didn't care about any of these losers.

He wanted to find Chiun.

Why did he feel that this was make-or-break time? He'd been offered a glimmer of hope that he could save his Little Father, and he really didn't have any other options.

Sitting unseen and unheard on the narrow steel beam high above the concrete floor, Remo felt himself fill with slow rage. The man on the roof and the ninja wanna-bes wanted to take Chiun's dragon—which was the same as trying to kill Chiun.

Well, Remo wasn't going to let that happen.

He was a stewpot simmering with anger as he fell

into meditation. He carried the anger into the meditation—the wrong thing to do but he didn't want to get rid of it.

The anger felt good.

"BUT WHAT IS IT that angers you so?" asked a Master of Sinanju.

Remo stood outside a cave, and from his vantage point he could see the twin pillars of towering, curved basalt. They were the Horns of Welcome. They greeted travelers arriving at the village of Sinanju.

The Horns, like the cave, looked too new. Remo knew the Horns and he knew this cave and in his time they were more worn by the passage of time. The cave and the Horns he looked at now had not suffered nearly as many bitter Korean winters.

"Have we met?" Remo asked, speaking in Korean as a show of courtesy to the other Master.

"What is it that angers you?"

"Obstinate Masters who ask questions but won't answer them."

"I may not reveal my name."

Remo was having a hard time focusing on the Master's face. It looked familiar. It looked like Chiun. But half the Masters of Sinanju whom Remo had met in the Void had looked enough like Chiun to be his twin. When he peered closely, he thought he detected a taint in the Master's eye color that was strange.

Remo recoiled as if slapped. "Kojong?"

"I know not a Master named Kojong."

"If you're not the forgotten Master, then you're a disgraced Master."

"Or a Master in hiding."

"Why would a Master of Sinanju go into hiding?"

"Why do you delight in carrying this burden of anger?"

Remo laughed bitterly. "Delight has nothing to do with it. I like having somebody to be mad at about Chiun's sickness."

"Chiun the Younger is ill?"

"Yes. But he'll never admit to it. And you didn't hear it from me. He's running around acting as if he's healthy, and he isn't. I haven't been able to do anything about, even talk to him about it, because the old goat's in complete denial. Now I can at least be mad at somebody about it."

The Master seemed surprised. "Who?"

"Some guys in the unloading building I'm sitting in right now." Remo had spoken to several Masters and he knew how their minds worked, and he knew what question was coming next. "No. They did not cause Chiun's illness. So why am I mad at them? Because they came to steal Chiun's dragon."

The old Master stepped away from Remo Williams, then he returned, his tainted eyes bright with emotion.

"Chiun the Younger has a dragon?"

"He will soon. Some bad people stole it and the bad people are going to give it back."

"Have you seen this dragon?"

Remo frowned. "I've seen the thing that Chiun thinks is a dragon. I want to believe it is a dragon."

"As do I."

This Master of Sinanju was almost jittery with excitement.

"What kind of a Master are you anyway?"

"A Master in hiding."

The words were still in Remo's ears as his meditation ended.

What had that been about? Remo had visited dead Masters before, but they were usually there to give him guidance or at least assurance. This Master did act like a Master who was on the run and in hiding. Why would a Master of Sinanju be hiding in the Void?

The very fact that he had gone to the Void was disturbing. Not that the Void was a frightening place—but he spent a considerable amount of time in the Void during the time of his Rite of Attainment, which fully vested him as a Master of Sinanju. It was during this time that he had dreamed of Chiun dying.

But the dreams were misleading. The dead Master in the dreams was not Chiun, but the forgotten Master himself, Kojong. Remo had rediscovered the remains of this forgotten Master, who came to North America centuries ago and established a tribe that still dwelt on a small reservation in Arizona. The Sun On Jo were Remo's tribe, as he discovered at that time of his life. His biological father was a member of the tribe, which meant Remo was descended from Sinanju. An amazing circumstance that was so astronomically unlikely it could not have been the work of chance.

This time, there was no chance of a mistaken identity. It was Chiun dying, no doubt about it.

The guys in ninja suits were getting nervous downstairs. They must have received some news about the dragon-dinosaur arriving soon.

Remo heard the squeak of air brakes, then a door at one end of the building swung open and a flatbed truck pulled in. The truck was big and its cargo was massive, but they were curiously dwarfed by the interior space. Water streamed from the bed and the door rolled shut.

The interior became a beehive of activity. The ninjas were moving around the empty space, taking up the best positions. Remo had to admit they were pretty skilled by American ninja standards. None of the five had been seen by the men who arrived in the flatbed. The man on the roof was working fast, too. He was opening gas canisters and Remo heard the angry rush of flowing gas.

Remo held his breath. Whatever that gas was, it couldn't be healthy. Remo would keep the good air inside and allow the carbon dioxide to trickle from his nose slowly, just like when deep-sea diving. Remo Williams could hold his breath for a very long time.

The men in black suits crept into the open as the block of ice was secured to an unloading crane.

"Hands up!"

The men with the dinosaur snatched at their weapons and turned them on the black suits. Two of the truckers went down at once, and an obese black suit slammed into the floor, head bursting. The ninja went into some sort of stealth behavior. Remo was impressed with their ability to cling to the shadows. He could see them but the surviving truckers were spinning in all directions looking for their foes. From the shadows the black suits opened fire, then ducked back into hiding. The place they shot from was overwhelmed with gunfire. The black suits popped up somewhere new and fired another precision volley. The last of the truckers went down hard.

The black suits stepped into the open and stood over a groaning trucker. The trucker's eyes blazed with agony and hatred.

"It's the Fizzer assholes," said one of the black suits. "I should have figured."

"I always hated you guys," the dying man croaked.

"'Cause we were always better than you," the black suit said before triggering a round point-blank into the dying man's head.

Remo went to ground as the black suits worked the crane controls.

"Something's wrong. I can't reverse it."

The block of ice continued to ascend.

The black suit banged the industrial control box.

Remo sneaked behind one of the black suits and yanked him off his feet from behind. The body jumped behind a box of machinery and died before it was settled soundlessly on the ground.

The steel skeleton of the building groaned.

"It's too high," one of the black suits said. "It's straining the crane."

"You figure it, you're so smart, Snate."

The block of ice was still ascending.

"Where's Hunnert?"

The black suits were extremely well-trained in the face of surprise. The instant they realized one of their members was missing, they returned to stealth mode. The one named Snate drifted into a dark place behind a brick support wall. Remo stepped out and gave him a wave hello. He was still holding his breath, or he would have thought of something insulting to say to the man before he poked a hole deep into his cerebral cortex. The man was dead before his knees buckled. Remo had moved so quickly his finger was unblooded—the measure of success in this move. Snate slumped against the wall.

The wall and the ceiling creaked like the mast of a wooden ship.

He felt the presence of the last two black suits on far sides of the room. He stepped quickly into the middle of the room and knocked on the fender of the flatbed cab. One black suit ran into the open just enough to line up the sights of his suppressed rifle. The second black suit triggered his weapon at Remo's chest and expected to see the gray T-shirt blossom with blood.

Remo moved out of the path of the bullets. It was a miraculous thing to see, especially for Camou-Nin 098, who had trained for all kinds of special-operations scenarios. Remo should have been an easy kill. Instead, Camou-Nin 098's rounds went beyond Remo and stitched across the front of Camou-Nin 096. One of the rounds caught good ol' Ninety-six right in the face, where he was unprotected by armor, and that was all for good ol' Ninety-six.

Camou-Nin 098 saw the son of a bitch coming right at him. He unloaded his rifle, but the assassin seemed to shimmy and skip away from the rounds. There was no way that was possible—unless you believed certain obscure legends that were repeated by very old-time Asian special-operations veterans.

One old ninja had repeated the legend to Camou-Nin 098 back in the days when he was just Herbert Oscar Jacobs. The man was giving a special demonstration to Jacobs's unit.

"Keep in mind, you will never be the best there is, so always keep improving," the old *sensei* said. Not very inspiring.

"Maybe I will be the best one day."

"You will never be the best."

"Why?" Jacob challenged him. "'Cause I'm not a ninja."

"Even the ninja are not the best." And the old ninja told him the legend about who was the best. About the level he would never come close to attaining, no matter how hard he worked.

Jacobs told the old ninja he believed it, but he wasn't sure he did until this moment.

Herbert Oscar Jacobs, now Camou-Nin 098, asked Remo Williams, "Are you Sinanju?"

Remo smiled and nodded and tapped Ninety-eight's rifle, sending it crashing through the shell of his head like a tire iron opening a duck egg.

When Ninety-eight slumped to the ground, the building began to scream. Every girder was protesting. Remo slipped to the controls and started punching buttons.

"What are you doing to my dragon?" squeaked Master Chiun.

"Jesus!" Remo cried. "I'm trying to get your dragon down from the ceiling is what I'm doing." He sniffed the air. "I thought there was gas."

"The only gas here is what swirls between your ears. Surrender the button box at once."

"Sure thing." The building shuddered. "Why's it doing that?"

Chiun jabbed at the stop button, then the down button. The block of ice did not stop and it did not come down.

"You have damaged this and it will not function," Chiun accused.

"Not me. It was that dead guy."

Metal screamed as pieces of masonry tumbled down along with the salty ice melt.

"This shouldn't be happening," Remo insisted.

"I have said this each day for thirty years."

"Hey, why's the blame getting laid on me? I'm just doing my effing job and without your help, I might add."

A cinder block plummeted from the ceiling and tumbled end over end. Chiun stepped aside and it smashed into dust where he had been standing. "It is I who have been scouring the land for my precious dragon."

"Well, I found him first. Maybe you should have stuck with me," Remo said, his blood boiling. He'd been eager to see Chiun since the middle of last night and now the old man was giving him holy hell.

"I have traveled with the dragon on his large truck since before dawn while you were here showing off to your unworthy and unskilled friends."

"They're not my friends. I just met them a minute

ago and then I assassinated them. That's not what friends are for."

"They knew you for what you were."

"What I am is pissed off."

"No more so than I!" Chiun squeaked, and he stamped his foot. The roof split apart. "Now what have you done?"

Remo said, "That was definitely you, Little Father." But Remo knew he was wrong. The pressure waves that had come down from the ceiling told him all he needed to know. The roof had been blown open with many small explosives.

He and Chiun drifted swiftly to the walls as tons of rubble crashed to the ground and daylight broke inside.

The frozen dinosaur broke out, its chain ascending to a cloud of shimmering, iridescent balloons. Each balloon was the size and shape of a tire-company blimp that is standing on its nose, and they all flowed together into a glimmering white plastic structure that looked like flimsy plastic—but it ascended with its forty tons of cargo.

Chiun wailed. "Aaeiii! My dragon!"

Remo climbed the walls fast on all fours, finding the microscopic indentations in the wall that helped him grip the wall. He took the bare, cold wall in his hands and in his mind he was pushing it down—and that made him go up. He slithered along a girder even as the girder was losing its hold on the roof and beginning to succumb to the pull of gravity. It bent and groaned like a dying monster, and Remo sprang off and snatched the first dangling scrap he came to, then yanked himself to the ceiling and clambered around the crumbling brick to the roof. The roof wave picked the roof up with Remo on it, then it fell away under his feet and another ton of pieces tore off.

The balloon rose with the breeze and the immense lift tore the block of ice free at last. Remo lunged and leaped but the roof was falling away underneath his feet and there was nothing to spring from. He sprang anyway, snatched at empty air. The forty-ton ice block spiraled into the heavens at incredible speed.

Remo was going the opposite direction, back to earth, and he was going even faster.

STREET THUGEE and Ivory Nyf leaned over the dashboard and were just able to see the thing that was hanging in the sky over the warehouse.

"Man, that is the biggest thing I ever saw ever," Nyf said.

"Man, that thing is bigger than the whole Astrodome," Thugee said. He was not exaggerating,

"Man, it's taking our damn dinosaur."

The roof caved in on top of them. Street's spine was compressed until it shattered but Nyf was popped out the door like a squeezed boil.

He jumped to his feet, amazed to be alive and unhurt.

What had crushed his car was a thin white man in black chinos and a gray, torn T-shirt.

"Wad you do to my Mercedes?"

"Getting rid of it. You're next." The man stepped down from the compressed roof of the Mercedes. He had the thickest wrists Nyf had ever seen on a human being, and he seemed to think he was some kind of tough guy. But this loser didn't have a bit of style or a speck of class, not to mention a total lack of gold accessories.

"Man, you know who I am?"

"A piece-of-trash dinosaur thief."

"Mostly I'm a rapper. I'm Ivory Nyf, man."

"Almost as bad as being a dinosaur thief."

"I sold a million records!" Nyf had never seen a man with eyes like the eyes of this white man. They were worse than wasted eyes; they were killer eyes. Devil eyes.

"You'll sell even more when you're a martyr." The man was coming at Nyf slowly and deliberately, and Nyf didn't think a tank would have stopped that white man.

Finally, Nyf had the good sense to be afraid. "But I wasn't the one who stole it."

Remo Williams snatched Ivory Nyf by the throat and said, "You meant to."

"Help!"

His boys came streaming out from behind every building. Guns were cocked. Music to his ears. But then Remo Williams disposed of him.

Ivory Nyf went up and up and just as he began to come down, he intersected with the needle point of a shattered steel girder that jutted from a corner of the wrecked building. It slid through Nyf like a finger through warm butter.

Nyf heard gunfire. At least they'd kill that white boy that dared go up against Ivory Nyf.

Another body was hooked on the steel and slid down, slamming into Nyf. It was one of his boys, and this was a most undignified way to die.

More of his boys were flung up on the piece of steel, smashing Nyf on the bottom. He could hear their groans and the shudders of their bodies as they shut down one after another.

Man, this was just an undignified way to die.

But die he did.

EIGHT SKEWERED RAPPERS dripped gore down the side of the building.

"Anybody else?" Remo demanded. His voice reverberated carrying out over the steely lake.

Two military troop transports rumbled to life and shot out from behind a scaling shed and raced recklessly away. Remo snatched the steering wheel out of the Mercedes and tossed it out the front gate. It tore through the driver's window of the front truck, obliterating the driver and sending the transport into a wild side skid. The second truck slammed into it, and the whole mess came to a noisy stop in the middle of the road.

Chiun noticed none of this. He eyes were locked on the glimmer of shimmering color.

"If you have finished playing at last…?"

"Yeah."

"Then let us go to fetch back my dragon."

24

"The rappers?"

"They have major interest in a pharmaceutical start-up," Mark Howard explained. "Somebody convinced them there was money to be made."

"If they were willing to bend a few rules," Smith added.

"The paramilitaries in the army transports were mercenaries hired by Glasgow-Hythair. Just one of their hired strongman teams. The flatbed operators who stole the specimen from the Meds-4-U operation were Fizzer LLC. The ninjas were from HAAC—some of the very individuals who were stationed in Pennsylvania to monitor the specimen when it was kept in the special-purpose research campus."

"Good Lord. Every major pharmaceutical conglomerate on the planet has dirtied its hands in this affair in just the past day. We don't even know how they're tracking this specimen."

"My guess is they are tracking each other. When one of them zeroed in on the specimen, the others were close behind."

"So which company commissioned the airship hijacking?"

Mark Howard could not answer that. "The balloons themselves were no great feat of engineering. The material for the gas bags is a two-ply polymer liquid-crystal polymer fiber that's widely available. A German company's been promising to build a fleet of airships using the same material to carry 160-ton payloads across the Atlantic for a fraction of the price of a cargo ship. What our friend did that was remarkable was fill his balloons from compressed tanks in a matter of minutes. I'm trying to track back the quick-fill-nozzles supplier, as well as the gas supplier. If he used helium, it was about a million dollars' worth."

"Not a promising avenue of investigation," Smith intoned. "The thief likely used hydrogen—better lift and easier availability."

"That's about all I've got to go on. Have you been able to narrow down the pharmaceutical companies that have shown interest in the apatosaurus?"

"I have." Smith sounded even less pleased. "I've narrowed it down to forty-seven. Airship-tracking results are not paying off, either. The airship is thermally neutral, optically camouflaged and virtually silent once it is in the wind stream. If and when they begin using these ships for transporting cargo, they'll need warning beacons and radar reflectors to keep other aircraft from flying into them."

"The transport airships will have engines," Mark Howard said.

"This one doesn't," Smith remarked. "That narrows its trajectory considerably, doesn't it?"

"HERE WE GO again."

Dr. Hedson sat back in his chair and folded his hands on his stomach.

"What's happening?" asked the director of the research center, rushing out of his glass-enclosed office.

"Relax, Jon. This won't take long. It's just the ghost." Dr. Hedson reached into his desk drawer and withdrew a sack of saltwater taffy.

"The whole place is shutting down!" the director cried as the researcher terminals went blank across the Mesoscale Dynamics Modeling Laboratory. A small knot of interns doing a postgraduate modeling routine began to panic. Like Jon Marchese, the new director, they didn't know what was happening. Several of the more tenured researchers threw up their hands in frustration, but not surprise. Several researchers gave small cheers.

"Ghost break," they announced to one another—and pushed back from their workstations. They reached deep into their desks and came up with bags of candy, then began strolling around offering the bags to their fellow researchers.

"Mmm," Dr. Hedson said, "Maple Nut Goodies." He took a healthy handful from a sack that was offered him by the chief resident climatological physicist. "Jon's never had a ghost break," Hedson mentioned.

"I love ghost breaks," the climatological physicist announced. "The ghost always knows. When he feels everybody getting wired on anxiety, he comes and makes us take a break. Shuts the whole place down. Takes over all the systems. Turns off the internal monitoring. Brings work to a halt in every room of the building. We call it the ghost in the big blue machine."

"The computer experts have tried to figure it out. They can't. They say we're being hijacked. Probably the federal government," Hedson said. "But I prefer to think it's the ghost. Whenever the ghost comes, we have candy. I started that tradition."

"But this is inexcusable!" Jon cried. "The government has no right to come in and take over our lab. We're privately funded."

"You want to make an issue of it, be my guest."

"It's not worth it," the climatological physicist declared. "So we lose a couple of hours of work every few months."

Jon shook his head. "We're running ninety-one trillion calculations a second on this machine. You know how much work we'll lose?"

"When the screens come back on, everything will be just the way we left it. No harm done."

"Besides," the climatological physicist said as he left to join a hackey sack game. "Look around. Ghost breaks are good for morale."

MARK HOWARD ALWAYS wondered what was going on in the research lab in Yorktown Heights when he did his meteorological modeling.

The fact was, he needed their machine. It was the third-largest mainframe on the planet. It ran 91.2 trillion calculations a second under typical meteorological-modeling conditions. And the modeling software was already there, in the machine. He just took control of the machine, locked everybody out and plugged in his data. The mainframe did the rest.

Soon he had a half-dozen models of the airship's possible path, but even using the world's most powerful weather-modeling tool, they were still just guesswork. There were too many variables that couldn't be pinned down, and the possible landing point could be anywhere within thousands of square miles of North America, the North Atlantic and beyond.

"Now what?" He tossed his maps on his desk, feeling defeated.

"Remo and Chiun are in the air now," Smith said. "In Chiun's chartered aircraft. I'll direct the pilot to keep a course central to your possible flight, and we'll let someone else find the specimen for us."

"Think they'll come through?"

"They knew where to find the specimen when it set down in the Pennsylvania mountains and they knew where to find it on the shore of Lake Erie. These people have clearly devoted a lot of resources to watching their competitions with regard to this specimen. They're all spying on each other," Smith said. "I think one or two of them will prove to be a step or two ahead of us. I have to admit, Mark, I'm caught off guard by the size of this phenomenon. To think of the investments made already—it has to be in the hundreds of millions of dollars."

"Yeah. If you think of it in terms of developing a single product, that apatosaurus is one of the biggest industries in America already."

"It's strange that any one drug could be worth it," Smith said.

"Not to me," Mark said. "You're talking about eternal life. At worst, extended youth."

"It's baffling that people would want it so much, that they would pay so much for it. These drug companies seem to think the market is there. Do you think it is?"

Mark nodded. "I think they could price it at a thousand dollars a pill and have trouble keeping up with the demand. I think whatever company owns it will become magnificently powerful and rich. This is the ultimate prize, Dr. Smith. Nothing counts for more than eternal life."

Smith nodded, but in all honesty, he found it hard to imagine wanting to live forever.

At the same time, he was troubled by Chiun's illness. It seemed wrong that Chiun, the great Master of Sinanju, would fall to a disease. He couldn't picture Chiun laid up and suffering the agonies of a lingering illness.

He couldn't imagine what would become of Remo—and CURE and himself—if Chiun died.

Remo would not take it well. Remo and Chiun had been closer than any father and son for all these years. They complemented each other; they balanced one another. Remo without Chiun would be—unbalanced.

Remo without Chiun would be harder than ever before to control. Remo had become more independent as his Sinanju skills increased, and had managed to drastically undermine the authority of CURE simply by disregarding it. After he became Reigning Master of Sinanju, Remo rebelled against the rules and limits set by CURE. At first, he did so unthinkingly, but then it began to dawn on him just how much sway he had.

He had come close to using his influence to ruin them all when he threatened to expose CURE. He did so in order to coerce CURE to protect his family on the Sun On Jo Indian reservation. Smith had bowed to Remo's demands. Smith had no choice, really. Remo was prepared to take unreasonable steps to protect his family, exposing CURE rather than subjecting the Sun On Jo to Smith's scrutiny. Remo would have exposed a huge scandal, decades of duplicity by the country's chief executive. It would have plunged the federal government into its worst crisis since the Civil War—and all to protect Remo's family.

Remo could be quite impulsive, and dangerously foolhardy.

It had been much, much easier in the early days, when Remo was just a skilled combat veteran with a lot of notches on his rifle.

It had been even easier—personally, for Smith—in the days before there was a Remo or a Chiun. For the first years of its existence, CURE was only an intelligence-gathering entity.

SMITH HAD NOT LIKED the idea of CURE from the moment he first heard about it. He recalled that one horrible moment, sitting in the Oval Office of the President of the United States of America.

The President at that time was a young man. An idealist. Some of his ideas were downright ludicrous. CURE ranked right up there with putting a man on the Moon.

It was more than just a crazy idea.

It was treason. Smith told the President of the United States that he ought to make a citizen's arrest, right then and there.

The President was a young man, compared to his predecessors, and he had one of the most engaging smiles in history. People loved this President. They would love him even more after he was martyred.

But, of course, Smith did not know then that he was talking to a doomed man.

"Think about it," the President said. "Take a week."

Smith insisted he did not need a week.

"Smith," the President said in dead seriousness, "you think about it. Whether the Constitution can survive."

"Survive? Survive what?" Smith demanded.

"Itself," the President said. "It gives all the people freedom, but that makes the criminals unaccountable for their actions."

"The Bill of Rights is the foundation of our freedom," Smith said.

"And it's a free pass for half the villains who come through the legal system."

"Better to leave the Constitution alone," Smith said.

"Better for what?"

"Better to keep the faith of the republic," Smith insisted.

"But not better," the President concluded, "to keep the republic itself."

Smith left the Oval Office in turmoil—and the turmoil arose from the tiniest suspicion that the President might be right.

What if the President was right? What if the United States was being undermined by the very freedoms it allowed its people? The social anthropologist inside Smith insisted that the U.S. should be allowed to fail, in that case, and something stronger was likely to take its place.

But even Harold W. Smith wasn't that cold of heart. And he was indiscriminately loyal to his country.

If someone were to take the reins of such a powerful, secret agency, who would be better than a man as dispassionate as he was? Smith knew himself, and he knew what he was capable of. Unflinching and logical action. He knew he was a man immune to the lure of power. He was a man with statistically insignificant sense of imaginative ambition—more than one psychiatric evaluation during his CIA years confirmed it. He was a man who could be trusted with such a grave responsibility.

And if not me, Smith thought, then who?

Smith knew most or all the men in the intelligence agencies of the United States who might be in line to receive the offer to head CURE, should Smith turn it down. They were all good men; they were all corruptible men. On this, Smith had no illusions.

Smith realized that he must take the reins of

CURE; to allow anyone else to do so would be an unpatriotic act in and of itself, because the consequences were most dire.

Only after he said yes and took control of CURE did it really occur to him that the young President must have thought this through himself. The man was less impulsive than Smith had thought at the time. Had the President known Smith was the only reasonable option to head CURE? Would this President have proceeded with CURE with someone else at the helm?

Smith never got the answers to these questions.

The young President took a bullet in Dallas.

His death shocked a nation—and energized it to his causes. NASA rose to the ridiculous challenge of landing a man on the Moon and bringing him safely back to Earth—and succeeded.

Smith carried on, as well. He wasn't sentimental enough to feel compelled to continue simply to honor the slain President. By then, he had come to believe in the righteousness of the cause. CURE did good work. There were only two of them who actually worked for the agency—himself and his only real friend, the drunken Conrad MacCleary.

Still, CURE employed people all over the world to serve as intelligence gatherers. These people thought they worked for the CIA, or the FBI, or the United States Postal Service or the Internal Revenue Service—or the Kremlin, the royal court of the nation of Togo, the laundry service of Buckingham Palace. Their numbers were legion, and they fed reams of intelligence to the offices of CURE, hidden behind the facade of Folcroft Sanitarium in Rye, New York. Using this intelligence, Smith was able to manipulate the criminals who would have manipulated the system.

In Boise, a killer of college students was set free because human body parts were found in his freezer during a search that was deemed to have been performed without probable cause. No evidence meant no grounds for arrest. The killer walked free and sued the city for false arrest. He stayed clean. The police were powerless.

CURE got to work and found fingerprint evidence from multiple crime scenes in Alabama—the kind of link that was rarely made in the days before there was an effective system for computer comparison of fingerprints. The killer couldn't be charged with murder in Idaho, but they locked him up for life in Alabama, thanks to CURE.

In Oklahoma City, a crime boss was in the wrong place at the wrong time. He was arrested in a raid—

him, two dozen of his boys and a kilo of heroin. The arrest was a sensation—and the mayor acted quickly to cast doubt on the effectiveness of his own police force. It seemed the crime boss had been making significant contributions to the mayor's personal campaign funds, with the understanding that the mayor keep the crime boss apprised of the progress of the city's antinarcotics investigations.

The timing of the raid was a screwup on the part of a city detective. The detective fell eight stories to his death within days, leaving a suicide note that admitted he had framed the crime boss. Nobody could explain why the suicide victim had fresh skin and blood—not his own—under his fingernails.

CURE found out. CURE blanketed the country until it found a medical facility in Oregon that treated a man with deep facial scars—a man who turned out to be an OKC hoodlum. CURE fed the information to law enforcement and media across the country until the case bulged at the seams and finally burst open.

More cases, more corruption was exposed by CURE—but CURE couldn't keep up and the criminals were too good. Especially the criminals' lawyers. For every case CURE busted, it wasted time looking for evidence on ten cases it could never bust.

For every guilty man CURE helped nail, ten guilty men walked free.

CURE was powerful, and ineffectual. It pointed fingers and let others handle the dirty work. It had turned into a passive-aggressive intelligence agency. Smith and MacCleary both understood that they needed to remove passive from the equation. "We need bite, as well as bark," MacCleary insisted. "We need claws. We need an enforcement arm."

Enforcement was a part of CURE's mandate from the very beginning, and Smith had chosen to ignore it. It was his own rebelliousness, perhaps, his way of showing that if he were forced into participating in an action he did not agree with, he would do it on his own terms.

But his terms hadn't worked. Smith finally and reluctantly agreed to take CURE to the next level. They would hire an assassin.

"I know just the guy," Conrad MacCleary said.

THAT HAD BEEN a long time ago. Conrad MacCleary had been gone for most of that time. Remo and Chiun had come on board. Years later, Smith had appointed an assistant—another CIA man but much younger than Smith. Mark Howard was just a kid.

The latest disaster had come in the form of Mark

Howard's fiancée, Sarah Slate. She had been exposed to Mark, and to the Masters of Sinanju. She knew the Masters for what they were, on sight. Her family had been world travelers and adventurers for generations, and they had known previous Masters.

Small world.

When Sarah came to Folcroft Sanitarium to nurse Mark through his recovery from a bad injury, she had assembled the puzzle pieces in short order. Almost carelessly, this young woman unraveled the basic structure of the world's most secure agency. But she had also taken some steps to ingratiate herself to the Master of Sinanju Emeritus—that was the title Chiun went by after Remo was named, officially, at least, the Reigning Master. Smith still didn't know what Sarah had done to earn the devotion of the old Master, but Chiun gave the girl a tiny gold medallion bearing the symbol of the House of Sinanju.

Once again, Smith was confronted with his own helplessness. In hiring the Masters of Sinanju, he had a tiger by the tail. All his common sense and intuition told him to have the Slate girl assassinated for what she knew of CURE, but her friendship with Chiun made it impossible. Yet again, the consequences of offending the Masters were too dire to risk.

But Sarah Slate had turned out to be a godsend herself. Even now, she was handling a special project for CURE. It was the same sort of job MacCleary had done years ago—recruitment. Maybe. But of a different sort. And if her efforts were successful, perhaps CURE could let go of the tiger tail once and for all.

But that was wishful thinking. It might be years before her efforts bore fruit. They were just as likely to fail as succeed. But if she did succeed, and developed a new kind of enforcement arm for CURE, it would be one that could surpass the Masters of Sinanju in its ability to remain unseen.

Then, maybe, Harold W. Smith could consider the possibility of retiring this post, once and for all.

But that was idle and foolish thinking. And retirement of any kind was years away, at best. Right now he had to keep a firm grip on the reins of the Masters of Sinanju.

And, God forbid, should Chiun succumb to his illness, Smith would see if Remo alone could even be managed. Maybe—most likely—not.

25

"Chiun, I've explained this to you before. Old Jack wasn't a dragon. He's just a big leftover dinosaur. Most of his kind became extinct millions of years ago, way before there were people. Old Jack and his family just got caught in their own little piece of real estate that protected them from whatever it was that killed off all the other dinosaurs. See?"

"I see nothing. Your words offer no illumination."

"Old Jack's not a dragon!"

"If one were to attempt to understand your babblings and accept, for the sake of incessant argument, that your bizarre scenario is true, then the question is begged, if the creature called Old Jack is not a dragon, then what is?"

"Nothing is," Remo said.

"Then what was?"

"Nothing was!"

"Something was, of course," Chiun remonstrated

gently. "It is written in the scrolls. There are many references, Remo, as you well know, to dragons. Do you even recall the story of Master Yong?"

Remo didn't know how they'd gotten into this argument again. He wanted to discuss other things. Like Chiun running off on a wild-thunder-lizard chase without so much as telling Remo where he was going, why he was going, why he refused to admit he had a terminal illness.

At least they were back together again. They were in Chiun's chartered executive jet. Whatever his reasoning, Chiun had to have some real motivation to go spend his own money on transportation when Smith would just as soon have made the travel arrangements. Remo had no idea where they were headed. Northeast, more or less.

"Sure. I remember Yong. I have a mind like a steel trap."

"You confuse your brain and your mouth. Please keep the steel trap shut while I refresh your memory."

"No need. My memory is good. I know all about Yong. Big disgrace. Yong the Gluttonous, they called him. Hey, I met the guy."

"You know little of Yong, regardless. Your dream-meeting in the Void taught you nothing of his character. What can a man learn from a momentary intercourse?"

"We just talked, I swear."

"And you know but some of the history of Master Yong," Chiun admitted. "The story is not in the scrolls."

"I know. Yong's one of those never-did-wells who doesn't get his own chapter—at least not in writing."

"There are many such stories that are a part of the oral tradition of Sinanju only."

"I just said that," Remo said.

"They have no remaining existence outside of the scrolls that exist inside my head."

"And mine," Remo reminded him.

Chiun cocked his head and examined the head of Remo Williams with such intensity it made Remo fidget in his airplane seat. "There is much history that is known only in the oral tradition of Sinanju. This head is doubtless gigantic enough to encompass all of the memories twice over."

"Thanks."

"And yet size is not everything. I doubt you could have retained the entire story."

"Let me see. Chinese emperor has dragon problems." Remo held up one finger. "Chinese emperor hires Yong to solve dragon problems." He held up a second finger. "Yong does." Third finger.

"What is your purpose for raising your fingers?" Chiun demanded.

"I'm ticking off the major plot points of the Yong story."

"For what reason?"

"So you'll know I know the story, why else?"

Chiun was aghast. "You feel that a list of these points of plot serve as evidence that you know Sinanju history? They prove nothing, this ticking off, and this is not how a Master of Sinanju tells a story."

"I'm a Master of Sinanju and it's how I tell a story."

Chiun said in a controlled tone, "Do you mean that this is how you intend to teach the lessons of Sinanju to your own student someday?"

"I guess I hadn't thought about it."

"Think about it now."

Remo rolled his eyes to the dingy ceiling of the 747. "No, I guess the story won't be much of a story if it's just the list of events. I see what you mean."

"This I doubt. Is it possible you know the way even to relate the history of Sinanju in a way that gives it meaning?"

Remo asked, "You mean, can I rip a good yarn?"

"Nonsense and prattle, that is all you are capable

of! How can you tell the tales of the Masters of Sinanju when all you know if the twaddle of the Western world?"

"'Rip a yarn' means to tell a story, Chiun."

"It means nothing! It means only that you are versed in the slang of the day."

"That counts for nothing?"

"Correct. Nothing."

Remo stewed silently, staring at the back of the aircraft seat in front of him. It was about the ten-thousandth airline seat back he had stared at in his life and about his ten-thousandth bicker with Chiun. Remo's simmering annoyance bubbled away enough for him to consider Chiun's point of view. He was getting better about seeing things the way Chiun saw them.

Remo was afraid. That's what did it for him. He was afraid of losing Chiun. He didn't want to lose Chiun. He didn't know how he'd keep on going without Chiun. Chiun was his best friend, even if the two of them did bicker like an old married couple from Hoboken. Chiun was his mentor and the source of all skill Remo possessed; everything that made him special and unique he owed to Chiun.

Even his wisdom. Chiun was undeniably wise and learned beyond anyone Remo had ever heard of, and some of that had come down to Remo. Remo, of all people, had managed to absorb some wisdom. And some understanding of history and the literature of Sinanju. All that came from Chiun, Master of Sinanju Emeritus.

If and when Remo was without Chiun at some point in the future, that source of wisdom and knowledge would be gone, and the only remaining repository of all that wisdom and knowledge would be—gulp—Remo Williams.

Wait. Not if. When. Remo Williams had to admit the awful truth of the matter—unless he, Remo, died before his time, then it followed that Chiun would be the first to go.

It was such an obvious, ugly truth that Remo had never felt the need to really admit it to himself, but lately that truth had been asserting itself in his thoughts. Remo without Chiun—and maybe in the not too distant future.

Remo shuddered.

Chiun felt his shiver and turned his eyes away from the window, where he habitually kept his gaze locked on the flimsy wing of the aircraft, and onto Remo Williams, his adopted son and the appointed heir to the legacy of Sinanju. He said nothing.

Remo said nothing. To raise the subject of Chiun's

illness would only lead to more of Chiun's denials, more of Remo's insistence, more bickering. That Remo could do without.

"You are troubled," Chiun announced at last, "because you cannot bring yourself to tell the story of Yong."

"That's not why I'm troubled, but thanks for adding insult to injury."

"You are most welcome. I shall tell the story of Yong."

"I know all about Yong," Remo grumbled.

"You know the facts of Yong," Chiun hissed. "That is not the same as knowing how to tell the story, and the facts have no meaning without the story, Remo. Without the story, the history dies in your arms."

Remo was slapped across the face with the image of Chiun slumped in Remo's arms, enfeebled by sickness and breathing his last breath.

CHIUN KNEW his son well, but he did not know the all of his son. Even one with the skills of a Master of Sinanju could not read all there was to a man, even a white man of America whose very breeding was base and crude.

Sometimes even Remo Williams gave him a surprise, and this was one of those times. For Chiun observed Remo's heart rate spike uncontrollably, and he saw the tightening of the muscles around his pupil's face, and he saw the sudden strain in his pupil's eyes. Then Remo said something offhanded and derogatory as he jettisoned himself from his seat.

"Go to hell, Chiun."

Chiun spent some time watching the wisps of clouds streak across the wobbling wings of the aircraft and considered his son's reaction, and Chiun was at a loss to explain it. Remo was not insulted, Chiun realized finally, but shocked with sorrow.

Then Chiun understood fully, and when his son returned to his seat after extended loitering in the lavatories, Chiun gave him a beatific smile.

"I'm ready to listen to the story of Master Yong, Little Father."

"I knew you would be, my son. I understand what you feel at this time."

"You do?"

"You feel sadness."

"Yeah?"

"You feel shame."

"Oh, really?"

"Shame, for in a moment of enlightenment you

have come to understand the breadth of your ignorance. You have seen a universe of understanding you do not yet possess, and which only I can give you. Is that not so?"

Remo folded his hands on his lap. "I guess it is."

"You know the meaning of the word *Yong*, at least?" Chiun tested.

"Yes. Sure. It's 'dragon' in Korean." Remo had come to be fluent in Korean during his many years as a Master of Sinanju. He hadn't really tried to become fluent; it just kind of happened. Chiun's question was akin to stopping a businessman on the streets of New York City and asking him if he could identify the animals in a barnyard scene. "I also know the words for 'cow,' 'pig,' 'chicken,' 'dog'—"

"None of which appear in the story of Yong," Chiun cut him off. "Yong was not the name of this ancient Master, but the name given to him by the Masters that came after him. It is a badge of disgrace for a Master of Sinanju to lose his name in the histories of Sinanju, and live on only with a false name. Yong the Gluttonous deserved his badge of shame."

"Isn't the gluttonous part shameful, too?"

Chiun exerted his supreme patience to overlook the rudeness of the interruption. "Yes."

"So he gets two disgraceful names?"

"Yes, and earned them both. In truth, his sin could be construed as one of the worst ever perpetrated by a Master of Sinanju upon the others."

Remo Williams knew the story of Yong, and he didn't know if he bought into Chiun's conclusion, but he kept his mouth shut and listened.

Chiun nodded as a signal that the tale was commencing in earnest. "In the Year of the Peacock, in the time before the birth of Wang, the assassins of Sinanju were without the Sun Source. The skills of the Sinanju were renowned in the world, but they did not have the far-reaching supremacy that would come in the time of Wang. It was at this time that Sinanju counted the factions of Cathay as its most profitable clients. The Middle Kingdom was a vast land of warlords and knights and pretenders to power. Sinanju profited from this political strife, naturally, for generations, but there came a summons to Sinanju for a different sort of undertaking than the usual royal executions and other such menial tasks as even a renowned Master was called upon to perform in those days. So the Master who would be known in later generations as Yong went to the emperor of Cathay."

"What was his real name?" Remo asked.

"His real name is not remembered. That is a part

of his shame. What would be the purpose in giving him a name of shame, only to retain his true name parenthetically?"

"'Parenthetically' doesn't sound Korean."

"'Parenthetically' was not his name," Chiun began, but then he could see that Remo was jesting him. Jests were never welcomed in Sinanju history. "This Master went to China with the Sword of Sinanju, which is a great and powerful weapon, the mere sight of which was awe-inspiring to those who would hire, or stand against, the Master of Sinanju who wielded it. It was capable even of slicing into the hide of a dragon."

Remo knew the Sword of Sinanju, and it was indeed a beautiful and deadly-looking piece of weaponry—if you went in for that sort of thing. The post-Wang Masters of Sinanju, those who had been blessed with the knowledge of the Sun Source, disdained weapons. Their only tools were their bodies. Still, the Sword of Sinanju was a symbol of the ancient history of the House of Sinanju and the time when it was much employed for executions. For centuries the House had languished without it. The great weapon had been stolen by Chinese foes and hidden there until Chiun recovered and returned it to its rightful owner—himself.

"A dragon was what the emperor of Cathay hired this Master to dispatch. The emperor was much distressed that his people were being consumed by this dragon," Chiun continued. "For the most part, they were rice farmers."

"Who'd grow the rice?" Remo commented.

"Exactly. Although growing rice is what nearly all Chinese did then, save for the occasional royalty and sword thief. Even if the lost rice was of no consequence, there was always a risk in leaving a dragon unchallenged. The beast becomes territorial. This inevitably attracts more dragons, who are always looking for new feeding grounds. They will fight the first dragon, to take his territory, or they will look for their own territory nearby."

"But the emperor wasn't worried about that, because this was the last dragon," Remo said.

"How would the emperor of Cathay have known such a thing?" Chiun countered.

"You're right."

"The dragon was named Wing Wang Wo."

"Who named him that?" Remo asked.

Chiun was annoyed. "How can I answer such an inane question? What does it matter? What matters is that it was the first dragon Yong had come across, but he had no doubt that he could slay the creature.

He told the emperor so, and asked for a most unusual form of payment. Instead of gold, Yong asked for the carcass of the creature as his payment. The Chinese emperor agreed without hesitation, for he did not know that a dead dragon was worth more than its weight in gold."

"If he was smart he would have asked for both," Remo observed.

Chiun's eyes lit up with rare paternal pride. "Yes, of course, Remo! Such good thinking!"

"Aw, gee."

"Yong found the dragon feasting on the rice paddies. It was a magnificent, raging wurm, scales flashing green and gold in the sun. Yong had not seen a dragon before, and he watched the beast, observing the swiftness with which it snatched up peasants and its magnificent gluttony as whole villages were consumed. Yong's patience was well rewarded, for after much time he had taken the measure of Wing Wang Wo, and by then Wing Wang Wo was sodden with his heavy meal. The dragon was weighed down, in body and in mind, like the corpulent ones who sprawl in the booths after they have consumed near to their own weight in horrid food in the American all-one-cares-to-eat restaurant. But a dragon is never slow. A dragon is never not dangerous, even when well fed."

"Just sort of slow," Remo agreed.

Chiun ignored the comment and said, "Then Yong appeared to the dragon and made a shape with his hands that was lewd and insulting in China at the time."

"What was it?"

"It does not matter," Chiun snapped.

"Did he flip him the bird? Give him the okay sign? That's an insult in some part of the world, right? The black-power fist?"

"I do not know nor do I care what sign language the Chinese used to insult one another forty centuries ago. Suffice it to say the dragon had Chinese sensibilities and he was insulted. Yong hurled further insults, and the dragon responded with his breath of fire, but Yong dodged the flames and the dragon pursued. Yong led Wing Wang Wo to a cave that he knew of, and the dragon followed the stalwart Sinanju inside. Now, this seemed to be the end of brave Master Yong."

"Yong was surely barbecued."

"How could he escape?" Chiun added.

"Holy St. George, it would take a miracle."

"Speak not of that faker. St. George is a fairy tale—those who promulgated his despicable legend paid for their crime. Yong knew that dragons were not strong on wits. They were easy to fool, and it took no great cunning for him to elude the dragon by hiding in a protected place in the rock that he had found when he scouted the hole earlier. The dragon trundled right by Yong where Yong was in hiding, and the fresh smell of sulphur rising from the dragon's own nostrils masked Yong's scent. The dragon went farther into the cavern and Yong went out. Yong perched above the cave entrance with the Sword of Sinanju. This great weapon was longer than you are tall, Remo."

"I know."

"It is brilliant in the flashing sun, as penetrating as the finest surgeon's needle, yet stronger than any sword ever to come out of the smithies of Japan. And the mark of Sinanju is upon it."

"I've seen it."

"Wing Wang Wo realized he had lost his prey. He returned to the daylight, but when his head came out of the opening of the cave, the Sword of Sinanju whistled in the air and cut into the dragon's neck. So powerful was the blow and so sharp was the sword that the momentum of the blade continued through the great fleshy neck, and the head of Wing Wang Wo rolled on the earth."

"Wow."

"Wing Wang Wo had further humiliations to come. Yong removed the flesh from the creature, until nothing was left but bones. These bones he crushed and scraped into powder, and from this powder he brewed an elixir, and this elixir gave him a life that never seemed to end. He outlived every Sinanju Master that came before him, and every Master that has come since."

"Why didn't everybody else eat dragons and live long? Why didn't St. George, for instance?"

"Speak not of that imposter. Georgus Gracchus slew no dragon. He was nothing but a Roman general whose petty assignments took him far to the east, where he heard the tales of dragons passed along from Cathay and the Hindu kingdoms and, yes, even Sinanju. This man heard the tale of Master Yong and promulgated the story in his missives to Rome. 'Believe not, Emperor, if you should hear fantastic rumors of my battle with a local beast on the borders of Asia,' he would write in one report. 'The gossip that spreads in this vicinity is untrue— I killed no such great creature,' he wrote next to his emperor. 'The thing was no dragon and not nearly the size that the local hearsay would have one believe,' he added in a following correspondence, and so on.

"This he wrote, and meanwhile when drunk on wine would tell the much exaggerated tale of Yong with himself as the hero, and pass it off as a mere fairy tale. These were repeated by the wounded men he sent limping back to Rome as he waged his petty campaign. Soon gossip became renown and Rome was convinced that this humble man had fought some strange creature in the reaches of Mesopotamia, on the very borders of the Roman Empire, a stone's throw from the lands the Romans called Asia. By the time Georgus Gracchus had returned to Rome, the populace was convinced he had fought the thing, and already predisposed to disbelieve his denials, and thus a tale of Sinanju was usurped by Rome."

"And this Roman, Georgus Gracchus, became St. George?"

"Yes. The West perverts all that is factual and truthful with grave casualness. This then can be seen as the cause of most European wars. This Georgus Gracchus fell in with the wrong peers and soon found himself cast in the public eye as a Christian. At this time, Rome was still putting Christians to death. It was a hundred years or more before the Christians took the throne of Rome and began putting all other religious practitioners to death. This

Georgus Gracchus was not believed when he denied he was a Christian. The Romans knew he was forever humble, and lied rather than admit to doing great deeds. Was not his slaying of the Persian dragon evidence of this behavior? It was assumed therefore that he believed in the greatness and truthfulness of Christianity and by denying his allegiance to it he was in fact proclaiming its glory."

"My head hurts trying to make sense of it all," Remo said.

"Liar. You get no headaches or I have taught you nothing. But I can understand your confusion. The Romans' convoluted logic condemned Georgus Gracchus to death by crucifixion. It is this same pool of thinkers, I might point out, that went on to write the backbone of all Western philosophy and literature."

"Poor sap, George."

"It was a just end to a man who would steal a Sinanju legend."

"But Sinanju doesn't want to be tagged to the legend of Yong. Otherwise, why not write it in the scrolls?"

"Regardless of how we feel about the legend, it is ours," Chiun sniffed, "to do with as we please. Not to be appropriated by a charlatan. Of course, he pleaded his innocence and groveled for mercy to his last breath, but this doesn't stop him from being a martyr to the Christians. All the truth of this man's character and deeds and even his name were forgotten a hundred years from his humiliating execution, leaving only the legend of his fight with a dragon and the fact that he died for the worship of a similarly executed carpenter.

"A millennium later, a busybody with no more credibility as a historian than ownership of a quill pen writes a sensationalistic bit of prattle about the lives of the saints, taking still more liberties with the tales he knew and stamping the legend of St. George and the dragon forever in the mind of the Europeans, who are incapable, it seems, of disbelieving anything they see in writing. It was called *The Golden Legend,* this irresponsible tome, and it was too widely dispersed throughout Europe by the time its existence became known to the Masters of Sinanju for the copies to be recalled. Still, a Sinanju Master went out of his way to pay a visit to this James of Voragine, who was an archbishop and who penned this trash, and educated the archbishop as to the truth of the legend."

"Poor James," Remo said. "Of course, we couldn't have him running around with a family secret."

"Of course we could not. The Master gave him understanding and took his life. And which Master did this deed?"

Remo scrambled mentally. "A bunch of bishops were assassinated by the Masters over the years. Not to mention a bunch of priests and a pope or two. But I don't remember James of Voyaging."

"Archbishop James of Voragine was not in the scrolls, because to record his name would be to record the purpose for his unpaid assassination."

"And that means putting Yong the Unmentionable in there. So how do you expect me to know which Master offed the archbishop?"

"Voragine was a Dominican, in Italy, in the thirteenth century."

Remo snapped his fingers. "Hun Tup."

"Yes," Chiun allowed. "Must have been right before the merchant of Venice paid Master Hun Tup to show Marco Polo the road to China. Now, there's a lesson for you. A Master of Sinanju should never work as a tour guide. Drops Marco at Kublai Khan's with a big payoff from the Khan, only to have the khan send out an ambush to steal it back. He wiped out the khan's soldiers, sure, but it nearly killed him."

Chiun nodded, and sighed heavily.

"What?" Remo demanded. "Did I get it wrong?"

"You did not present your facts incorrectly, Remo, but you presented them poorly."

"Says who?"

REMO KNEW that the Masters of Sinanju were exceptionally long-lived. Barring violent death—they were, after all, in a violent profession—a Master could reasonably expect to live at least a century. Many Masters lived to be 120 or more, but Yong had gone on to be 148 years old. Remo knew that Yong had brewed the dragon-bone elixir every month, although Chiun said it was needed but twice a year to keep the body strong.

Chiun himself was born, when? Some god-awful long time ago, and Chiun himself was inconsistent on this little detail. The closest he had ever pinned the year down was 1891, and that meant Chiun was closing in fast on 120. After that—nobody could reasonably be expected to live longer than that.

Not even a powerful Master of Sinanju.

Remo had heard the tale of Yong and dismissed it out of hand. There never were dragons. Right? And Chiun brought up the tale when he was slavering over a newly discovered, nonextinct brontosaurus living in the jungles of Africa.

The brontosaurus was about as un-dragonlike as

any dinosaur Remo could imagine. The thing was waddled like a land-locked walrus and ate mangoes morning, noon and night. Remo had seen manatees that were more frightening than Old Jack the brontosaur. Old Jack—or, as its handler liked to call the creature, Punkin—did not match any of the dragon-like characteristics Chiun described in his stories of Yong the Dragon Killer. No fiery breath, no arrow-shaped tail, no tendency to eat rice farmers. In fact, Punkin was known to have eaten just one human being in its entire life, and even then it had taken some serious abuse.

But Chiun seemed to believe the thing was a real, honest-to-goodness dragon.

And what was the deal with all the drug companies? Why had they been taking such drastic measures to get their mitts on Punkin for all these years? They seemed to think that maybe there was something inside the bronto bones that could really and truly prolong human life.

And now Punkin was dead and frozen solid and his weighty carcass, and all his precious life-giving bones were being tossed around like some gigantic hot potato.

26

The news of the murdered, stolen dinosaur had leaked, then exploded everywhere.

All of a sudden, everybody cared about Punkin again. Once he had been a sensation. A real dinosaur, found alive, sixty million years after the scientists claimed they had all died out. Punkin attracted twice as many visitors to the zoo in Philadelphia during his debut season.

But it seemed the more people got to know Punkin, the less popular he was. He didn't live up to the hype.

Some customers wanted their money back.

Irate weekend dads jostled to be interviewed on the evening news. "They're trying to pass this off as a living, breathing dinosaur? I know dinosaurs and my kids know dinosaurs and this is no dinosaur. The Philly Zoo should be ashamed of themselves."

The problem was, Punkin wasn't scary—he looked pretty much like a reptilian cow, complete with doughy cow eyes. He didn't eat people. He was a vegetarian, for crying out loud. The public was disappointed.

Interest waned. A few well-placed comments from the scientific community cast official doubt on the legitimacy of the zoo claims. Without dinosaur DNA to test against, there was no way of confirming that Punkin was, beyond a shadow of a doubt, a survivor of the Jurassic Age. This confirmed what the ticket-buying public suspected already—Punkin might really be just some sort of bloated, deformed walrus or some such thing.

The drug companies had been behind the discrediting of Punkin's hereditary claims. They had read the white paper by Dr. Nancy Derringer and they saw the enormous potential in harvesting Punkin's biochemistry. Once Punkin lost his marketability, and he was moved into seclusion, the drug companies assumed his bones would be easy picking.

What a surprise when their efforts failed. They still couldn't understand the forces at work to protect the specimen. More than one supplements and pharmaceutical company had risked everything on getting a chunk of Punkin, and that collapsed under the reprisals of Punkin's protectors.

The public heard very little about any of this.

There was low-level chatter in the media about the scientific community's interest in the chemistry of the specimen, whatever the specimen was. But when the specimen was actually in the hands of one of the drug companies, the other drug companies became catastrophically spiteful. The news spread worldwide in minutes.

"The World Health Union is claiming to have research study reports that say therapy from the dinosaur enzymes will create permanent hormonal changes that can be passed on to offspring," Mark Howard said as they watched the outcry grow. "You live longer, and your progeny live longer."

Smith nodded. "That is probably true. That's what Dr. Derringer found initially. Nobody really understood the implications at the time—including Dr. Derringer."

"The chance to grab hold of immortality is enough to make people seriously crazy," Mark observed. "Now you're talking about creating a longer-lived bloodline. A superior lineage."

"I'm afraid so. Survival instinct is the foundation of the human psyche, and the chance to enable the survival of your own kind, whatever that kind is—I think that's an extension of the same instinct. We've seen what happens when it becomes an obsession.

God forbid any one creed or group or race succeeds in making long-lived supermen."

"They would become a dominate, distinct race," Mark said.

"Inevitably. Which is why the carcass must be destroyed."

The media were in a frenzy of coverage by the middle of the day. One fringe group after another came out of the woodwork, driven by the impulse to preserve their race or clan or family for all time.

We Own Punkin, shouted the headline above the photo of men in white bedsheet robes and pointy white hoods, standing in a wedge formation, while a lawyer with a briefcase stood alongside the hooded leader waving some sort of legal paperwork. They were the Native American White Race Warriors. Their leader was descended from the red man, specifically from the Pennsawauskee Indians who had been cheated by the U.S. government out of their hereditary lands. Specifically, they owned the southeast corner of the state of Pennsylvania and everything in it, and by the legal definition of ownership in the state they owned everything that had resided on their land for the past seven or more years. That included the dinosaur. Their lawsuit sought an injunction against all further business activity in the city of Philadelphia and surrounding environs while the courts decided on their claims. Or, the lawyer said, they would settle for just the dinosaur.

"Pennsawauskee Indians?" Smith asked aloud.

"They can't possibly make anything of it," Mark Howard observed. "The claims are ludicrous."

"All it takes is one stupid judge willing to listen. If they succeed in getting an injunction of any kind to put in place any sort of a legal injunction, even for one day. Even for a few hours. It will cost the state billions in immediate losses. Then every big corporation will try to recoup its losses by suing the city or the state or the federal government, and the cost will triple. You think somebody in the state government won't want to try to appease these people?"

But the Native American White Race Warriors were just one of the claimants. There was also the Former Slaves of Gondwanaland Ancestry. They were standing in a wedge formation in another front-page photo, in robes made of Afro-print bedsheets, holding what was said to be a ritual spear of Gondwanaland but looked much like the rubber-tipped spears sold in pioneer-village gift shops across the country.

"The creature was stolen by whites from the Gondwanaland—just as we were stolen by whites from Gondwanaland and brought in chains to this country," their leader decried. "We demand the return of our property!"

The government of Gondwanaland itself was demanding the return of its stolen specimen. It declared a state of war against American terrorists and jailed the U.S. ambassador to Gondwanaland as an enemy combatant.

Every drug firm on earth was making public claims to the apatosaurus. Judges in eight states, under the urging of their state's wealthiest corporations, passed emergency injunctions against removal of the carcass, which had never actually entered their state, and its immediate return to the state if the illegal removal had already occurred. Once news of the theft spread, it became evident that the drug companies were all extremely keen, even desperate, to get their hands on the carcass—then the me-too factor kicked in. Companies and individuals across the country and around the world began to make claims to the carcass.

The UN secretary general said only the UN had the global mandate to handle a crisis of such worldwide proportions, and ordered the carcass brought for safekeeping to his home country of Egypt. The U.S. immediately stopped payment on its recently mailed check to cover its 2002-2003 UN membership dues.

The public battle raged over the ownership of the frozen carcass, but who knew where the carcass even was?

Many people, as it turned out.

27

Serge Perouse let the idiots with the machine guns kill each other. Americans on one side—obstinate cretins. British on the other—filthy troglodytes. Better if they simply exterminated one another.

They were well on their way to doing so. Bodies from both sides littered the floor of the cargo depot. Now the survivors were stationed on second-level platforms on either side of the station, while the dripping ice sculpture sat between them on a flatcar. They were making no headway toward claiming their prize, just picking one another off methodically. It was anybody's guess which side would still have a man standing when all was said and done.

Perouse would be long gone by then, when the depot would be bursting into flames.

He stepped among the slaughter on black crepe-soled shoes, in tight black slacks and a tailored suit jacket over a black shirt. He wore supple black leather gloves, with which he held a strand of razor wire.

The apatosaurus was looking at him. Its mild brown eyes were frozen open. Its mouth hung slightly agape. The ice was clear as fine crystal. Most of the insulating outer coating had dropped off in chunks around the base of the ice block.

The mercenaries from competing pharmaceutical companies were more worried about killing each other than they were about protecting the specimen. The depot was heated by big electric radiant elements on the roof—there was no way the depot could have operated without heat during half the year. Ammassalik was toeing the Arctic Circle.

This made the work much easier for Serge Perouse. Perouse was after a small chunk of the specimen. A few pounds of tissue would be more than sufficient for analysis and synthesizing the immortality compounds. The rest of the carcass would melt and burn in a phosphorous conflagration.

The Americans and the British companies were all trying to get the whole carcass. How like them. Big and blundering and stupid. Perouse was French. The French were intelligent and efficient, as Perouse was about to prove.

He thumbed the power switch on his hip. The elements in his palms blazed hot, but his hands were protected.

The wire did not change color, but it smoked slightly—and it hissed when he sawed into the ice.

Then the light changed, and Perouse hunched down.

"Cease, Frenchmen!"

The tiny Asian man in the garish robe was coming to a landing atop the frozen carcass. A taller man in a T-shirt alighted beside him—and the mercenaries on both sides held their fire momentarily.

Then they let the newcomers have it all.

Perouse was astonished that the two men didn't immediately wither under the barrage. The white man leaped away and seemed to be doing a dance that took him from the floor to the stairs to the walls, and avoiding the stream of bullets that came at him form both sides. The Asian man simply stepped to the floor alongside Perouse, where the shadows hid them from the gunmen.

Perouse struck at the old man with both hands, pulling the razor wire taut. It would burn and cut into any living flesh it contacted.

"An amateur's tool," Chiun mocked, and snatched the two wrists in his own ancient, bony hands and maneuvered the hands up over Perouse's shoulders. The taut wire sliced easily through his neck flesh. Chiun cocked his head, allowing the odiferous air to seep into his nostrils. There was a mix of unpleasant smells, and the least pleasant of them all was the Frenchman at his feet.

Then he knew the smell. "Remo! Save my dragon!"

"Give me a second," Remo said as he landed atop the dinosaur and leaped to the platform.

"There is no second to give," Chiun retorted. "A fire is coming."

"Where?" Remo asked.

"Everywhere," Chiun snapped as he heard the tiny fizz of detonators, then the incendiaries hissed to life on all sides. Fragments of burning chemicals burst from the bombs like fiery pustules. Chiun avoided the burning bits but was helpless to stop them from catching ahold on the plywood walls of the depot. At once the walls crawled with flame and the heat escalated as if the Master of Sinanju were inside a furnace that had just been turned on.

Remo ignored the remaining soldiers, who had been pocked with burning chemicals that bored into their flesh and bone, inextinguishable until the chemical was consumed. Those dino bandits were as good as dead. Remo stepped to the ground and put his shoulder against the rear of the flatcar as Chiun yanked off the hand brakes and demolished the wooden chucks with quick snaps of his toes. The flatcar lurched on its tracks. Remo increased the speed of the car, finding himself staring down the doleful eyes of the frozen apatosaurus.

"He pleads with you to quit stalling and save him," Chiun said, clambering onto the car. "See, he burns!" A tiny dot of blazing white phosphorous could be seen burrowing into the ice like a fiery worm. As if guided, it zeroed in on the dinosaur's doughy-looking head. Chiun stiffened his hand and jabbed at the ice, cracking off the burning and slapping it away. The flatcar hit the double exit doors and burst into the frigid air of east Greenland. The buzz of aircraft was coming close.

"More dragon robbers," Chiun announced, then he shouted, "I shall hunt you all to extinction!"

He was answered with a volley of machine-gun fire. Remo felt the pressure waves zeroing in on his back and he moved briskly from side to side, allowing the rounds to dance under his feet and ricochet on the tracks.

"Quit dallying."

"I'm going as fast as I can." Remo had the train car moving at a respectable twenty miles per hour, and a growing slope was helping him out. Chiun was not helping at all. He snapped a part of the retaining rail and sent it spinning skyward.

The pilot of the bubble-headed helicopter couldn't quite believe it when he saw the little old man skip around his bullet and lob a hunk of scrap metal at him. The metal flew fifty yards, passed through the bubble and through the pilot's head.

Remo heard the uncertainty of the helicopter, then the unmistakable stall and fall. More aircraft winged at them over the stark subarctic land. The slope was getting steeper, and he had the railcar clacking along at highway speeds. Chiun sent another scrap-metal boomerang flying out over Remo's head. At the same instant a rocket flashed out of its pod and slammed into the earth a few paces to the side. Remo flung himself onto the bed of the car and used Punkin as protection from flying shrapnel.

He was alone on the car.

"Chiun!" Remo leaped to the tracks and raced back until he came to Chiun, who stood stiff and bent at the waist, one hand digging deep into the flesh under his rib cage to hold in the pain.

"Little Father?"

"See to my dragon."

"I want to help you," Remo pleaded.

"Do so by protecting my dragon!" Chiun stomped his foot. "I see I must do it myself." He raced up the tracks with Remo close behind. Chiun ran with a limp, as if he had a stitch in his side, but he lost the limp as the pain passed on. Remo couldn't stand to see it. He knew the old man could withstand pain that would kill a human being. If it hurt Chiun bad enough to stop him in his tracks, it must be very bad. And that meant Chiun's sickness was more advanced than Remo had imagined.

They weren't catching up to the fleeing dragon. The rail followed the slope to the sea and it gained momentum by the foot. Remo passed Chiun and ran on, then he turned his head.

"Go on!" Chiun cried.

Remo swallowed the lump in his throat and poured on every ounce of speed in his body.

Two miles downhill a helicopter came to a violent crunch on the earth alongside the tracks and the copilot jumped out. He hauled on the track-switching lever, then leaped back into the cockpit of the chopper as a gang on dirt bikes climbed to intersect him on knobby tires. One of the bikers triggered a fat-barreled weapon that he shouldered with one hand. The bulbous projectile arced too low to strike the rotors as the chopper rose fast, but burst under the craft, giving it a nudge on the bottom. The chopper spun on its side and peppered the dirt bikes with gunfire. Two bikers were cut to the ground, but the survivor pulled his bike into a dirt-spitting one-eighty and started downhill. A shotgun blast pushed him off the bike.

"Oh, now what?" Remo demanded.

A band of grungy Inuit unloaded their hunting rifles into the low-flying helicopter before one of them pushed to the front with a shoulder-slung weapon that hung at waist level and looked as if it were meant for lobbing bowling balls. It spit a mound of wire that expanded into a cloud of metallic strands. The helicopter tangled up in it and fell on its side on the earth. It chewed up soil, the rotors shattered, and the engine smoked.

Punkin careened down on them and the Inuit raced for the track lever. Remo cursed. He couldn't run any faster than this. Why didn't everybody just leave Chiun's dragon alone?

An Inuit hauled on the lever but he was a half second too late. Instead of continuing north for a long journey along the east Greenland shoreline the dragon took a roller-coaster hillock, squeaked through a turn and plunged downhill toward the Denmark Strait.

The excited Inuit shot at the railcar. They chipped ice from the frozen dinosaur and shouted at one another, then spotted Remo Williams streaking at them faster than any human being had any right to move.

So they shot at him, too.

"I've had enough of all of you," Remo said, meandering to bypass the flying bullets. The big gun *pooted* again and a cloud of barbed wire netting floated down over him. Remo slipped out from beneath it, snatched it by the edge and whipped it furiously at the gunners. The little barbs peeled away skin wherever the wire touched.

Remo was closing the distance, but he wasn't closing it fast enough. Punkin was running out of rail in a hurry. Men on the cargo dock were fleeing the runaway apatosaurus. It was still traveling more than fifty miles per hour when it hit the curve in the tracks where the posted speed limit was five miles per hour. The railcar left the track and the wheels tore wooden dock planking and came to a halt.

Even after all that melting, Punkin and his icy cocoon weighed better than thirty-five tons, and there was no stopping them. Punkin cut a trench in the planks until it came to the edge of the dock. The boat that had been waiting for Punkin got Punkin. The frozen block slammed into the deck, obliterated the deckhouse, rolled off the nose of the vessel and lodged there. The vessel's nose sank ten feet while the rear end left the water entirely.

Another boat raced in, leveling gunfire at the survivors on the dock, and swung itself broadside into the nose of the wrecked vessel.

Punkin tumbled onto the deck of the second ship, which hunkered down in the water, then churned up the ocean and headed away.

"Chiun," Remo said. He turned around and headed back the way he'd come.

There was no sign of Chiun.

Remo checked the rocky places where a little body might fall and lie hidden.

"Chiun!"

There was nothing except the thrum of another helicopter, which sunk down to the ground nearby. "Come, Remo!"

Chiun sat in the second seat of a little Bell helicopter, one hand grasping the pilot gently by the earlobe. The pilot had been exposed to Chun's special pain-in-the-ear technique, and now he was extremely cooperative.

"You may sit in the back," Chiun said. "You may sit upon the lead acid battery that is there, and it is better than you deserve."

"I did my best, Little Father."

"Then where is my dragon?"

Remo sighed and compressed himself into the tiny space in the rear of the Bell. "That way," he said, waving vaguely at the cold ocean.

28

The helicopter got them to within sight of land, then hit the water. Remo and Chiun stepped out a moment before the splash and ran across the water, their feet finding the surface tension and balancing on it without breaking it.

The dragon-thieving pilot, who did not know how to walk on water, tried to swim through it and didn't last five minutes.

They came ashore and Remo used the phone at a tiny hovel that was, he was told, the only store of any kind within fifty miles.

"We're in Iss-afford-a-her," Remo reported. "Where's Iss-afford-a-her."

"About an hour from Bolungarvik," the clerk said helpfully. She was in her fifties, platinum blond and nearly seven feet tall.

"We're an hour from Bolungarvik. What's a Bolungarvik?"

"Iceland," Smith informed them.

"Iceland?" Remo said.

"Where else did you expect to end up when traveling southwest from Greenland?" Smith asked.

"Call me an idiot."

Chiun did so.

"How come you don't know you're in Iceland?" the clerk demanded.

"Can you move elsewhere to speak? Out of earshot of the proprietor?" Smith asked.

"No. It's her phone," Remo said. Chiun began conversing with the Nordic giantess in a language Remo could not understand, although he recognized it as sounding a lot like some other languages he did not understand. He did catch a reference to someone's "gigantic head," which caused the clerk to giggle.

Remo gave Smith a sketchy report. "Remo," Smith said, apropos of nothing, "I must remind you of your duty. The specimen must be incinerated."

"I never said I would do that. It's not going to happen."

"It must happen."

"It's Chiun's dinosaur."

"He has no right to it."

"The lady who owned it gave it to Chiun."

"She did not own it and she had no right to promise it to him."

"Smitty, you've got no claim to Punkin. Nobody has any claim to Punkin except Chiun. You can't go taking stuff away from us just because we're working for you."

"Remo, this business is bigger than the terms of our contract," Harold Smith said sourly.

"You're right about that. It's about Chiun's survival and the whole history of Sinanju. You're my boss, and I'll do what you say, but that doesn't extend to claiming my property."

"Now it belongs to you?" Smith said, irritated and short of patience.

"Yes, dammit. I'm the Reigning Master of Sinanju. It's my dinosaur. If you try stealing my dinosaur, you get the same treatment the other dinosaur stealers get."

"And I say this creature is not your property—not yours, Chiun's or anyone's."

"Bulldookey."

"You won't find the specimen without me, Remo," Smith said. "Iceland is a big island."

Remo felt a moment of panic. He had to find the dinosaur. He had to save Chiun.

"Our friend Dabba knows where the dragon may be found," Chiun said, using his slow and friendly voice. When he talked like that, you could believe he was the kindliest, gentlest Korean grandfather you never had.

"Our friend Dabba knows where the dino is," Remo said, and hung up.

THEY DID NOT SPEAK of their weariness. Remo was tired. He had slept little in two days. Chiun must be exhausted, but he didn't ask.

"All I'm saying is Punkin doesn't look like a dragon. Even most dinosaurs don't look like dragons. They don't have wings, most of them. They don't breathe fire."

"You speak as if the differences were meaningful when they are not. You know the elephant of Asia and the elephant of Africa. Any child can see the difference in these animals. The African pachyderm is greater in girth, more fetid of breath and more expansive in its ears. It is the same with the Chinese dragon and the African dragon."

"Punkin looks more like a platypus."

They were skimming over the rocky, fjord-like barrenness at a restorative pace, heading into the highest peaks on the peninsula. Dabba claimed there was a place that was the hub of much activity. Chiun seemed confident this was the place.

"It was you, as I recall, who pretended to have knowledge of dragons. You recognized the breed when first we laid eyes upon the creature in Gondwanaland in Africa."

"Matter of fact, I do know a thing or two about dinosaurs," Remo said. "When I was a kid, I was so into dinosaurs I actually read about them. Can you imagine, me, reading up on something by choice? There was dimetrodon. They tried to fake dimetrodon in *Journey to the Center of the Earth* by gluing fins on a bunch of Mexican iguanas. Then we found out dimetrodon came way before the real dinosaurs. This was way before *Jurassic Park*. This was even before *Land of the Lost*. We hadn't even heard of a velociraptor, or a Sleestack back in those days."

"You speak on and on and yet no intelligent words seem to be forming. It is a miracle."

"Our favorite was T-rex, of course. Now, that was a real dinosaur."

"Describe this T-rex," Chiun ordered.

Remo did. Big, strong back legs, small front legs, huge head, huge teeth.

Chiun understood. "I have seen this creature depicted often. It is regarded as the king of all of its kind for its ferocity and carnivorous nature. It was the favorite to what group of which you were a part when you say 'our'?"

"Me and the other kids at St. Theresa's. Dinosaurs were always cool at the orphanage. Even the fat, wobbly ones like brontosaurus. Or apart-of-a-saurus, I guess they call it now."

"But this T-rex is a ridiculous, lumbering creature. Its weight is all on its hind end, while its front legs are useless little feelers. A true dragon, with its breath of fire and its lithe body and wings, could make quick work of such a foe."

"That's my point," Remo said. "If you think the T-rex is un-dragon-like, then you gotta admit that Punkin is totally wrong for a dragon. It does not breathe fire. It doesn't eat rice farmers or any kind of farmers. It couldn't fly without the help of a cliff. It isn't a dragon."

Chiun smiled thinly, but with absolute assurance. "A dragon," he said, "it is. Despite its bulbous body and clown like behavior, it is a dragon, and the life-giving properties in its bones are the same as in the bones of its brothers. Our dragon's bones will be as efficacious as the bones of Wing Wang Wo, the dragon slain by Yong."

"Yong got a bad deal," Remo grumbled.

"No, this was not among his list of sins," Chiun

said. "The deal itself was adequate, for the prize was worth more than its weight in gold."

"I don't mean he got a bad deal from the emperor of Cathay, but from the holier-than-thou Masters of Sinanju that came after him. What he did was not such a bad thing, especially when you think about when he lived. Keep in mind that he lived in the old Wild West days of Sinanju."

"Bite your tongue! Sinanju once was an uncivilized place, with many assassins vying for mastery of the village and the wealth, but it was never Westernized."

"Sinanju was uncivilized then. Lots of assassins, all of them wanting to be Master, all of them wanting to be the one who controls the gold. Yong lived in a different sort of Sinanju. Where honor was put lower on the list than survival. It was all about who could get the power and keep the power. Keeping the dragon bones and keeping himself alive the longest was just natural for him to do. Maybe any of the other Masters from those days would have done the same thing. Maybe he's no better and no worse than any of the pre-Wang Masters. But he was the one who happened to get called in to kill the dragon, so he's the one who suffers for it. All the other good things he may have done for the village are erased because of it. His real name? Buried with his bones. He's remembered with a double-dog-insult of a nickname and he spends all eternity standing around in some soggy, after-life rice paddy getting rained on."

"This is just."

"Who says?"

"Did Yong offer complaint, when you met him in the Void?"

"No," Remo admitted. "But after four thousand years, he's probably kind of resigned himself to it. Did anyone ever consider that Yong kept some bones for himself, but hid most of it away?"

"If Yong hid the bones of the dragon away, then he hid them too well. They have never been found in the four millennia."

"But has anyone ever looked?" Remo insisted.

Chiun looked at him sharply. "My son, the village and the traditions of Sinanju have endured with great tenacity. No civilization or tradition or institution has gone on as long as Sinanju. Only the Kingdom of Kemet even came near to lasting so long, and even in the land of the pharaohs the memory faded and the people of later dynasties were mystified by the stone monuments of the earlier dynasties.

"In Sinanju, our memory did not fade, but you have yourself just proved how the passage of time cannot but help to leave its mark. All things, physical and spiritual alike, are affected by the passage of time. A statue of the most resilient stone, even held in a shelter, will show the signs of age after four thousand years. Where in Sinanju could Yong have hidden the bones of a dragon where the passage of time would not have revealed them, through the erosions of great floods and the devastation of fires?"

"Hole in the ground," Remo said.

"Then they rotted away even before the coming of Wang."

"In oilcloth."

"The oil would have dispersed into the soil in a thousand years and the water would have soaked inside. The result is the same—the bones do not exist today."

"Maybe he put them somewhere safer," Remo insisted. "Maybe in China. In a Chinese tomb or in the same cave where he did his trick on the dragon."

Chiun chose not to answer. The air was brisk in Iceland. There was grass, but not a tree in sight.

"There is no tree in all of Iceland, Remo," Chiun said. "The followers of Odin arrived on these shores one thousand years ago, and there were many trees then, but they burned them for fire. Burned them to keep themselves warm and never considered what the future generation would burn. By the time of Saemundur the Wise—who is considered wise only by the Icelandic standards—the trees were gone. The Icelanders are like Yong the Gluttonous."

"What did they burn, then?"

"Dung."

"Yech." Then he said, "Yong was the Reigning Master of the village at the time he slew the dragon, but this was in the pre-Wang days. There were lots of other assassins in the village at the time. So even if he did share the dragon bones, wouldn't he have been sharing them with the other assassins?"

"No. The bones of the dragon are fit only for the Master."

"But back then, before Wang, before the Sun Source, being the top dog in the village wasn't that big a deal, right? The leader of the assassins might be nothing more than a warlord who had a lot of friends at any given moment. He could lose his position and status and his life at a moment's notice. The leader wasn't really anybody special until Wang came along and got the Sun Source and set up the one-Master tradition. I know I am right about that."

"You are," Chiun agreed. "But those who were the leaders before Wang still regarded themselves as supreme. Were Yong to share the bones of the dragon, he would have shared them with the leaders of the assassins that came after him. And yet, this is speculation."

"Just thinking things through, is all," Remo said. "Now, what if there was some sort of village intrigue going on and Yong knew that the Master that came next was unworthy of the bones of the dragon? A bully or a jerk. Wouldn't be right to give the soup bones to that guy. So he has two choices. Drink them all up himself, or hide them away."

"To his shame," Chiun concluded, "his choice was the selfish one."

"How do you know?"

"Our history says so."

Remo grinned. "Little Father, I have a lot of respect for the history of Sinanju. I've read them all and you know it. One thing I know for sure, they don't always agree with each other. One of them says one thing and then another one says something else about the same thing or the same person and both scrolls can't be right, right?"

"The scrolls are sacred to the Masters," Chiun said.

"And they're sacred to me," Remo said so seriously that Chiun believed him. "But there are inconsistencies in the details."

"If so, then this is true of all great history."

"Probably. It's the only history I ever read. Except from a textbook in school when I was a kid. That stuff never quite stuck in my head. But the point is this."

Chiun waited.

"Oh, yeah, here's the point. Depending on which of the scrolls you read, some of the Masters were good guys or jerks. In the case of Yong the Gluttonous, we don't even have scrolls with him in it, just these stories that have been passed down. And you know how it is with stories that get passed down. They change. A little bit here, a little bit there."

"I do not like your casual assertions of carelessness by legions of your forebears."

"Yong was one of the first known Masters, so who knows how much his story got changed—it was like four thousand years ago," Remo said.

"The Masters protect the accuracy of their histories!" Chiun snapped. "I can recite the tale of Yong word for word as it was told to me!"

"But you're Chiun the Wise," Remo said, without a hint of mockery. "You're one of the greatest of all the Masters. No Master of Sinanju has done so much for Sinanju, including passing along the history perfectly."

Chiun was usually amenable to flattery, but now he was suspicious. "I have done my duty and it was the duty of all Masters who came before me."

"You're the most modest person I've ever met. But we both know that you've done way more than that. You've done a better job than the average, run-of-the-mill, adequate-but-nothing-special Master, let alone the poor performing Masters. Take Master Sam for instance."

Chiun's face colored. "Do you seek to shame me by airing so much soiled washing?"

"Hey, it's my dirty laundry, too. I'm trying to make a point. Master Sam is so dim-witted that he gets outfoxed by a Japanese king who learns some of the secrets of the Sinanju Sun Source, and that brings about ninja, and then Japanese martial arts come into being until today, so you could say Master Sam is directly to blame for every Jackie Chan movie ever made."

"What of it?" Chiun snapped.

"If Master Sam was standing here right now, would you trust him to carry your trunks?" Remo asked.

"They would doubtless become scratched or dented."

"Would you trust him with the history of your people?"

Chiun pursed his thin lips until they were white. "No."

"There's been a freakin' lot of Masters and there's been a few Master Sams along the way and who's to say the stories didn't get messed up now and again?"

Chiun nodded unhappily, then his eyes opened wider and he regarded his pupil with a puzzled look.

"What?" Remo asked.

"Your point is well made," Chiun said. "You have used the history of Sinanju to make evident what you desired to make evident. I am pleased."

"You are?"

"It took much time. It was overlong in the telling."

"Sorry."

"But it was well done, Remo." Chiun nodded and turned his head away, nodding still, and said as if to himself, "Well done."

"Wait, I'm not through yet," Remo said. "My point about Master Sam was leading somewhere else."

Chiun waited expectantly. Remo was thinking that maybe he should leave well enough alone. He had achieved something here, and Chiun had approved in a way Chiun rarely approved, and why risk ruining this small success by taking it too far?

"But, see, that was just a point that gets to the real

point," Remo said. "The real point I was trying to get to was about Master Yong. We don't know that much about him and we don't know for absolutely certain that he even deserves to be named what he was named. Maybe he didn't consume all the dragon bones for himself. Maybe they just disappeared and the jerk Masters who came after him were ticked off when they couldn't find the bone stash so they blame Yong and that's how it all started. So we're dealing with what Yong's rivals and maybe his enemies thought about Yong."

"This is unlikely."

"Not impossible," Remo declared triumphantly.

"And not provable," Chiun added. "So what is the point of entertaining the notion?"

Remo felt the wind go out of his sails in a big hurry. "Yeah. I guess so."

"And there is the matter of the long life of Yong," Chiun insisted.

"But it wasn't all that long," Remo stated. "Yong only lived to be 148. That's old enough for a yogurt commercial but it's not that much older than a lot of the Masters. Most of them live to be a hundred. Lots of them live to be 120, like you. That's pretty close to Yong. You're almost as old as Yong was when he died, and you've never had a dragon bone in your life, right? Wouldn't Yong have lived a lot longer if he had an entire dragon skeleton to brew up?"

Remo turned to Chiun and said, "Do you remember when Sunny Joe almost died?"

Chiun nodded. "A tumultuous time."

"To say the least. I'm going through my Rite of Attainment. You finally tell me you know who my biological father is, and when we stop in for a visit he's dying of some sort of rat plague that's wiped out half the reservation of the Sun On Jo Indians, which we also happen to discover is descended from a long-lost Master of Sinanju, which makes you and me cousins, of all things, and we also happen to find the old Master himself mummified in a nearby cave. Crap, I get tired just trying to think back on all the bedlam. So I'm going through the Rite of Attainment—which, by the way, I had no warning about. You wake me up one morning and go, 'By the way, your Rite of Attainment starts—now!' But I'm not still carrying it around with me or anything."

"Of course not. What was the purpose of your example?"

"I forgot."

"Perhaps you were referring to the near death of the one who sired you, and the treatment that brought him back from the brink of death."

"Yes!" Remo said. "And I was having visions. I was getting to meet many of the Masters of Sinanju as a part of the rite. They kept appearing to me in my dreams. That's when I met Yong. I called him a jerk for using up all the dragon bones, and he said, no, not all, I saved some for you. He gave me a little piece of bone."

Chiun looked impassive, waiting for more.

"When I came around, and we were trying to nurse my dad, you happened to mention that a piece of dragon bone might help Sunny Joe. Why'd you mention that, Chiun?"

Chiun shrugged. "It was merely an observation."

"Kind of coincidental, you just happening to mention something like that for the first time in all our years together, and it just happens to be when I actually have a chunk of dragon bone in my pocket."

"Exactly. Coincidence."

"No. Not a coincidence," Remo said. "I was set up."

"Remo," Chiun said, "you do not know of what you speak."

"You're right about that, Chiun. I have got no clue what happened that day. It was a long time ago and there was a lot going on but now I can look back and see that it was a setup. But here's the part I don't know, Chiun—who set me up? Was it you? Or was it Yong? Or both?"

"What leads you to this conclusion in the first place?" Chiun demanded.

Remo nodded seriously and laid it out the same way it was laid out in his brain. "You could have planted it there. You could have laid some sort of hints that made me dream about meeting Yong and maybe it was you talking to me when I was sleeping, playing the part of Yong."

"Remo, you accuse me of trickery?"

"Also, you plant the piece of bone in my pocket. Then you act out the little scene. 'If only we had a piece of dragon bone we could save Sunny Joe,' you say. 'Well, as it so happens,' I say, and then we cure Sunny Joe."

"Where would I have come by this piece of dragon bone, and to what end would I perpetrate this charade?" Chiun demanded angrily.

"Where you got it? I have no idea," Remo said. "Why you planted it on me? Just another part of the wild and wacky Sinanju rites. Maybe all my visions during the Rite of Attainment were in reality you talking to me while I was sleeping, like some sort of subliminal Sinanju."

"And in this scenario in which I am a duplicitous and conniving priest, is the bone a true dragon bone? Or is it an important fragment of some other creature's skeleton? And in either case, what would be the purpose, Remo?"

Remo had thought all this through, too. "The purpose is to reinforce the faith of the newly attained Master. Makes a sort of sense. It's like putting sooty footprints on the living-room floor on Christmas morning to prove to the youngsters that Santa Claus really did come down the chimney."

"You insult us all with this supposition. Myself. Yong. All the Masters who came before you."

"Well, don't blow your top yet, Little Father, 'cause I have more to say on the subject. If it wasn't you who set me up, it had to be Yong himself. He didn't just set me up—he's been fooling all the Masters of Sinanju that followed in his footsteps. Me, you, Wang, Lu, Can-Wi, Sam. Everybody."

"How? And to what end?"

"I don't know how. It's all supernatural afterlife stuff. But I think I'm right about this. You can help me prove it. Tell me one thing, Little Father, when you went through the Rite of Attainment, did you meet Yong in the Void, and did he give you a piece of dragon bone?"

Chiun stared straight ahead, but after a long moment, his lips barely moved and he said, "He did."

"And the Masters that came before you?"

"I do not know. It is not spoken of."

"It's a test, isn't it?" Remo said. "Yong gives the new Master a piece of the dragon bone during the Rite of Attainment, and the way in which the new Master disposes of the bone is a signal to all the Masters of the Void, and maybe to the Master who came before the Master who is undergoing the Rite of Attainment. Is this not so?"

"This is your fantasy. Do not ask me to confirm it."

"You just did," Remo said. "So Yong gives the bone to the new Master, and when the new Master returns to the real world, he finds the bone in his pocket. If he is a considerate student who is not selfish and who holds his own trainer in high regard and in a position of honor, he would not think twice before giving it to the elder Master, who, naturally, needs it more. But I didn't do that, did I, Chiun? I failed the test."

Chiun heard the strangeness in Remo's voice and was surprised to see that Remo's eyes were bright and moist. The Reigning Master of Sinanju was on the verge of tears.

"I could have given you the dragon bone, Chiun. I could have given you more life and I didn't do it."

"My son, you do not even know if this is true—"

"It is true. This is the way. Yong is not a glutton. Yong did not drink the elixir but stashed it away and now he doles out the fragments from the Void and that is the way of it. I don't know if he knows he is maligned in the traditions of Sinanju and I don't know if he cares and I don't care, Little Father. I just want the goddamned truth and there it is."

Remo waved at the empty floor as if he had just deposited something vile there. "Yong is noble and keeps the precious dragon bones to present to the new Master, who in turn will present them to his Master, and thus the honor of the Sinanju Masters is preserved in deed and symbol, for generation after generation and in this I have failed."

Chiun's aged mind was a storm of thoughts, but what he thought first and foremost was this: he had never heard Remo Williams speak with such eloquence and feeling.

This was a Master who would know how to tell the tales of the history of Sinanju, and tell them correctly.

"Remo, my son," Chiun said, "there is much that is unsaid in the history of Sinanju, and no Master knows what is true about Yong. And Yong does not say. But this much is true and known and told to the most senior Masters—Yong does give the bone to the newly attained Masters and it is a test of the new Master's esteem for his mentor. But this is true, too—no Master was ever tested as you were tested. You had two fathers upon which you might have bestowed the honor of the gift of the dragon bone, and one of them needed it far more than the other. It was right of you to give it to Sunny Joe of the Sun On Jos. It may have saved his life. And in truth, I wished you to give it to him—that is why I suggested it."

"But you need it now."

Chiun said nothing.

Remo stopped on the rocky escarpment with nothing but the stony crags of the ancient land as far as could be seen. "Will you lie to me again, Chiun, and tell me you don't? Are you going to tell me one more time that you're not sick? You're not dying?"

Chiun colored. "I will tell you that one dose of the elixir taken then would have done little. It cured Sunny Joe because he had the vermin plague. It was a fever to be broken. Not a cancer that devours the innards."

"And one dose today, Chiun?"

"My son, you scheme of trying to contact Yong,

to get another piece of the bone he has in safe-keeping, to save my life? You, and every good son that has come before you, when he learns that his Master is dying."

"Yet another Sinanju rite, Little Father?"

"No. Just a foolish act of affection and honor. Fated to fail—Yong is stingy with his bones."

"So he ticked somebody off. And he got a bad rap."

"Don't be quick to exonerate Yong, Remo. What you have guessed is true enough, that Yong presents the dragon bone to the new Master, that the Masters have come to read much into how the new Master dispenses with his dragon bone. But this was not planned, least of all by Yong. The stories of his gluttony are true enough, as far as I am concerned and as far as the spoken history of Sinanju is concerned. Count the fragments of dragon bones he has gifted to the new Masters, and it adds up to little more than a single rib or half a shin from a creature as big as a dragon."

29

"Are you sure they're all dead?"

"They're all dead," Scott Wrought promised. He waved to the aluminum tube that protruded from the hard-packed ice. "We need to hurry. We've got less than an hour before the ice shifts enough to seal our entrance. The cavern entrance was completely blocked in the cave-in."

Jeremy Landis bit his lip.

"Want me to go first?" Wrought asked.

"No. I'll go."

He stepped into the narrow tube and started down. The steps were aluminum, flimsy and loud. His steps reverberated ahead of him. "If they're not dead, there's no sneaking up on them, is there?"

"They're dead. I swear," Wrought said behind him.

Wrought was right. Nothing in the hollow place under the Korpudalur glacier was alive. The tight little ice cave contained more bodies than he could count. There were Asians and Caucasians and Africans. There were men in black suits, men in mountain-climbing gear, men in enclosed haz-mat suits with their own breathing units.

"They mostly killed each other," Wrought explained. "You know who came out as the winner?"

"Who?"

"The Fizzer guys!"

Wrought showed Landis a pile of disfigured corpses with bulging eyes.

"Then we gassed them." Wrought shrugged.

Landis gagged slightly, but he was a happy man as he ran his hands over the gleaming surface of the frozen apatosaurus.

"We'll have to get this out piece by piece, you know," Wrought said.

Landis was in a dreamy place. "It's mine."

"No, it is not."

Landis turned around quickly. Wrought gargled, then fell on his face, a finger-size hole in his temple.

"Who are you?" Remo demanded.

"The wealthiest man on Earth," Landis said.

"Well, that doesn't count for much," Remo said, tapping Landis on the sternum.

The man who would never be a trillionaire fell on his back and grabbed his chest. His heart had lost its natural rhythm; it was beating faster, too fast. Landis pounded his own chest, trying to beat his heart into submission. His heart didn't listen. It galloped until it burst.

The icy covering around Punkin's neck gave way at last. The big dinosaur head flopped on the floor and gazed up at the Masters of Sinanju.

"It's dead, right?" Remo said.

"If not yet, then soon," Chiun declared delightedly as he sized up the thirty-ton specimen, then stepped to it with his talons extended like an eagle preparing to gut a salmon.

30

They camped out alongside the ice. The night was brisk, but Remo willed his body to adjust to the temperature. Chiun had an inner pocket that bulged with fresh dragon bones—the skeleton of an entire foot. It was enough, Chiun assured Remo, to last years.

Chiun had been carrying a tiny iron pot in the sleeve of his kimono. Remo was amazed when he produced it. "You mean you have been carrying that since we left Folcroft?"

"It is from Dabba's store. See?" Distastefully, Chiun displayed the legend on the bottom of the pot, where it was stamped Made In Reykjavík.

Remo collected lichen and moss, and on the stony bluff overlooking the ice field he worried stones until they became red-hot. The lichen burned under the pot, melting the ancient ice of the Korpudalur glacier. When the water boiled, Chiun dropped in the bloody fragments he had extracted from the foot of the last dragon.

When the brew was done, Chiun tasted it. He sipped until the pot was half-empty, and then he held it to Remo.

"No, thanks."

"You must know this brew to be able to recognize it when you taste it again. One day, if you are lucky, your son shall give you the elixir, and you shall know you are honored as I am honored."

Remo took the tiniest sip. He felt his tongue dance. He swallowed, and it seemed as if his body came alive from the inside out.

"I am tired," said Chiun. "It has been two days since I slept last."

He stretched out on his back, with only arctic moss as his mat, and closed his eyes.

Down on one side of the hill were the gathered engines of all the dragon thieves who had come to do battle in the cavern under the ice. They had eventually brought down the very rock, sealing the way out. The air-dropped tubing had penetrated the ice through heat, but now the shifting ice was causing that to close up, too. The metal tube creaked and groaned under the weight of the moving ice.

Chiun slept, breathing easily.

Remo wished the old man would give him a good, healthy snore.

But Chiun slept in silence.

Remo finally allowed himself to stretch out on the cold rock, as well, dreading the coming of the morning.

THE HORNS OF WELCOME looked fresh, as if the sculpture was just completed.

Remo was at the cave again—the familiar Sinanju cave, but this was centuries before his time.

The same Master of Sinanju was waiting for him there.

"You're Yong, right?" Remo said.

The Master cocked his head.

"Did you know Chiun and I have our dragon?"

"And put it in a most convenient place," the Master said agreeably.

"Under a glacier in Iceland is convenient?"

"From the Void, it is as good as any other place."

"Like a cavern in China?"

The Master did not answer. Remo still couldn't make his eyes focus on the Master's face. "I know you're Yong," Remo said. "I want you to do me a favor. I want to know your real name."

That stymied the Master. He put his hands in his crude robe sleeves and said, "Perhaps."

"Chiun!" Remo said, and leaped past the Master and down the side of the cliff. Remo had seen another Master pass by—it was a small man with a pale white skull and ears like shells, with thin yellow tufts of hair over his ears.

But if Chiun was in the Void, it could only mean Chiun was dead.

"Little Father."

He had lost the little man. There was no one in sight. He reached the cliff bottom and stood on the shore.

There was a sound of collapsing metal. Part of Remo knew that the glacier had finally crushed the metal tube that led to the tomb of the dragon, but he was still in the Void, on the shore of a Sinanju of another age. He trembled from the awful sound.

"Chiun," said Remo Williams, "I am sorry." He let his voice travel over the steely Korpudalur glacier and the slate-gray sea along the Sinanju shore, and he struggled to find words that would be pleasing to the ear of an old and revered Master. "I am sorry that I did not give you the dragon bone years ago, during my Rite of Attainment. I know my other father needed it more at that moment, but still I wish that I could have honored you, as a good son should, by presenting you the dragon bone as a token of my respect and affection."

"But, my son."

Remo sat up, disoriented. He was on the stony bluff in Iceland. It was nearly dawn, and Chiun sat smiling beside him, hazel eyes sparkling.

"But, Remo," Chiun said, "you have given me more than any Sinanju son has ever given his mentor. You have given me an entire dragon."

James Axler
Outlanders®

**An ancient Chinese emperor
stakes his own dark claim to Earth…**

HYDRA'S RING

A sacred pyramid in China is invaded by what appears to be a ruthless
Tong crime lord and his army. But a stunning artifact and a desperate
summons for the Cerberus exiles put the true nature of the looming battle
into horrifying perspective. Kane and his rebels must confront a four-
thousand-year-old emperor, an evil entity as powerful as any nightmare
now threatening humankind's future….

Available November 2006 wherever you buy books.

Or order your copy now by sending your name, address, zip or postal code, along with a check or
money order (please do not send cash) for $6.50 for each book ordered ($7.99 in Canada), plus
75¢ postage and handling ($1.00 in Canada), payable to Gold Eagle Books, to:

In the U.S.	In Canada
Gold Eagle Books	Gold Eagle Books
3010 Walden Avenue	P.O. Box 636
P.O. Box 9077	Fort Erie, Ontario
Buffalo, NY 14269-9077	L2A 5X3

Please specify book title with your order.
Canadian residents add applicable federal and provincial taxes.

GOLD
EAGLE®

GOUT39

TAKE 'EM FREE
2 action-packed novels plus a mystery bonus

NO RISK
NO OBLIGATION TO BUY

SPECIAL LIMITED-TIME OFFER

Mail to: Gold Eagle Reader Service™

IN U.S.A.:
3010 Walden Ave.
P.O. Box 1867
Buffalo, NY 14240-1867

IN CANADA:
P.O. Box 609
Fort Erie, Ontario
L2A 5X3

YEAH! Rush me 2 FREE Gold Eagle® novels and my FREE mystery bonus. If I don't cancel, I will receive 6 hot-off-the-press novels every other month. Bill me at the low price of just $29.94* for each shipment. That's a savings of over 10% off the combined cover prices and there is NO extra charge for shipping and handling! There is no minimum number of books I must buy. I can always cancel at any time simply by returning a shipment at your cost or by returning any shipping statement marked "cancel." Even if I never buy another book from Gold Eagle, the 2 free books and mystery bonus are mine to keep forever.

166 ADN DZ76
366 ADN DZ77

Name _____ (PLEASE PRINT)

Address _____ Apt. No. _____

City _____ State/Prov. _____ Zip/Postal Code _____

Signature (if under 18, parent or guardian must sign)

Not valid to present Gold Eagle® subscribers.
Want to try two free books from another series? Call 1-800-873-8635.

* Terms and prices subject to change without notice. Sales tax applicable in N.Y. Canadian residents will be charged applicable provincial taxes and GST. This offer is limited to one order per household. All orders subject to approval.
® are trademarks owned and used by the trademark owner and or its licensee.
© 2004 Harlequin Enterprises Ltd.

GE-04R

a priceless artifact sparks a quest to keep untold power from the wrong hands…

AleX Archer
SOLOMON'S JAR

Rumors of the discovery of Solomon's Jar—in which the biblical King Solomon bound the world's demons after using them to build his temple in Jerusalem—are followed with interest by Annja Creed. Her search leads her to a confrontation with a London cult driven by visions of new world order; and a religious zealot fueled by insatiable glory. Across the sands of the Middle East to the jungles of Brazil, Annja embarks on a relentless chase to stop humanity's most unfathomable secrets from reshaping the modern world.

Available September 2006 wherever you buy books.

GOLD EAGLE®

GRA2